MORE THAN A HERO

BAYTOWN HEROES

MARYANN JORDAN

Cover by: Graphics by Stacy

Cover photograph: Eric McKinney 612Covered Photography

ISBN ebook: 978-1-965847-16-9

ISBN print: 978-1-965847-17-6

AUTHOR INFORMATION

I am an avid reader of romance novels, often joking that I cut my teeth on the historical romances. I have been reading and reviewing for years. In 2013, I finally gave into the characters in my head, screaming for their story to be told. From these musings, my first novel, Emma's Home, The Fairfield Series was born.

I was a high school counselor having worked in education for thirty years. I live in Virginia, having also lived in four states and two foreign countries. I have been married to a wonderfully patient man for over forty years. When writing, my dog or one of my two cats can generally be found in the same room if not on my lap.

Please take the time to leave a review of this book. Feel free to contact me, especially if you enjoyed my book. I love to hear from readers!

Facebook
Email
Website

Author's Note

Please remember that this is a work of fiction. I have lived in numerous states as well as overseas, but for the last thirty years have called Virginia my home. I often choose to use fictional city names with some geographical accuracies.

These fictionally named cities allow me to use my creativity and not feel constricted by attempting to accurately portray the areas.

It is my hope that my readers will allow me this creative license and understand my fictional world.

I also do quite a bit of research on my books and try to write on subjects with accuracy. There will always be points where creative license will be used in order to create scenes or plots.

All books have errors, no matter how many author, editors, proofers, and readers have looked at the manuscript. If the errors are minor and do not affect the story, please forgive and ignore. But, if you find errors that you deem necessary to report, please send me an email with your notations and do not try to report to Amazon. Be kind to authors… we are human!
authormaryannjordan@gmail.com

1

Angie Brown barely waited for the sliding glass doors to open before she burst through the front of Stuart's Pharmacy. Her breath came in short pants as she made a beeline for the prescription counter near the back.

"Oh my God, you're a lifesaver!" she gushed, her purple-framed glasses slipping slightly down her nose as she grinned at the pharmacist behind the elevated counter.

Thomas chuckled as he glanced down at her from his perch, his smile wide. "No worries, Angie. You know I've got you. We've got a couple of folks ahead of you, but give me a few minutes, and I'll have it ready."

Relief flooded through Angie as she exhaled a grateful breath. "Thank you, thank you, thank you," she said dramatically, pressing a hand to her heart before stepping aside to make room for an older couple waiting nearby.

She inhaled deeply, catching the comforting scent of vanilla and antiseptic—an odd but familiar combination in the small hometown pharmacy. Stuart's was more than just a pharmacy—it was a staple of the community. The short aisles brimmed with everyday essentials, saving residents a trip out of town to one of the stores scattered along the main highway that cut through the Eastern Shore.

When vacationers hit the town during tourist season, they perused the sections filled with Baytown souvenirs, flip-flops, and brightly colored T-shirts. But what Angie loved most was the attached old-time diner that served simple yet mouthwatering meals, from thick milkshakes to their iconic sweet potato pancakes.

Just thinking about those pancakes made her stomach rumble, and she made a mental note to come in next weekend for a big breakfast.

She wandered down the aisles, checking her list. "Band-Aids? No. Vitamins? Yes. Deodorant? No. Toothpaste? Yes," she murmured to herself, her arms filling quickly with her selections. Rounding the final aisle, she stopped short, eyes landing on the feminine hygiene products. "Shit... yes." She grabbed a box of tampons and a package of pantyliners, but then remembered she needed ibuprofen.

Juggling her haul, she turned the corner and collided with something solid and unyielding.

Her breath whooshed out as her grip faltered, sending boxes and bottles tumbling to the floor. A pair of strong hands shot out, gripping her upper arms, steadying her before she could crash to the ground.

"Oh my God! I'm so sorry!" she gasped, clutching onto the person she'd just barreled into.

"No apology necessary," replied the deep, steady voice.

Her head snapped up, eyes locking onto familiar stormy-gray ones. His soft brown hair was long enough on top that it was brushed back, giving him a slightly tousled appearance. His neatly trimmed beard framed a perfect mouth. When he smiled, his lips curved higher on one side than the other. To many, it would appear as a smirk, but in the few times she'd talked to him, she knew he was quiet.

Introspective. And the smile? Not a smirk, but more of a shy grin that captured her attention from the first time he'd shared it in her presence.

Detective Pete Bolton. Of course. The man who'd put her off when she'd asked him to dinner and never called back. "Detective Bolton?" she managed to squeak out, pushing her glasses up the bridge of her nose.

"Ms. Brown," he acknowledged with a nod. His hands, still lightly grasping her arms, flexed for a moment before he let go. "I wasn't looking where I was going."

"It wasn't your fault," she assured, offering him a bright smile.

Truthfully, she liked the feel of his hands on her more than she cared to admit. Since meeting him weeks ago, he had crossed her mind far too often. Something about his serious, reserved nature intrigued her.

"Here, let me help," he said, crouching to retrieve her scattered purchases.

She dropped to her knees beside him, reaching for the toothpaste. A sharp twinge shot up her knee, but she barely registered it when she realized what Pete had in his hand.

Tampons. *Oh hell.*

She lunged, grabbing for them, but he had also picked up the package of pantyliners. Her face burned with unnecessary blush. She wasn't embarrassed but assumed he would be when he realized what he held. *Great. Of all the ways to run into him, it had to be in the pharmacy, mid-PMS, with him holding the evidence. Only me.*

He stood smoothly, holding the items in one large hand while offering the other to help her up. Without hesitation, she slipped her smaller hand into his, letting him pull her to her feet, wincing slightly at the pain in her knee.

"I'm so sorry, again," she said with a breathy chuckle,

brushing nonexistent dust off her skirt. "I'll take those from you."

He handed them over without the slightest hint of discomfort.

"I'm glad you weren't embarrassed to pick those up." She leaned closer. "Some men get really weirded out."

"No reason to," he said with a shrug. "All normal stuff."

She tilted her head, studying him. "You have a sister."

His brows rose slightly. "Uh… yeah, I do."

She grinned. "I can tell. Men with sisters tend to be more comfortable with these things. That, or men with strong mothers."

His expression shifted, something flickering in his eyes before he looked away. "No, I surely didn't have one of those."

The air changed, a subtle but noticeable tension settling between them. She had unintentionally wandered into unwelcome territory. "I'm sorry," she murmured, sincerity in her voice.

His gaze swung back to her, sharper this time. He shook his head. "You don't have to be sorry. I… just—"

"Peter Bolton?"

They both turned at the sound of the pharmacy cashier calling his name. He exhaled, giving her an almost sheepish nod. "Sorry, Ms. Brown."

"Angie, please."

A small, almost imperceptible smile touched his lips.

"I hope to see you again soon, Pete," she said, meaning it.

"Same," he replied, his voice low, before turning away.

She watched as he paid for his purchase, her gaze trailing him when he walked past her toward the door. He gave her a simple chin lift in goodbye before stepping outside.

Her shoulders sagged with a sigh. The one man who sparked something inside her was also the one who seemed utterly immune to her charms. She thought back to the first time she'd met him. She had first met Pete a few weeks ago when her friend Karen, the lead home health nurse, had called her.

"Angie? Hey, it's Karen. I have two detectives here with questions about some of the people who drive older patients around. Can they come talk to you now, or are you out in the field?"

Angie laughed and teasingly asked, "Are they single?"

She heard Karen relay the question, then return with, "They said yes. Anything else?"

"Are they hot?" Angie had chuckled.

Karen had laughed. "Yes, I can definitely say they're nice-looking."

"Well, if they're handsome, I'll make time to see them this afternoon. And if they're single, you can send them right over."

When the detectives arrived, both men had been tall, well-built, and clad in full tactical gear with the ES DTF insignia. But it wasn't the outgoing Jeremy who had captured her interest —it was the quiet, enigmatic Pete.

During the meeting, Jeremy had done most of the talking while Pete remained mostly silent, only speaking as he handed her a list of names. His voice had been steady, his words polite.

"Take your time, Ms. Brown. We know you're busy and appreciate you seeing us on short notice."

When she had teased him about being mysterious, batting her lashes dramatically, he hadn't cracked a smile—but he had blushed from the collar of his shirt to his ears.

A few days later, he had called for more information, and on a whim, she had invited him to dinner. His answer had been noncommittal. "I'll have to check my schedule."

Normally, Angie would have let it go, but Jeremy later messaged her with a simple, "Don't give up on my partner."

She sighed once again as she blinked, realizing she was staring at the door through which Pete had left and was now long gone.

"Angie?"

She blinked, turning to see Thomas waving her over to the counter. Squaring her shoulders, she pushed Pete Bolton from her mind. *For now.*

By the time Angie pulled into the narrow driveway in front of her townhouse, a deep, familiar ache had settled into her knees, radiating with each subtle movement. She gripped the steering wheel tightly for a moment, inhaling deeply before letting out a slow breath. Long shifts were always hard, but today had been particularly brutal. Her limbs felt heavy, exhaustion woven into every fiber of her body.

With a slight wince, she leaned over, gathering her belongings—a well-worn leather satchel that housed her laptop, a crinkling pharmacy bag with the latest medication refill, and her purse, its strap slipping slightly as she shifted. Pushing open the door, she eased herself out of the car, careful not to jar her stiff joints too much.

The evening breeze cooled her skin as she made her way toward her front porch, the scent of freshly cut grass and the soft, lingering aroma of someone's grilled dinner drifting on the breeze. The glow of a porch light flickered to life next door, and before she reached her steps, the familiar creak of a screen door opening caught her attention.

A warm smile spread across her face. "Hi, Grandma," she called out.

Her grandparents Dorothy and Stan stepped out of their townhouse, their presence as comforting as a well-loved quilt. Dorothy, with her short silver bob and ever-present floral cardigan, extended her arms, and Angie didn't hesitate to close the short distance and accept the warm hug.

"Angie, dear! We haven't seen you in several days!"

"I know, Grandma," Angie sighed, squeezing the older woman lightly before stepping back. "Work's been crazy, but we're almost to the weekend. I promise I won't stay late tomorrow." She turned her gaze to her grandfather, whose eyes twinkled behind his thick glasses. "And I see someone's been busy. My flower bed looks better than it did yesterday."

Stan chuckled, wiping his hands on his khaki pants. "I was already pulling weeds from my walk, so I figured, why not? It's no trouble, really. I like keeping busy and knowing how much you love your flowers."

Angie smiled, warmth blooming in her chest. It wasn't the first time her grandfather had done little things like this for her, and it certainly wouldn't be the last.

"Can we offer you some dinner?" Dorothy asked, her tone hopeful.

"Not tonight, thank you." Angie shook her head gently. "I had a big lunch, so I'm just going to have some soup and put my feet up."

Her grandmother gave her a knowing look but didn't push. "Well, you know where to find us."

With a final wave, Angie stepped a few feet to her front door and let herself inside, relishing the quiet comfort of home. She loved having her grandparents living next door. Dorothy and Stan were her dad's parents. Her mom's dad had passed a few years ago, and her maternal grandmother was in a local nursing home. Her parents lived in a house just down the street.

The scent of lavender and vanilla lingered in the air, a fragrance from the candles she often burned in the evenings. The townhouse, while older, had a charm she adored—warm wood floors, a soft sage-colored couch piled with mismatched but inviting throw pillows, and bookshelves filled with well-loved novels and little trinkets she'd collected over the years.

The living room to her right was cozy but open, leading seamlessly into a small dining area separated from the kitchen by a breakfast bar. The kitchen itself, though compact, was her sanctuary—its deep blue cabinets and cream-colored countertops gave it a homey, welcoming feel. A sliding glass door at the back of the house revealed a small patio adorned with twinkling string lights and a pair of cushioned chairs, where she often curled up with a book on warm weekend mornings.

Upstairs were three bedrooms, though one was barely large enough to be considered a room at all. She'd converted it into a multipurpose space with her yoga mat and small set of weights tucked neatly against the wall, and a corner bookshelf holding everything from workout guides to old college textbooks.

Sighing, she dropped her bags onto the entryway bench and made her way into the kitchen, pulling open the fridge with sluggish movements. The truth was, she hadn't eaten a big lunch like she'd told her grandparents. In reality, her pain had been so persistent today that she'd spent her lunch break leaning back in her chair, eyes closed, willing her body to find even a fraction of relief.

Opting for simplicity, she poured a can of soup into a pot, stirring as it warmed on the stove. She grabbed a slice of bread, quickly assembling a simple sandwich, and within minutes, she settled onto the couch with her modest meal, the heat from the soup soothing her from the inside out.

As soon as she finished, she took her medication, washing it down with the last sip of water from her glass.

The weariness in her bones urged her toward the stairs, and she didn't fight it. After making sure the doors were locked and lights dimmed, she let the promise of a hot bath lure her upstairs.

The steaming water worked its magic, easing the tension from her muscles and joints as she sank beneath the fragrant bubbles, her eyes drifting shut. By the time she crawled into bed, her body felt marginally lighter, the weight of the day slowly fading. But as she lay there, wrapped in soft sheets and darkness, her mind refused to rest.

Pete.

The enigmatic detective had been creeping into her thoughts more and more even though she barely knew him. She'd seen the surprise on his face when she invited him to dinner. There had been something else, too... a flicker of hesitation that left her second-guessing herself.

She was good at reading people. But when he said he had to check his schedule and never called back... *ugh. I thought he'd been interested... I guess I was wrong.*

Rolling onto her side, she exhaled deeply, willing herself not to overthink. Solving the mystery of Pete could wait for another day.

2

Pete climbed into his SUV but didn't start the engine. Instead, he sat, gripping the steering wheel, his gaze locked on the wide picture window of the pharmacy. Through the glass, he could see Angie standing near the counter, talking to the pharmacist. Her head tilted slightly as she listened. She faced away from him, but if the grin on the pharmacist's face was anything to go by, he knew she must be smiling. The way she interacted with people was so effortlessly warm that she tugged at something inside him.

A long sigh left his lungs as he rubbed a hand over his jaw. What the hell was it about Angie Brown that turned him into a bumbling idiot? He was a man of precision, a man of action. Words weren't usually his forte, but they had never completely failed him—until her.

His snort of amusement had him shaking his head. Jeremy would get a kick out of this. His partner never struggled to talk to anyone, whether they were suspects, fellow officers, or even strangers at the American Legion. He had that easy, affable charm, the kind that made people trust him within minutes. And women? Christ, Jeremy was a natural.

Pete, on the other hand, didn't have the gift of gab. He wasn't a man who talked just to hear his own voice. He was direct and focused. It served him well in his line of work. But with Angie? He'd been damn near useless.

His mind drifted back to the first time he'd seen her. It had been Karen, the head home health nurse, who had suggested they talk to Angie Brown. She'd made the call while they were in her office, and he remembered how she'd laughed as she relayed Angie's response.

"Well, she wants to know if you're single and good-looking," Karen had reported.

Jeremy had chuckled, but Pete had simply raised a brow, unsure of what to expect when they walked into Angie's office.

And then she had stepped out to greet them, and he'd been gobsmacked. Warm brown eyes had met his from behind the frames of purple-rimmed glasses, her gaze curious and bright. Sandy-blond hair, thick and unruly, fell in soft waves past her shoulders. She looked nothing like the buttoned-up, no-nonsense woman he'd expected.

Instead, she had been colorful. A deep purple blouse hugged her curves, its silky fabric catching the light as she moved. Her multicolored, flowing skirt swayed around her calves, giving her a kind of effortless, bohemian beauty. And he hadn't known he had a thing for women's boots, but something about her ankle boots clicking lightly along the hallway as she led them to her office made his pulse hasten.

Then there was her floral scent, delicate but not overpowering. Whatever it was, he remembered thinking he would follow that scent anywhere.

But it wasn't just her appearance that had caught his

attention. It was the way she spoke, her expressive hands moving as she described her work with the older people, her passion evident in every word. Yet what had shocked him the most was that Angie had been focused on him.

Pete had spent the entire conversation waiting for the moment she'd inevitably shift her attention to Jeremy, but it didn't happen. Her eyes lingered on Pete. She asked him the most questions. She smiled at him. Angie's interest felt genuine.

She even teased him about being a man of mystery when they left. He never felt mysterious—just a man doing his job. But her offer to "stop by anytime" had thrown him. Had she meant it? Or was she just being polite?

With a jolt, Pete snapped out of his thoughts, his eyes zeroing in on the scene inside the pharmacy.

Angie had stepped closer to the counter, her hands resting lightly on the surface as she talked to the pharmacist. The guy smiled broadly, and Pete's stomach twisted as he watched the man wink at her. From this angle, he couldn't see her reaction, but something about their easy familiarity made him wonder just how friendly they were.

Was that the kind of guy she liked? Someone neat, professional, the kind who spent his days in a climate-controlled environment rather than chasing criminals through back alleys and wading through crime scenes?

She turned, waving goodbye to the pharmacist, and Pete moved quickly. He started his engine, not wanting to look like a creep sitting in the parking lot, watching her.

As he backed out, he caught sight of her in his rearview mirror.

She was juggling her purse and the pharmacy bag, shifting her weight slightly as she walked. That was when he noticed the limp again. It was subtle, but it was there.

And when she'd knelt earlier to pick up what she'd dropped, she had winced.

The memory of her fingers wrapped around his flashed through his mind. She had accepted his help without hesitation, and that simple gesture stuck with him for some reason.

As he drove home, he found himself thinking about their brief encounter. She had babbled when he handed her the items she'd dropped, clearly embarrassed, but he hadn't lied—little fazed him. Certainly not women's hygiene products. But she had him completely off balance.

He pulled into the driveway and cut the engine, staring momentarily at the small house before climbing out. It wasn't fancy, but it was enough. He had rented the house for the past several years. He knew many people thought renting was just throwing money away, but he hadn't found a house he cared about enough to become tied to a mortgage.

His landlord considered him a perfect renter. He kept up the yard, handled the small repairs, and even split the cost on bigger ones. In return, she hadn't raised his rent.

He was proud that he'd stayed in this house since moving to the Shore years ago. His parents had never put down roots. They would stay in one place until the rent money ran out and the eviction notices stacked up. Then they snuck out in the dead of night, looking for another barely affordable place to start the cycle all over again.

Shaking off the weight of old memories, he climbed out of his SUV and stepped inside. The front door opened into a combined living room and kitchen, a space that had likely been two separate rooms once, before a former owner had knocked down a dividing wall. A hallway cut through the middle of the house, leading to two modest bedrooms and a single bathroom. Nothing fancy, but comfortable. Lived-in. A door off the kitchen led to the side deck, where he'd built a small patio and firepit—his one real indulgence. Sometimes he had friends over, but mostly, it was just him, a cold beer, and the quiet of the night.

He did little in the way of making it personal. The windows had no curtains, just basic mini blinds. His furniture leaned toward function over aesthetics. Nothing was old or broken, but there were no designer touches or decorative flourishes. He'd never really thought about it before, not until now. Not until her.

A soft thudding sound caught his attention, and he glanced down at his overweight, aging cat as she waddled toward him. He smiled indulgently. "Hey, Queenie." He held up the small paper sack from the pharmacist. "Got your meds. Give me a few minutes, and I'll fix your dinner."

He headed to his bedroom, secured his weapon, and took off his protective gear, setting it on the chair for the next day's duty. Peeling off his jeans and shirt, he stepped into the shower and hastily washed off. Dressed in sweatpants and a T-shirt, he hustled back into the kitchen.

Once there, he dissolved the pill and mixed it into Queenie's food. She ate with enthusiasm, tail flicking lazily as she chewed.

While she ate, he pulled a container of homemade chili from the fridge. Over the weekend, he'd made a big batch, freezing most of it but keeping a few servings handy for quick meals. He didn't love cooking, but he was decent at it. While growing up, he and his sister, Sally, had learned early that if they wanted a real meal, they had to make it themselves.

He heated the chili and some boxed mix cornbread,

then settled at the small kitchen table, eating while Queenie finished her dinner.

But his mind wasn't on the food. It drifted instead to her. Angie.

The few times he'd been around her, she'd worn something bright and colorful. She appeared full of energy, yet if he hadn't been trained to watch for telltale signs in suspects he questioned, Pete might have missed the thin lines bracketing her mouth when she'd knelt or when he helped her up to stand.

He wondered if she had an injury. And then he wondered who he could ask. Leaning back in his chair, he scoffed. Jeremy would never let him live it down if he went sniffing around her without actually asking her out.

Shifting his thoughts, he tried to imagine her home compared to his. Hers would be filled with cheerful colors, soft blankets, and candles that smelled like the ones he'd noticed in the gift section of Stuart's Pharmacy.

Would she take one look at his place and find it dull? *Hell, how could she not?* Then an unbidden thought hit him. *Would she go out with me and think the same?*

He shook the thought away, finishing his meal before rinsing the dishes and wiping down the counter. Queenie had wandered back into the living room, settling in for a bath in the middle of the floor. He followed, flipping on the lamp beside the sofa. The music channel hummed softly from the TV as he grabbed his book off the end table.

It was quiet. Peaceful. Just the way he liked it. Another thing he and Sally learned early was to stay quiet or suffer the consequences. No music. No TV unless their dad had it on. No playing loudly. The noise that came and came often was from his parents' fights. Their dad yelled about their mom spending too much money, and she screamed about the gambling and women he spent his on.

Even though he lived alone and could make as much noise as he wanted, he craved peace and enjoyed his time alone. But for the first time in a long time, he wondered what it would be like to have something more.

Pete tried to focus on the mystery novel in his hands, but the words blurred together, his mind stubbornly refusing to stay on the case unfolding on the pages. Instead, it wandered down a different path—one lined with golden hair, warm brown eyes, and a smile that reached places inside him he hadn't realized were lonely.

He wasn't usually a man who stumbled over his words around a woman. But even his partner, Jeremy, had picked up on how he seemed to lose the ability to form a coherent sentence whenever Angie was around. Hell, the man never let him hear the end of it.

Jeremy had been pushing him to call her, and Pete wanted to. He'd sat more than once, phone in hand, thumb hovering over her number. But he never pressed the button.

A few weeks ago, he'd had a legitimate reason to call when he needed information for a case. And then, just as easily as breathing, she asked him to dinner.

His heart had slammed against his ribs, his stomach twisting in that unfamiliar way that only she seemed to cause. He wanted to say yes. But he had some commitments he wouldn't miss. Instead of taking the chance and figuring it out, he'd hesitated, muttered something about checking his schedule, and left it at that. *God, what an idiot.*

He hadn't been able to tell from her voice if she was disappointed, if she thought he was blowing her off, or if she was glad he'd prevaricated.

When he'd told Jeremy, his partner had nearly torn his

head off, cursing him out and telling him to get off his ass, check his damn schedule, and call her back.

And now, every day that passed made it seem even more ridiculous to reach out. She'd probably moved on. But then, there was the way his entire body had come alive when he touched her. Just the simple brush of his fingers against hers when he helped her to her feet.

That wasn't normal. That wasn't just an attraction. It was something more. Something different. Something that made him feel both unsteady and completely anchored all at once.

Exhaling, Pete closed his book, setting it carefully on the coffee table. Queenie had hopped onto the couch, kneading his thigh with determined paws before curling up against him. His hand drifted absently over her soft fur, patting her rhythmically until her purring slowed into the steady rhythm of sleep.

His thoughts drifted back to the last time he'd actually been on a date. And not just a night with an out-of-town woman he'd met at a bar, something that ended in a hotel room and left him feeling empty by morning. That had been months ago. Maybe longer, considering one-night stands weren't his thing. He didn't judge those who enjoyed that type of release, but he didn't like the hollow feeling of emptiness that followed.

The last time he'd tried to date was almost two years ago. She'd lived in Virginia Beach but wanted more commitment than he could give. He'd liked her well enough but hadn't felt the pull he needed. They'd parted amicably, but he knew she'd been hurt. And that fact had hurt him in return.

His life now was work. Come home to an empty house, except for whatever foster animal the local shelter needed cared for. The kids he worked with. *Rinse and repeat.*

His sister had found love, something neither of them had ever truly understood growing up. Their parents hadn't modeled anything other than what love was not. He witnessed love with many of his friends and knew it was real. Yet it always just seemed outside his reach. *Maybe it's not for me.*

But then there was Angie. Even after he'd left her hanging, she'd greeted him at the pharmacy with warmth, without any frustration or irritation in her expression. Maybe she didn't care. Perhaps she'd never really been that interested in the first place. Or maybe... maybe it wasn't too late to ask her out.

His mind conjured an image of her—her hair catching the sunlight, her colorful clothes standing out against the dark uniforms he wore. His imaginings wandered to an old picture he once saw of a young woman in the 1960s—she was blond with flowers in her braids, bell-bottom jeans, and a bright red shirt with a peace sign printed on the front. Her head was thrown back in laughter, and he could easily see Angie in that pose.

The thought barely had time to settle before his phone rang. He glanced at the caller ID and grinned. "Hello, Jalen."

"Hey, Mr. Pete. Just checking to see if we were still on for tomorrow. Mom is starting to work an evening shift and wanted to know what my plans would be."

"Yep, we're still on. Between my vehicle and Mr. Richard's van, we can get everyone home. Tell your mom that I'll make sure you get in safely."

"Thanks, Mr. Pete. See you."

Disconnecting, Pete tossed his phone to the side and winced as it startled Queenie out of her slumber. "Sorry, ol' girl. But it's time for bed anyway." He scooped her up and placed her on the floor. Securing the house, he walked to his bedroom, grinning at Queenie, already curled on her fluffy pillow on the floor. He shucked the sweatpants, leaving the boxers.

Sliding into bed, he abandoned reading more in his book. With the covers pulled up, he lay on his back, trying to push the thought of Angie from his mind. He thought of the cases he and Jeremy were working on, the kids he would meet the next day, and even resorted to making a mental grocery list. But nothing worked. The beautiful smile of Angie Brown settled firmly in his mind and then, later, in his dreams.

3

Pete sat at his desk, facing his partner across the cluttered space of reports and half-empty coffee cups. The Eastern Shore Drug Task Force had its own section within the North Heron County Sheriff's Office. They were close to the large area where the local detectives had their desks. The setup allowed easy collaboration, especially since cases often bled into one another.

Right now, Pete was knee-deep in paperwork, his focus drifting as he slogged through the tedious report on the discovery of drugs taken from a routine traffic stop. The endless documentation was a necessary evil, but today, his mind refused to stay on task.

Across from him, Jeremy's phone buzzed, and his partner grinned before answering. "Hey, Mom. Yeah, I got the birthday cake. I can't believe you ordered it from Bess's bakery. You know she's the best in the area. She dropped it off at the station yesterday, and we destroyed it."

Pete half listened as Jeremy continued chatting, his face relaxed, his voice filled with easy warmth as he talked to both his parents. He could practically hear his partner's mom fussing over him, reminding him to eat, asking about work, probably slipping in a not-so-subtle hint about wanting to visit to meet Jeremy's new girlfriend, Cora, the local medical examiner.

Pete was happy for his friend. But he was also honest enough to admit to himself that there was a dull ache beneath his ribs, a flicker of envy curling through him like smoke.

Birthdays hadn't been a thing in the Bolton household. No cakes. No presents. No halfhearted attempts at singing Happy Birthday. Just another day on the calendar, ignored or forgotten. Except for him and Sally. They had celebrated each other, scraping together what they could, even if it was just a piece of candy they'd saved or a promise of a wish on a shooting star. Until he was fourteen—then, everything had changed.

"You ready for lunch?"

Pete blinked, surprised to see Jeremy was off his call and looking at him.

"Sorry. Mind was miles away, I guess."

Jeremy laughed. "I'd say you were. Let's hit up Stuart's." Jeremy stood, stretching his arms behind his head. "I'm dying for a burger and fries."

"I was there last night. They had a sign up for cherry and apple fried pies," Pete said, pushing back his chair. "I've been craving one ever since."

"What'd you go in for?"

Pete chuckled. "Queenie's pills."

Jeremy let out a booming laugh. "Damn, I forgot about your new pet."

"She's just the latest one." Pete shrugged as they made their way to their DTF vehicle. "Her owners passed away, and she ended up at the shelter. Older, sick—practically unadoptable."

Jeremy gave him a sidelong glance, all traces of humor gone. "You know, man, I really admire that about you. Most people wouldn't take that on."

Pete shrugged again, not needing to explain. Jeremy already knew. A few years back, over beers and a crackling fire at Pete's place, he'd opened up about his past—at least as much as he ever did. His partner understood him probably better than anyone.

The drive to Stuart's was quick, and soon, they were perched on the swivel stools at the diner's counter.

"I haven't seen you two in a while," Charlene called out from behind the grill. "Burgers and fries?"

"You know it, darlin'," Jeremy replied with a grin. "And Pete here tells me you've got fried pies."

Charlene chuckled, flipping a burger before turning to them. "Marcy's been experimenting with those, and we can't keep 'em stocked. Apple and cherry. Pick your favorite, and it's on the house."

"Apple," Jeremy said without hesitation.

"Cherry for me," Pete added.

He twisted in his seat, absently scanning the street outside. His gaze landed on the pharmacy in the back, and just like that, Angie was in his head again. Bright and colorful, her laughter still somehow echoed in his mind.

And then, like he had conjured her out of thin air, there she was. His pulse kicked up as he spotted her walking out of the pharmacy, pushing a man in a wheelchair toward a waiting van. Without thinking, Pete shot to his feet, moving toward her.

She jumped slightly at his sudden approach, but the moment her gaze met his, a slow, radiant smile spread across her face.

"Pete! Twice in two days?" Her voice was light, teasing. "How lucky can I get?"

He huffed out a quiet laugh, watching as she expertly maneuvered the van's wheelchair lift. She had things under control, but he still stepped in, offering his assistance. He noticed the faint hitch in her step, the way she favored one leg.

Still, she moved with practiced efficiency, ensuring her patient was secure before returning to him. "Thanks," she said, her eyes warm.

He wanted to linger and find an excuse to keep talking to her. But she sighed, glancing down at her phone.

"I'd love to stay and chat, but I need to get Mr. Jackson home. His regular driver couldn't come, and he was completely out of his meds."

Pete nodded toward the pharmacy. "You sure you don't need a hand? Jeremy can grab my lunch, and I can follow. Make sure you're good."

She reached out, placing her hand on his arm. His breath stilled, his skin burning where she touched him. "That's really sweet, Pete, but I just got a text. His son is home now. He has a ramp, so we'll be fine."

She squeezed his arm, lingering just long enough to make his heart thump, then stepped back, giving a little wave before climbing into the driver's seat.

He stood on the sidewalk, watching her drive away, before finally turning back inside. By the time he slid onto his stool, his plate was in front of him, and Jeremy was giving him the look.

"What?" Pete muttered.

Jeremy crossed his arms. "Please, for all that is holy, tell me you asked her out."

Pete groaned. "It wasn't the right time."

Jeremy huffed. "Man, you are clueless."

"You just started dating Cora," Pete shot back. "Don't act like you've got all the moves."

Jeremy smirked. "I have enough to know Angie's into you. And I know you're into her. So what's the damn holdup?"

Pete grumbled something unintelligible before taking a massive bite of his burger.

Jeremy just shook his head. "Unbelievable."

They let the conversation drop, focusing on their food, but Pete knew his partner wasn't wrong. The real question was, what was he going to do about it?

They'd barely finished when they got a call. Heading out, they drove about twenty minutes north on the main highway, then turned off and traveled several more miles out into dense woods at the back of an old dirt lane.

"Who owns this?" Jeremy wondered aloud.

"I don't know. The farm hasn't been worked in years. Probably, the farmer died off, and there are no relatives to give it to, or they are letting it go to seed," Pete said, looking down at their GPS. They soon came upon many county vehicles, including state police. The firemen were in hazmat suits and moving carefully in the vicinity of an old trailer.

Climbing down, they approached Elizabeth Perez and John Sullivan, two detectives for the county. "What do you have?" Jeremy asked.

"Two men were crabbing in the marsh just behind here. They unwittingly discovered an old meth lab."

"At first, the men thought the bad smell just came from the boggy mud. They had moved as close to the shore as possible and were digging for clams as well as having their crab pots away from the shore. They didn't even notice there was a trailer here right away."

"They must be new to the area," Pete said, glad he wore a mask. "The sulfur smell we sometimes get from the water is nothing like the ammonia coming from that rat trap."

Jeremy had walked over to speak to the firemen and the state police hazmat team. Pete looked up as he approached. "What did they say?"

"It doesn't look like anybody has been out here for ages," Jeremy reported.

"I wonder if it's safe enough for us to check for prints?"

John spoke up. "I already asked about that. The chief will let me and two of our deputies inside to see if we can snag any fingerprints or anything else that would help discern who might have been out here."

Pete nodded. "Let us know what you need."

Elizabeth said, "I hate to say it, but you know more about this than I do."

"What were they using?" Pete asked.

"There are still plastic cat litter containers inside and scattered behind the trailer. It's an off-brand, so I'm unsure who carries it around here."

Jeremy exhaled, shaking his head. "Cat litter means they were likely using the ammonia method. We'll want to check for bottles with tubing, camping fuel, cold packs, and lithium batteries—common household stuff but deadly when put together."

John glanced at the hazmat team, who were still scanning the site. "Yeah, and if they were using the red phosphorus method, we need to see if there's any iodine or matchbooks around. If they cooked inside, the walls are probably coated in residue. We'll swab and test for methamphetamine, but I bet hazmat's already getting high readings from their sensors."

Elizabeth frowned. "Best case, we're dealing with a dump site. Worst case, this was an active lab, and they left in a hurry."

Pete looked toward the rotting trailer, its windows coated in a sickly yellow film. "You'll need to find out where they got their supplies. Hardware stores, farm supply places—hell, even gas stations sell some of this stuff. If someone bought in bulk, we might get a lead."

Jeremy nodded. "I'll reach out to the local stores, see if anyone's bought a shit ton of pseudoephedrine or drain cleaner lately."

John looked toward the evidence team, who had just finished setting up a collection station near the entrance. "We should also check the ground for burn pits. They probably ditched the used lithium strips somewhere close. And if they were shaking bottles instead of cooking over heat, they could have dumped them in the water."

Jeremy cursed under his breath. "Take care and warn the others. Have some deputies check the marsh for discarded bottles, but treat them carefully. They might explode if you handle 'em wrong."

"Fuck," John said grimly.

One of the deputies approached, holding up a clear evidence bag. Inside was a scorched, rusted canister. "Found this near the back. Could be an old anhydrous tank."

Jeremy took a step back. "Shit. That means they were pulling ammonia from fertilizer. We need to see if any local farms had thefts."

Pete turned to Elizabeth. "See if you can cross-check recent reports. Anhydrous ammonia is too dangerous for some backwoods cook to be hauling in bulk. If someone stole it, it's gotta be on record."

Elizabeth nodded, already pulling out her phone.

Having gathered all they could at the site, Pete and Jeremy returned to the station. Even with Elizabeth and John taking charge, Pete and Jeremy would stay active in the case, especially if it seemed as though the meth cookers had just moved to a new location.

4

Angie sighed as she glanced at the clock on the wall, the steady ticking a reminder of how endless this day felt. The morning had been swallowed by a mountain of paperwork, including budget reports, funding allocations, and discussions, that left her with a throbbing headache. As the director of the Eastern Shore Area Agency on Aging, she knew these meetings were necessary, but that didn't make them any less draining.

She leaned forward at the conference table, smoothing her hands over a stack of documents. "I want to get something in the local newspaper that clearly outlines what we do," she said, her voice firm despite the exhaustion creeping in. "Public awareness is key to ensuring we have enough volunteers and community assistance."

"I can handle that," Shelby, one of their newest hires, chimed in. "I'll draft a list of our services and include ways the public can get involved."

Charlotte, a seasoned director with silver-streaked hair and a sharp mind, nodded in approval. "Excellent idea. We used to do this annually, but considering the current financial climate, we might need to do it twice a year."

"I agree," Angie said, flipping open the annual report she had been compiling. "When you see it all on paper, it's astounding what we accomplish. These figures will go to the County Board of Supervisors and then to the State Board. Take a look at some of these numbers."

She passed the reports around, and a low whistle came from Sam, another executive member. "Meals on Wheels—almost twenty-seven thousand meals served last year. Nearly a thousand vouchers for seniors to use at the farmers' market."

Diane, one of the nurses leading their personal care program, tapped a finger on the report. "And our seven CNAs provided nearly seven thousand hours of in-home care."

The discussion continued, but Angie's mind drifted momentarily. She was proud of their work and proud of her team, but there was always more to do. When the meeting finally wrapped up, she felt a flicker of relief.

Shelby walked with her toward their offices. "I'm heading to the Careway Assisted Living home to check on two clients."

"Tell Belle Simmons I said hello, and remind her she still owes me lunch," Angie joked. "Or maybe I owe her lunch... I can't remember!"

Shelby laughed before they parted ways. "I'll also check on your grandmother while I'm there."

Angie smiled her thanks. In her office, she packed up quickly, tucking her laptop into her satchel before heading down the hall to the equipment storage room. She checked out a wheelchair, rolling it smoothly toward her car. The next stop was Joe's Diner, where Josephine greeted her at the door with a warm smile and three bags of prepared meals.

"Oh, thank you!" Angie gushed, taking the bags from her.

Josephine waved her off. "No thanks necessary. It's the least we can do."

Her next delivery took her to a quiet trailer park where the late afternoon sun cast a light over a freshly built wheelchair ramp. The American Legion volunteers donated the supplies and worked tirelessly to ensure the ramp blended seamlessly with the home. They even planted flowers along the edge. She knocked on the door, and a round-faced woman quickly opened it with a welcoming smile.

"Come in! Dad's been waiting on you."

Angie stepped inside, the scent of fresh-brewed coffee filling the cozy space. The older man in the recliner looked up, his eyes lighting up as they fell on the wheelchair she brought.

"Oh, what have you brought me, Ms. Angie?" he asked, grinning wide.

"It's not brand new, but it'll make life easier for you and your daughter," she said warmly. "Trips to the doctor, strolls through the neighborhood—you name it."

"And what's in those bags?" he asked, grinning.

"I stopped at Joe's Diner for lunch and thought I'd bring some for you two as well."

"Oh my word," his daughter exclaimed. "I was just fixin' to make dad a sandwich."

The three sat at his table and enjoyed their BLT sandwiches, piled high with bacon and no skimping on the tomatoes. As they finished, his daughter patted his shoulder. "I promised him that if he got a wheelchair, I'd take him across the bridge to a shopping center in Virginia Beach."

Angie laughed, charmed by the twinkle in his eyes. "Be sure to send me a picture when you do."

After finishing her deliveries, she returned to the office just long enough to grab the keys to one of the ESAAA vans. With the help of Carina, a nursing assistant, she made the rounds to pick up five seniors, each eager for their outing to the YMCA. Some used canes, others walkers, but all shared the same excitement.

At the YMCA, she guided them inside, ensuring everyone was signed in before a cheerful volunteer led them to the class space. The room was bright and welcoming, filled with seniors settling into chairs for a yoga session. Angie helped her group find their spots before sinking into a chair herself.

"Oh, are you joining us?" Rosetta, a bespectacled woman with a sharp wit, asked with a teasing smile.

Angie nodded. "I figure I could use some joint loosening myself."

George, seated beside Rosetta, chuckled. "I was never into exercise when I was younger. Now I look back and wonder why on earth I didn't take better care of myself."

"I remind myself of that every day," Angie replied, stretching her arms.

The session flew by, and by the end of it, Angie's muscles were pleasantly warm. She helped the seniors gather their things, watching as they laughed and chatted on their way to retrieve their walkers and canes. There was no rush—she enjoyed these moments of connection. But as she lingered, something unexpected happened.

Her mind wandered, and Pete's name drifted into her thoughts. It wasn't the first time that had happened lately.

And that thought, more than anything, left a quiet ache she wasn't sure what to do with.

5

Pete stepped into the Baytown YMCA, the familiar scent of rubber mats, sweat, and faintly lingering chlorine from the pool wrapping around him. The large facility buzzed with energy—basketballs thudding against the polished hardwood in the gym, sneakers squeaking against the floors, and the low hum of conversation from various members weaving through the air.

Just inside the lobby, a group of his boys hovered near the front desk, their energy barely contained as they shifted restlessly, checking their phones or bouncing on the balls of their feet.

"Sorry I'm a little late, guys," Pete called, lifting a hand in greeting as he strode toward them. He threw a nod to the man behind the registration desk before scanning his group, doing a quick headcount. One of the boys' moms worked for the county, driving one of the buses. She would drop the boys off and then, along with a friend, Richard, they would get them back to their apartment building at the end of their time.

"Everyone's here except Mike," Jalen reported, his voice

carrying over the din. "He came with us but went to the bathroom—"

"I'm here!" came a hurried voice. Mike jogged up, slightly out of breath, his sneakers skidding a bit on the tiled floor as he rejoined the group. At eleven, he and Darius were the youngest of the bunch, just barely making the age cutoff for Pete's mentorship program.

Pete grinned. "Alright, guys... remember what we talked about last week?"

Caleb, one of the older boys at thirteen, straightened slightly. "Treat the equipment and the other people using the space with respect."

Pete nodded approvingly. "That's right. We're here to work, talk, and enjoy our time together. What we're not here to do is be a distraction or make the staff or members feel like they have to manage us. Everyone in this building has paid for their membership, and they deserve to use the facilities without dealing with nonsense. Understood?"

A chorus of nods and murmured agreements followed, just as Richard jogged into the lobby, his face lined with urgency. "Sorry, sorry! One of the teachers couldn't get her car to start, so I had to jump her."

A couple of the boys snickered, and Pete immediately caught the glint of mischief in their expressions. He exhaled, lifting his brows.

"Boys, cut it out. We may be near a locker room, but we're not going to entertain locker room mentality."

That was all it took. Their smirks faded, and their postures adjusted slightly, shoulders squaring as they redirected their focus. Pete had worked hard to build a sense of discipline and respect in these young men—something too many of them weren't naturally given in their daily environments.

With that, they moved into the main gym area, where

the scent of perspiration mixed with the steady hum of treadmills and clanking machines. Pete had found that starting with physical activity worked best. Some of these boys struggled in school, and their bodies brimmed with restless energy after sitting in classrooms all day. Giving them a chance to move, exert themselves, and work through some of that tension helped them focus later when they sat down for homework.

By now, they knew the routine. They spread out, instinctively scanning for available equipment rather than monopolizing one area. Pete had drilled into them the importance of gym etiquette—waiting their turn, using the machines properly, wiping them down after use, and not crowding out the paying members.

While Richard took a few of the boys to the side for a body-weight circuit, Pete observed as several others moved toward the free weights. He stepped in to spot where needed, ensuring their forms were correct. These kids ranged in age from eleven to thirteen, and many had never been in a structured fitness environment before Pete started working with them six months ago.

It had all started with Rasheem. Nearly a year ago, Pete had arrested a gang member who had begun running drugs. On the fringes of that world was an eleven-year-old boy just hanging around. Rasheem wasn't in yet, but Pete knew the signs, and without intervention, it was only a matter of time before he got pulled into something he couldn't get out of.

Pete had visited Rasheem, spoken to his mother, and found her more than willing for someone to take an interest in her son. That had been the beginning. As Pete spent more time with Rasheem, he realized there had to be more boys like him—kids who needed guidance and someone to show them another path.

Richard Pendleton had been an easy recruit for another male role model. Pete had met him at an American Legion meeting and, upon learning he was a middle school teacher, floated the idea of starting a mentorship program. Richard jumped at it.

"I know I have a huge influence over my students," Richard once told him. "But with twenty-five kids in each class, six periods a day, there's only so much of me to go around."

Together, they'd worked with the middle school's counselor to identify kids who would thrive in the program. Pete had met with each of them and their parents or guardians, ensuring everyone was on board. Once a week, the bus dropped them off at the YMCA, where Pete and Richard met with them. The first half hour was all movement—lifting weights, running if the weather was nice, or shooting hoops on the outdoor court. They headed to the locker room for quick showers. Pete and Richard monitored the time, also ensuring the boys knew about personal hygiene.

Then came academics, where they reviewed homework. The third part of their time together was spent in conversation—about life, about dreams, about anything the boys wanted to bring up. They asked about Richard's time in the military, about Pete's work on the Drug Task Force, about what it meant to be a man who made a difference.

As the gym session and showers wrapped up, the boys gathered their bags, still buzzing with the energy of their workout as they filed toward the conference room for the next part of the afternoon. That was when Pete heard a woman's laugh. It sounded so familiar that it made his chest tighten before he even turned around.

And sure enough, when he did, his hunch was right.

There was Angie, her bright yellow blouse flowing over a pair of light blue leggings. Her thick hair, the color of sand on a sunny day, was pulled into a high ponytail, tied back with a multicolored bandanna. Bracelets jingled with every step. She moved alongside a group of older adults, her steps slow to match their pace. A warm smile lit her face as she spoke to the woman in scrubs beside her.

Without thinking, Pete called out, "Angie!"

She turned, surprise flashing across her face. For a second, Pete regretted the sudden ambush—he hadn't meant to put her on the spot. But then, her gaze found his, and her smile widened, radiating warmth that rivaled even the vibrant colors she wore.

Angie was still smiling at Pete as she turned slightly, checking on one of the seniors she was assisting. The woman was steady on her feet, giving Angie a reassuring nod, but Angie still placed a gentle hand on her elbow before shifting her attention back to Pete.

Realizing she was clearly working, he hesitated. "I can see you're busy—"

"Yes, but what a nice surprise to run into you here!"

The fluorescent lighting of the YMCA hallway cast a harsh light, but it still managed to create a golden glow around her, catching the wavy tendrils of blond hair that had slipped free from her ponytail. They floated about her face like a halo, and her cheeks were slightly flushed. Had she been exercising, too? He felt an odd twist in his stomach at the thought, imagining her moving through stretches, laughter in her eyes, and wishing he could have been close to her.

Determined not to waste this moment, he cleared his throat. "I owe you an apology. I didn't get back to you about having dinner. Not because I didn't want to, but because I... I..." The words faltered as his brain scrambled for an excuse. He sure as hell wasn't about to admit he'd chickened out.

She waved a hand, her fingers moving gracefully through the air. "It's fine, Pete."

"Ms. Angie," Carina, the woman in scrubs, interrupted. "Take your time. I'll get everyone settled in the van."

Grateful for the reprieve, he nodded at Carina, but Angie looked momentarily torn as she glanced at the group of seniors grinning at her with open curiosity. Her blush deepened. "Thank you, Carina. I'll be right out, I promise."

Carina simply waved her off and then, to Pete's amusement, winked at him before ushering their group toward the front doors. Now that they were alone in the hallway, he breathed a little easier without an audience.

"I won't keep you, Angie," he said, his voice softer now. "But I really would like to take you to dinner."

She cocked her head to the side, lifting her chin slightly to hold his gaze. She had an expression he couldn't define, but her hesitation gave him pause. Finally, she said, "Please don't feel that you need to extend an invitation—"

"No," he rushed to interrupt whatever she was getting ready to say. "I want to take you to dinner. I'm just embarrassed that I didn't do this… ask you earlier."

"Really?" Uncertainty still filled her eyes.

"Yes. That is, if you're still interested," he added.

She laughed gently. "Of course I am."

Now it was his turn to express doubt. "Really?" He felt his ears burn at the sound of his less-than-suave attempt to secure a date with her.

"Yes. Why wouldn't I? After all, I asked you first."

"Okay." He smiled. He almost said he would call to set up the time and place, then realized that would sound too much like the last time.

"Mr. Pete!" Rasheem's voice rang out as he burst

through a nearby doorway, grinning widely. "Are you going to help me with my math?"

Pete opened his mouth to respond, but Rasheem's gaze swung to Angie, and the boy's eyes widened comically. "Actually, come to think about it, I don't have any math homework, so you can… um… don't hurry on my account… um… you can keep talking… to… um… you know… her."

The boy turned on his heel and practically ran back into the room, and a moment later, the muffled sounds of snickering and whispered words filtered into the hallway. Pete chuckled, shaking his head.

"It seems like you're working, too."

"And I have my youth group once a week."

She lifted a shoulder in an easy shrug. "I have my group of older folks one evening a week."

For a beat, they stood there, sharing something that felt just a little deeper than small talk. He reached behind his neck, rubbing at the tension there, wishing he could think of something smooth or clever to say. Instead, he said, "Good. That's nice."

Angie laughed, her amusement bubbling over in a way that made his stomach tighten. Then, as if she sensed his discomfort, she reached out, her fingertips lightly pressing against his forearm. The warmth of her touch shot through him like a live wire.

"At least, since we now know that we have something happening on the same night each week, you can check your schedule and let me know if or when you'd—"

"Do you trust me to call this time?" he asked.

"Absolutely," she declared with surety. "Because now you know that I'll be waiting by the phone." She turned to walk toward the lobby.

"How about tomorrow?" The words tumbled out of his mouth before he could stop them.

She stilled and turned back toward him, her smile wide. She blinked, her chin jerking back slightly. "Tomorrow?" she squeaked.

His heart fell. "Oh, it's Friday night. You probably have plans."

"No, I don't have any plans. And I would love to take you up on a dinner invitation for tomorrow night."

Relief flooded his body so fast he was surprised he remained standing. "That's perfect, Angie. Good. Yeah, that's perfect."

She laughed again, and he swore it was the best sound he'd ever heard. "Well, since we have a date, how about a time and place?"

He hadn't even thought that far. It should be someplace nice. Maybe somewhere she could get a glass of wine. Wasn't there a new Italian place in Baytown?

"Do you like barbecue?" she asked, breaking through his inner debate.

His head jerked slightly in surprise. "Absolutely."

"How about the barbecue place just outside Baytown on the highway? I've only been there once, but I really liked it. It's Friday night, so it might get a little loud, but the food is good, and we can't beat barbecue and beer."

His brain short-circuited. Barbecue and beer... perfect. She had just made this the easiest first date ever. He nodded. "Can I pick you up?"

She tilted her head slightly, considering. "Tell you what, Pete. I think we're going to have a great time. But for a first date, I want to put you at ease. I'll meet you there, and if we have a good time, we'll make more plans. And if one of us doesn't feel a connection, then we don't have an awkward drive home."

She leaned in just a fraction closer, her smile now giving her an impish look. "But I have a feeling we'll have a fabulous time."

His heart thudded in response, a bead of sweat slipping down his back. He wanted to argue, to insist on picking her up, but her logic was sound. And right now, he'd agree to anything just to make sure he didn't screw this up.

"Okay, how about six o'clock?"

"I'll be there. And if something happens and you can't make it, you've got my number."

Thinking quickly, he pulled out his phone, found her number, and texted her. "There. Now you have my number, too."

She squeezed his arm lightly, her smile still brightening the hallway. "I'll see you tomorrow."

His chest felt lighter than it had in a long time.

With that, she turned and hurried toward the exit, and he watched her go. With the faster pace, a slight limp was still evident. He had no idea why, but all he could focus on was the fact that tomorrow night, she wouldn't be walking away from him.

She'd be walking toward him. And he was determined that she wouldn't regret saying yes.

6

"That was a mighty fine-looking man you were talking to," Carina said, her voice carrying a teasing lilt.

Angie laughed, shaking her head. She should have known she wouldn't be able to rejoin the group at their Eastern Shore Area Agency on Aging van without someone already stirring up gossip.

"Yes, I have to admit, he is definitely fine-looking," she agreed, unable to hide the smile tugging at her lips.

"When are you going out?"

Angie turned, narrowing her eyes playfully at Rosetta. "How do you know we're going out?"

Rosetta snorted. "It's not like you to shy away from a question."

Rolling her eyes, Angie twisted in her seat, glancing at the six pairs of eyes watching her expectantly. Each face was split into a wide, knowing grin.

With a sigh, she relented. "We're going out tomorrow night."

Carina, driving the van, grinned. "And before you ask— yes, he's employed. He's a detective."

"Oh, how nice!" George said with a pleased nod.

"We actually just met recently," Angie explained, tucking her purse against her lap. "He's kind of quiet, and I wasn't sure he was interested in asking me out. To be honest..." She exhaled a small laugh. "I asked him out first. But he never called me back, so I figured nothing would happen."

Hannah, sitting closest to her, leaned in, fiddling with her hearing aid. "You know... some men are very confident with themselves and don't have to talk a lot to make their point. They have nothing to prove to anyone, so they are more introspective."

Angie's shoulders relaxed as she stared at Hannah. "You're right." She smiled, then leaned over and kissed Hannah's cheek.

Hannah chuckled. "And you just happened to run into him this evening?"

"Yes! It was a complete surprise. He seemed to be there with some young people."

"Oh, a nice man with a good job, and he works with young people?" Marty nodded approvingly. "I like him already."

Angie chuckled, shaking her head as they pulled up to the Careway Senior Apartment building. Once an old motor lodge, it had been repurposed into cozy one-story apartments for seniors. The building wrapped around a patchy garden in a U-shape, its center full of benches and bird feeders. Once purchased by the company running Careway Assisted Living and specializing in senior housing, it had undergone a much-needed refresh. The open-concept design made it easier for residents with walkers or wheelchairs, and there were even grants available to help those who needed assistance with rent.

It wasn't directly associated with ESAAA, but given the

residents, Angie was well-acquainted with just about everyone who lived there.

Tonight's group had all agreed to participate in a chair yoga class for seniors at the YMCA, on the condition that they had some assistance getting there. It was only one night a week, and Angie had been thrilled to help. She wasn't always able to be the one who accompanied them, but when she did, she had to admit that easy yoga felt great on her joints.

After helping them to their apartments, she and Carina returned the ESAAA van, parking it in the parking lot. Walking to their cars, they waved goodbye before parting ways.

By the time Angie arrived home, she felt a pleasant weariness settle into her limbs, but before heading inside, she detoured to her grandparents' door. The second she knocked, the door swung open. "Hey, Grandma. Grandpa. Just wanted to let you know I was home."

Dorothy beamed, stepping aside to let her in. "How was yoga?" She settled back onto the sofa while Stan muted the TV program they'd been watching.

"It was good," Angie said, stepping into the cozy living room. "I had six who went, and I know you would like it." She shot her grandfather a grin. "Marty and George were there, so we definitely need more men."

Stan chuckled, shaking his head. "Well, you might talk me into it. But if not, you've got your grandmother convinced."

Dorothy stood, moving toward the kitchen. "Do you want something to eat? I saved you a piece of my chocolate pecan pie."

Angie's smile widened. "Mom sent over some lasagna, and that would be perfect."

With a pleased nod, her grandmother retrieved the pie

plate, the wedge of chocolatey, nutty goodness wrapped neatly in plastic. Handing it over, she gave Angie a searching look.

"Are you doing okay, sweetie?"

Angie softened, balancing the plate in her hands. "I'm fine, Grandma. Really." Leaning in, she whispered, "I have a date tomorrow night."

Dorothy's eyes twinkled. "Oh, do tell."

Laughing, Angie backed toward the door. "It's with a detective in the county. We've met a few times professionally, and he asked me to dinner." She crinkled her nose. "Well… in all honesty, I asked him first. But whatever— we're finally connecting."

Her grandmother smirked. "Well, if I don't see you tomorrow, have a good time. And come over Saturday and tell me everything."

"You know I will."

Blowing a kiss to both of them, she headed to her townhouse. Once inside, she grabbed a fork and sat at the kitchen counter, sighing in delight as she took the first bite of pie. Perfection. Greedily gobbling the rest of the slice, she groaned in delight. After rinsing the dish, she made her way upstairs, slipping into her nightly routine, but her mind refused to settle.

She was excited about this date. *Oh God, what if we end up hating each other?* The more she thought about it, the less likely it seemed. She was pretty good at reading people, and everything she'd surmised about Pete made her smile.

She couldn't imagine the kind of mental weight he carried —walking into work every day, facing dangers that could appear at any moment. She liked that he was quieter, more introspective. The last couple of men she'd gone out with had been so absorbed in themselves, she'd barely gotten a word in.

She ran a warm bath, letting the delicate scent of bath oil ease the last bit of tension from her muscles.

Tomorrow was Friday. As she leaned her head back against the tub, she mentally reviewed what she needed to get done at work. Thankfully, it wasn't an overly busy day. That meant she'd have plenty of time to get home and prepare for her date.

By the time she crawled into bed and turned out the light, anticipation continued to move through her. She drifted off to sleep with a soft smile, excitement stirring deep in her chest.

———

Angie prided herself on being punctual, but as she pulled into the parking lot of Roy's Barbecue, a pang of guilt twisted in her stomach. She glanced at the time glowing on her dashboard and winced. Two minutes late. It was hardly a crime, but still—she didn't want Pete to think she didn't care enough to be on time.

She threw open her car door and stepped out, the warm evening air wrapping around her as she smoothed the fabric of her ankle-length skirt. The scent of smoked meats and tangy sauce drifted through the air, teasing her appetite as she hurried toward the entrance. Her steps faltered when she saw the long line snaking out the door. Great.

Pulling out her phone, she fired off a quick text. **I'm here! Just waiting in line to get in.**

She had barely slipped her phone back into her purse when a voice called over the crowd. "Angie Brown!"

She blinked and glanced up. "That's me!" Angie lifted her hand, feeling the weight of curious eyes on her. The hostess stood just inside the doorway, scanning the line, her gaze landing on Angie with an inviting smile.

"Your party is already inside and waiting. Come on through."

Angie hesitated only a second before weaving past the waiting diners, offering a few polite smiles as she slipped through the entrance. Hopefully, no one thought she was getting special treatment—though, if she was being honest, she wasn't about to complain.

And then she saw him. Pete stood near the hostess station, hands in his pockets, looking relaxed yet alert, like he had been watching for her. The second their eyes met, his face broke into a slow, easy smile, one that sent warmth unfurling through her. His gaze swept over her, head to toe and back again, something unreadable flickering in his expression before he stepped forward.

Without a word, he reached for her hand, lacing his fingers through hers in a way that felt natural even though they were still getting to know each other. The heat of his palm and the quiet assurance in the way he held on sent a pleasant hum through her senses.

"Come on," he murmured, leaning in slightly as he guided her through the crowd. He stayed close, his presence a protective barrier against the bustle of the restaurant, keeping anyone from jostling her.

They reached a cozy corner table, away from the noise but close enough to feel the lively atmosphere. She slipped into her seat, glancing around before her gaze landed back on him.

"Oh wow," she breathed, eyes wide with surprise. "How did you score this table?"

Pete chuckled, resting his forearms on the table as he grinned. "I might have pulled a few strings. Got here early, checked in, and—turns out—a server here is the son of a deputy I work with. I coached the kid in baseball a few years ago, so I asked if he could hook me up with a good table for my date." He tilted his head slightly, watching her reaction. "This one just happened to be opening up."

Angie laughed, shaking her head in admiration. "That is some serious dedication. But I have to say, I approve."

"Good." His smile softened. "Perfect for you."

Before she could reply, a young man stopped at their table to take their drink orders. Pete introduced him as their server, and once their drinks were settled, they turned their attention to the menu.

Angie groaned, pressing a hand to her stomach as she skimmed the options. "I want everything."

The server grinned. "Then you might want to go with the sampler platter—it's got chicken, pork, and beef barbecue."

Her eyes lit up. "Done!" She handed over her menu without hesitation.

Pete smirked and passed his over as well. "Make it two."

As the server walked away, Pete lifted his beer, tipping it slightly toward her in a silent toast. Angie clinked her glass against his, meeting his gaze.

"To an amazing first date," she said, smiling. "With barbecue, beer, and getting to know each other."

Pete studied her for a moment, his expression unreadable before he took a slow sip of his beer. Setting his glass down, he murmured, "Like I said. Perfect."

Her breath caught in her throat as she worked to steady her breathing. So far, he was right… this was perfect.

7

Pete immediately realized why he'd been nervous about this date. It was because he genuinely liked what he already knew about Angie, and he really wanted the night to go well.

There was always that underlying tension when dating someone you might run into professionally or even at the grocery store. A bad date meant awkward encounters. That was one reason he'd been relieved when his last relationship hadn't been with someone from the Shore. When it ended, it ended cleanly. No unexpected run-ins or lingering awkwardness.

But as he stared at Angie, watching the way her lips curved into an easy smile, something settled in him. He wasn't nervous anymore. She had an ease about her, a quiet confidence, as though she wasn't trying to impress him or put on any kind of act. Angie was simply herself. And damn, if that wasn't incredibly sexy.

"Have you been on the Shore for long?" she asked, tilting her head slightly.

Shaking his head, he replied, "No. I didn't grow up here. I'm from Newport News."

"Oh, that's not far. I'm from Williamsburg, but I've been out here for about five years."

"I remember visiting Colonial Williamsburg once as a teenager," he said. "It was on a senior trip. I'm embarrassed to admit that at the time, I wasn't all that interested in it. But I must've paid attention because I still remember being impressed with the restored buildings."

Her eyes lit up. "I love Colonial Williamsburg! I was such a history nerd." She grinned, shaking her head. "I haven't been back in years... well, I mean, not to the historic district. But I still visit Williamsburg because my brother and his family live there."

She lifted her beer, taking a sip, and when she pulled the bottle away, her tongue darted out to catch a stray drop lingering on her bottom lip.

Pete's breath hitched. His gaze locked onto her mouth, the soft sweep of her tongue, the slight glisten of moisture against her lip. For a second, he almost missed that she was still speaking.

"Now that I think about it, I need to make a trip back to the colonial area next time I visit."

He wanted to ask about her family, wanted to know everything, but he hesitated. If she didn't have a great home life, he'd have just led them into an awkward conversation. And if she did have a good relationship with her family, that meant she'd likely turn the question back on him.

And his family? Not exactly something he wanted to get into over barbecue. Before he could figure out how to navigate that landmine, their food arrived, and Angie's eyes widened as the server set down the massive platter in front of her.

"Oh my God!" she gasped, staring at the overflowing plate of barbecue. "I thought we'd get tiny portions of pork, chicken, and brisket. I had no idea it was this much food!"

Pete chuckled. "Dig in and enjoy. If you can't eat it all, at least you know it'll make for some great leftovers."

"You're right about that." She picked up her fork, eyeing the platter with delight. "Barbecue is always just as good the next day."

They fell into a comfortable silence as they ate, and Pete couldn't help but appreciate how Angie really dove into her meal—no tiny, polite bites just to impress him. She took full, satisfied forkfuls, humming in appreciation after the first taste.

And damn if those little sounds didn't make his brain go in a completely inappropriate direction. He forced himself to focus on his own plate, pushing away thoughts of what else might make her moan like that.

He was nearly finished with his meal when she slowed down, leaning back in her chair with a contented sigh. "I have to tell my grandparents about this place. My grandfather loves a good barbecue, and I don't think he's ever been here."

Her comment caught him off guard. He'd been curious about her family but hadn't considered the possibility of her grandparents still being in the picture.

Before he could stop himself, he asked, "Do they live out here on the Shore?"

"Oh yes," she said, laughing. "In fact, they live in the townhouse next to mine."

His eyes widened.

She grinned at his reaction. "It's my dad's parents. They lived in Maryland, but when I moved here, they decided they wanted to be closer. I was renting a townhouse duplex at the time, and the other side was available. They sold their house and moved in."

He hesitated, now really wanting to know more but still unsure if he should ask.

As if reading his mind, she smirked. "I can tell you're dying to ask if it's a pain having my grandparents as my neighbors." She shook her head, her eyes full of warmth. "And I can honestly say—not at all. They're such cool people, and having them close means I never have to worry about them. Plus, my parents live just down the street."

Pete's head jerked back slightly. "Your parents live here, too?"

"Yep." She popped the "p," clearly amused by his reaction. "And it's all good. I'm close to my parents and my grandparents." Her expression softened. "My mom's dad passed away several years ago, and my grandmother needed a lot of care. Once I saw how great the Careway Assisted Living facility was, we moved her in. I don't know if you know Belle Simmons, but she's the head nurse administrator. They take such good care of my grandmother."

"I do know Belle. Her husband is a detective I work with occasionally."

"Oh, that's right! I forgot about that." She shook her head. "That's one thing about the Shore, isn't it? It doesn't take long before you start making connections."

By the time they finished most of their food, the restaurant had gotten even louder with the Friday night crowd. When the server stopped by, Angie asked for a to-go box.

Pete found himself stalling, not wanting the date to end. If people weren't waiting for tables, he would've suggested ordering another beer. But before he could figure out what to do, Angie leaned forward, her fingers toying with the edge of her napkin.

"I feel like we were just starting to really get to know each other." She held his gaze. "I hate for this to end."

The breath he'd been holding rushed out. He grinned. "I was just thinking the same thing."

Her lips curved. "Then... how about you follow me home? We can have another beer there. No noise, no crowd."

His smile turned slow, easy. "I'd love that, Angie."

The server returned, setting the to-go box in front of her. Pete watched as she carefully boxed up the extra food, biting her lip in thought.

"You're gonna have enough for another meal," Pete said.

"That's true if it was just for me." She scrunched her nose. "But I was going to take this to my grandparents. Now I'm realizing it's not enough for both of them."

Pete signaled the server. "Add another triple barbecue meal for takeout. Put it on my bill."

The server grinned. "Yes, sir."

Angie's mouth dropped open. "Pete, please let me—"

"Nope." He smirked. "Don't even suggest it. My treat."

Her lips pressed together, but she didn't argue. Instead, she just shook her head, her expression softening. "That's really sweet of you."

He shrugged, but the look she gave him made him feel ten feet tall. When they walked out, he placed a hand lightly on her back, guiding her toward the door. The drive to her townhouse was short, but Pete found himself appreciating the extra minutes to process how much he liked being around Angie. It had been a long time since he'd felt this way on a first date—comfortable, intrigued, hopeful.

He followed her car through the quiet, tree-lined neighborhood, pulling into a spot in front of her home. The townhouse was charming, just like her—brick exterior, a welcoming front porch with a cozy-looking swing, and warm light glowing from the windows.

She parked and slid out of her vehicle with a smile, giving him a little wave as he stepped out of his own SUV.

"Come on in," she said, leading the way to the door. "I can put the leftovers in the refrigerator and get us another beer."

He followed her inside, taking in the space as she disappeared into the kitchen. The place felt like her. It wasn't just a house—it was a home.

A woven throw blanket was draped over the arm of the sofa, and a book lay open on the side table as if she'd been reading it before she left for work. The scent of something light and floral lingered in the air, barely noticeable, but enough to make him think of her.

She reappeared a moment later, two bottles in hand.

"Here we go," she said, offering him one as she kicked off her shoes. "Make yourself comfortable."

He settled onto the sofa, and she curled up beside him, tucking her feet underneath her.

"This is nice," he murmured, glancing around again.

Her brows lifted. "You like my place?"

He took a sip of his beer, then nodded. "Yeah. It looks like you. Feels like a home."

Her smile softened as she looked around, as if seeing it through his eyes for the first time. "Thanks. It is home. I've lived here long enough now that I can't imagine being anywhere else."

He let his gaze linger on her. Her hair was slightly tousled from the night air, her lip gloss gone after the meal, and her eyes held a touch of fatigue, but she was beautiful. Even more so now, sitting here, relaxed in her space, with a beer in hand and an easy smile on her lips.

"So," she said, twisting slightly to face him. "Honest thoughts on the date so far?"

He huffed out a short laugh. "You really just jump in and go for the goal right away, don't you?"

Her lips twitched. "Would you rather I dance around it?"

"Not at all." He let his arm drape across the back of the sofa, his fingers brushing lightly against her shoulder. "Since you asked—yeah, I'm enjoying myself. A lot."

Her eyes searched his face, something quiet and unreadable flickering in their depths. Then she smiled again. "Good. Me too."

For a moment, they just sat there, the hum of the refrigerator in the background, the faint tick of a clock on the wall. The silence was comfortable. Pete had been on enough dates to know this feeling didn't come often. And if he had his way, tonight wouldn't be the last time he sat beside Angie, in this home that already felt like one he could come to know.

8

_____

Angie couldn't believe how well the date was going.

Under normal circumstances, she never would have invited a first date to her house. But something about Pete had her throwing her usual rules out the window. Maybe it was his quiet confidence, the way he didn't try too hard but still made her feel like he genuinely wanted to be there. Or perhaps it was simply that she trusted him. And when she had told him she didn't want the night to end, she'd meant it.

From the moment she had spotted him at the restaurant, her gaze had taken him in, and she was just as mesmerized as when she'd first seen him in uniform. Tonight, he wore dark jeans and a navy blue button-up with the sleeves rolled to his forearms, the fabric stretched just right over lean muscle. A charcoal-gray sports coat had completed the look, giving him that effortless put-together but not too put-together appearance.

But looks could be deceiving. Just because she was attracted to a man didn't mean they were meant to be. That was why she had been cautious, why she'd suggested they take separate vehicles and meet at the restaurant. An escape route was always good to have. But now, sitting next to him in the warmth of her home, she didn't feel the need for one. She wanted time. Time to get to know him. Time for him to get to know her. And, hopefully, for both of them to like what they discovered.

She took a sip of her beer, settling into the sofa, and turned toward him, one knee tucked onto the cushion to face him more fully. "Tell me about the young people you were with at the YMCA."

Pete shrugged, rolling the bottle between his palms. "I just saw a need in the community and thought I could do some good."

She arched a brow. "That answer was good, but it feels a little… incomplete."

He chuckled, his thumb absently peeling at the label of his bottle, his eyes dropping for a second.

"Pete?" she prompted gently. When he lifted his head, she held his gaze, speaking carefully. "I don't want to make you uncomfortable. And I certainly don't want you to feel like you owe me anything. But I do want you to feel like you can share things with me. Anything. Because I really want to get to know you."

This time, he didn't look away. Instead, he studied her, and something serious and contemplative moved in his dark eyes before he nodded slowly. "I didn't exactly have the same upbringing as you did."

She blinked but kept her expression neutral. His words surprised her. But more than that, she wanted to know more.

"You grew up with parents you speak highly of," he continued. "You're close to your grandparents. I'm sure you know how lucky you are."

She bit the corner of her lip and nodded. "I do. There

are times I probably take them for granted, but I know how incredibly fortunate I was growing up. And how lucky I am to still have them close."

His jaw flexed slightly, and when he spoke again, his voice was steady, but there was a weight behind his words. "I'm not sure either of my parents was ever really interested in having kids. Or if they were, maybe it was just because that's what they thought they *had* to do. Good parenting was never something they understood how to do."

Her heart ached at the quiet way he spoke, and before she could think better of it, she reached out, her fingers lightly resting on his arm.

The warmth of his skin seeped through their touch, sending a charge through her system, but she ignored it. She didn't want to be sidetracked by the sexual energy she felt around him.

"I'm so sorry," she murmured. "Please, share anything you want."

He hesitated, and then, without releasing his beer bottle, shifted his free hand over hers, wrapping his fingers around hers, holding tight.

"I wasn't physically abused," he said, his voice low. "But my parents were so unhappy that it spilled into everything with our family." He exhaled, as if gathering his thoughts. "My dad worked, but he also liked to gamble. He was always sure he'd hit it big. But he never did. And every time he lost, he grew angrier. He drank a lot. I could usually tell how much money he'd lost by how drunk he was."

Angie swallowed hard, tightening her grip on his arm.

"My mom worked part-time," he continued, his tone even. "But she always felt like having kids had taken away her 'big break,' as she called it. When my dad would drink, she'd get mad, say she could have made it big if it hadn't been for him... and then for us. They'd scream at each other until he left to gamble more, to drink more, to sleep around. And she'd drink, too. Get upset. Then turn on my sister and me, yelling about how we had ruined her life."

She saw it then, the ghost of old wounds flickering across his face.

He took another sip of beer, then gave her hand a gentle squeeze.

"I remember you have a sister," she said softly. His head tilted as though in question, and she hastened to remind him, "From the night we ran into each other... literally, in the pharmacy."

A slow, genuine smile crossed Pete's face, softening the hard edges that had formed as he spoke about his past. "That's right. Yeah. Sally was just one year older than me. We protected each other growing up. Or at least... until I became rebellious."

There was warmth in his voice when he said her name, an unmistakable affection that contrasted with the heaviness of the conversation.

"She left home when she was eighteen," he continued, his gaze momentarily distant as if recalling a long-faded memory. "She got pregnant but moved in with a friend, kept a job, built a life. She was *everything* to her daughter that our mother wasn't."

Angie's heart clenched at the way he said it. There was no bitterness, just quiet reverence, as though his sister's strength still amazed him.

"When she was twenty-five, she met and married a really good guy who treats her like a queen," he said, a small smile playing on his lips. "He adopted her daughter, and they had a son together. She's such a great mom." He let out a small chuckle, shaking his head. "I always tell her that, and she laughs and says she just did everything opposite of what our parents did."

Angie smiled, touched by the story. "That's probably the best thing she could have done."

His grin lingered for a moment before he exhaled, nodding. "Yeah. It really is."

Her original question had been about the kids at the YMCA, but now, she could see so much more. His past, his family, and the reasons he was drawn to mentoring those kids. It was all connected. And he was trusting her with it… something she didn't take lightly.

"Anyway," he said, shifting slightly as if suddenly self-conscious. "I'm probably going on too much—"

"No!" She cut in quickly, shaking her head. "I love learning about you, Pete."

His eyes searched hers, lingering long enough that she could feel the weight of his scrutiny. He was testing her sincerity, trying to determine whether she really meant it. Whatever he found in her expression must have satisfied him, because he slowly nodded.

"By the time I was twelve, I was getting into trouble." His voice was quieter now, more reflective. "I didn't care much about school, but I had a group I hung out with. Most of them were older, and I was too dumb to realize they were just using me." He let out a short, humorless laugh. "I must've still had an innocent look about me, because they figured out pretty quickly that I could get away with things they couldn't. So they got me to start shoplifting for them."

He shook his head, his grip tightening slightly around the beer bottle still resting in his lap. "I thought I was slick," he muttered. "But I was such a dumb fuck."

Angie leaned in slightly, her fingers still wrapped around his. "In case you didn't know this, Pete," she said, her voice light but sincere. "We're all dumb fucks in middle school."

For a second, he stared at her in surprise, then barked out a laugh, the sound sudden and full. "Yeah," he said, nodding. "I guess you're right."

The laughter faded into something quieter, something that hummed between them like an unspoken thread of understanding. And then the air shifted. She could feel it, the way his nerves passed through their connected hands, how his body seemed to hold just a little more tension. His story wasn't over. And she could tell that they were getting to the part that really mattered.

"I had just turned fourteen when I finally got caught shoplifting in a grocery store by the police. It was an older cop," he said, his voice thoughtful, distant. "I don't know what the hell he thought he saw in me, but he must've looked deep and found something decent."

She wanted to tell him that finding something decent in him wouldn't have been difficult. That it was probably always there, just waiting for the right person to notice. But this was his story, so she remained quiet.

Pete took a sip of beer, then exhaled, his thumb idly rubbing over the rim of the bottle. "Instead of arresting me," he continued, "he told me that if I was willing to work at the grocery store for free to pay off what I'd taken, he wouldn't haul me in."

Angie swallowed, her chest tightening. "He gave you a choice. And therefore, he gave you a chance."

He held her gaze again and nodded. "That's a perfect way to put it."

"I take it you took him up on his offer?" Angie asked, tilting her head as she studied him.

Pete let out a chuckle, low and rough. "I might've been a dumb fuck, but I wasn't that dumb. No way I was turning him down." He shook his head, a smirk tugging at the corner of his mouth. "The store owner agreed, and that was the beginning of the next phase of my life. I worked after school, stocking shelves, sweeping floors, and unloading deliveries. And the cop, Frank, would check on me regularly. Not in a 'keeping an eye on a troublemaker' way, but more like… he wanted to make sure I was sticking with it."

Angie leaned forward, absorbed in every word. "And when you'd worked off what you stole?"

"The store owner let me stay on," Pete said, his expression shifting to something quieter, more thoughtful. "Offered to pay me a paycheck, but I told him it wouldn't do me any good. I'd just get home, and my parents would take it. So instead, he paid me in cash but locked it up in the office for me. Let me take out what I needed when I needed it."

Angie's stomach twisted at the thought that a fourteen-year-old *couldn't* take money home because his own parents would steal it.

"Did that surprise Frank?" she asked, already suspecting the answer.

Pete snorted. "Not at all. By that time, Frank had told me exactly why he wanted to help me. He'd put my dad in the drunk tank plenty of times. He knew what I was up against."

"Oh, wow." Angie exhaled, shaking her head as she wrapped her mind around everything he'd just shared.

Pete took another sip of his beer, rolling the bottle between his fingers. "Frank became a mentor. So did the grocer. Frank and his wife even started having me over sometimes, just for dinner. That was the first time I ever saw what a healthy relationship looked like." A small smile ghosted across his lips. "They once took me to the

Eastern Shore for a fishing trip, and I fell in love with the area."

Angie's eyes softened. "So that's how you ended up here."

"In a roundabout way," Pete admitted. "I graduated, joined the military, and thanks to Frank's influence, I went through military police training. I liked the structure. I liked knowing the rules. Hell, I needed the rules. And it wasn't hard to fall into a role where I helped others keep them, too."

Angie let out a slow breath, shaking her head with admiration. "For a quiet man, you really know how to weave an amazing story that holds my rapt attention."

Pete threw his head back and laughed, the sound deep and genuine. "Yeah, well... I don't know if I've ever told anybody all of this."

Her brows lifted. "Really?"

He shifted, turning slightly so he was facing her more fully. "Really," he confirmed. He hesitated, then shrugged. "I don't like talking about myself. But I like spending time with you, Angie. And eventually, if we keep seeing each other, some of these things would come out anyway."

She studied him for a long moment, warmth settling in her chest. "So now you pay it forward, right?"

His brow furrowed slightly. "What do you mean?"

She gestured toward him. "Frank and the grocer helped you when you were young and impressionable. It made a difference in your life. Hell, it probably made the difference between you ending up in jail and becoming the man you are now. And now you're doing it for others."

Pete was quiet for a beat, then let out a slow exhale. "Yeah," he admitted. "I guess that's right. I was already helping out with the American Legion and coaching the ball teams, but I started realizing we had some kids slipping through the cracks. Gangs have started creeping down from Baltimore, and there are a lot of young guys who are ripe for the picking."

His fingers absently played with the label on his bottle, his expression unreadable. "One of the middle school teachers and I started meeting with some of them at the YMCA once a week. We help them work out, get some homework done, and just talk." His jaw flexed. "I don't kid myself into thinking I'll get through to all of them. But if I can help some? Then it's worth it."

Angie's throat tightened, emotion pressing against her ribs. "I think you're amazing," she murmured.

His gaze snapped to hers, sharp, searching.

"I mean it," she continued, her voice steady. "I can't remember the last time I was so fascinated... not just on a date, but just getting to know someone. I'm so glad you shared all of this with me."

Pete nodded slowly, his gaze never leaving hers. "Me too."

Silence stretched between them, thick with something unspoken. Something undeniable. She could feel it in the air, in the weight of his gaze, in the way his hand still lingered near hers. After a moment, she inhaled deeply, shifting slightly. "Do you still see your parents?"

A muscle ticked in his jaw. "My dad died while I was in the military," he said, his voice measured. "I came home for the funeral, and my mom stayed drunk the entire time."

Angie's stomach twisted.

"She died a few years later," he continued, exhaling sharply. "Liver disease. My dad had it, too. They drank their way into an early grave."

She squeezed his hand, not knowing what to say, only wanting to offer something.

But Pete didn't dwell on it. Instead, he tilted his head, his lips curving into something softer.

"What about Frank?" she asked.

A genuine grin spread across his face. "He's in a retirement home in Virginia Beach. I try to see him at least once a month."

Angie smiled widely, giving his hand a gentle shake. "Maybe next time you visit him, I can go too."

Pete's brows lifted slightly, as if the suggestion had caught him off guard.

She shrugged, smiling. "I'd love to meet the man who helped you become who you are."

His expression shifted into something warm. And when he spoke, his voice was quiet but firm. "I can't think of anything better."

The space between them had shrunk without either of them acknowledging it. Pete's arm rested along the back of the sofa, fingers grazing the ends of her hair as they sat facing each other. Their voices had quieted, the air between them charged with something unspoken.

Angie could feel her heart beating a little faster, her pulse fluttering at the base of her throat. Pete had spent the last hour telling her things he hadn't told many people. And she had hung on every word, drawn to the way he spoke, to the pieces of himself he had entrusted to her.

Now, he wasn't speaking at all. Neither was she. But the silence felt alive.

Her gaze dipped to his mouth for half a second before she dragged it back up to meet his eyes. His dark, steady gaze told her he'd noticed.

Slowly, Pete reached up, fingers brushing a strand of hair from her face, tucking it behind her ear. His touch was light, careful, as if giving her time to pull away.

She didn't. Instead, she let herself lean in, just enough

to feel the warmth of his breath against her lips. And then he kissed her. A slow, searching press of lips, warm and unhurried. Angie sighed into it, her hand drifting up to rest against his chest, feeling the steady beat of his heart beneath her palm.

Pete tilted his head, deepening the kiss ever so slightly, and a pleasant shiver ran through her. His hand slid to her waist, anchoring her to him, and she let herself sink into the moment. The quiet hum of attraction. The softness of his lips. The heat of his palm through her shirt.

But just as the kiss started to tip into something deeper, Pete slowed, pressing one last lingering kiss to her lips before pulling back.

Their breaths were uneven, their eyes locked. A slow, lazy smile curved his lips. "I should probably go."

Angie exhaled a quiet laugh, her own lips curling at the edges. "Yeah… probably." Neither of them moved right away.

Then, with a reluctant sigh, Pete pushed off the sofa and stood, holding out a hand to help her up. She took it, letting him pull her to her feet, their fingers lingering before she laced hers loosely through his. She walked him to the door, not letting go until he reached for the handle.

But before he could open it, he turned back to her, his expression softer now, his gaze dipping to her mouth again. This time, she met him halfway.

Their second kiss was just as sweet, just as unrushed, but something was different about it. Something that whispered this wasn't the last time.

When they parted, Pete traced his thumb over the back of her hand. "Can I see you again this weekend?"

Her stomach gave a little flip. "I'd like that. Um… I have a family thing tomorrow. But…"

"Sunday?"

"Sunday," she confirmed, smiling up at him.

He gave her hand one last squeeze before stepping outside. "Good night, Angie."

"Good night, Pete."

She watched him walk to his SUV and waited until he drove off before closing the door. Her cheeks were warm, her lips still tingling as she climbed the stairs, changed into her pajamas, and slid into bed. Just as she was settling under the covers, her phone buzzed. **Home now.** A second message followed. **Good night, Angie.**

Her smile was immediate, and her fingers moved over the screen. **Good night.** She set her phone on the nightstand, rolled onto her side, and closed her eyes. And for the first time in a long time, she fell asleep smiling.

9

"How did your date go last night?"

Angie glanced up from the loaf of bread in her hands, catching her mother's expectant gaze. A slow grin tugged at her lips, but before she could answer, her gaze flickered to her grandmother, whose bright blue eyes twinkled with mischief. Angie shook her head, feigning exasperation.

"What?" Grandma Dorothy asked, her laugh light and knowing.

"Were the two of you gossiping about me?" Angie teased, arching a brow.

Her grandmother's smile only widened. "I just might have mentioned something," she admitted, eyes brimming with amusement. "But when we talk about you, dear, it's not gossiping."

"Oh?" Angie challenged, biting back a smile. "Then what would you call it?"

Her mother smirked as she added another slice of turkey to a sandwich. "Caring conversation."

Angie lost the battle and laughed aloud, shaking her head. The three women stood in her mother's cozy kitchen, the scent of fresh bread and peanut butter, jelly, lunch meats, and cheese lingering in the air as they worked. Twice a month, they gathered here to make bagged lunches for older shut-ins. The Easy Breezy Lunches program had been Angie's idea. It was a way to bridge the gap for those shut-ins when Meals on Wheels couldn't fully cover their needs.

Before she could offer details about her date, the back door swung open. A crisp breeze drifted in as her father and grandfather entered, each carrying stacks of bread.

"More supplies!" her father announced, setting the loaves on the counter.

Grandpa Stan clapped his hands together. "Let's get to work. Can't have our friends going hungry."

Within moments, the five of them fell into a well-rehearsed rhythm of spreading condiments, layering meats, bagging up sandwiches, chips, cookies, and apples. The warm, familiar chatter filled the kitchen like a melody Angie had known all her life.

"I'm still waiting on an answer," her mother reminded, breaking the hum of activity.

Her father looked up from sealing a sandwich bag. "An answer to what?"

"Mom was asking about my date last night," Angie said, suddenly feeling every pair of eyes turn to her. She hesitated, then shrugged, attempting nonchalance. "It was fine."

Her mother stopped mid-reach for a bag of chips, narrowing her eyes. "Just... fine?"

Angie smothered a chuckle. "Okay, okay. Actually, it was perfect."

Grandma Dorothy's brows lifted with interest. "A perfect date? Well, now, that's something worth talking about."

She grinned, tucking a strand of hair behind her ear.

"We met at Roy's Barbecue—Oh! That reminds me, I have leftovers for you and Grandpa. Pete ordered an entire extra meal just to be sure you had enough."

Grandpa Stan's eyes widened with approval. "Well, I like him already!"

Laughter rippled through the kitchen as they continued their work, their easy companionship surrounding Angie like a soft embrace. She glanced around, taking in the simple beauty of the moment—the warmth of her parents' home, the love and familiarity woven into every shared meal and teasing remark.

She had this. She had them. She had a family who loved without conditions. One that gathered on Saturdays to give back, to laugh, to be together. She had what Pete had never known. And maybe, just maybe, she had found someone to share it with.

Angie jolted at the sound of her mother's voice, blinking as she pulled herself back into the present. "I'm sorry, did you say something?"

Her mother gave her a knowing smile. "I just wondered if there was anything else you could tell us about him, besides the fact that he's a detective."

A warmth spread through Angie's chest before she even realized she was smiling. "He works with at-risk youth," she blurted out, the words tumbling free before she could filter them. It wasn't the first thing she'd planned to say, but somehow, it was the first thing that came to mind. Maybe because it had left such an impression on her. He had so effortlessly stepped into their lives, offering guidance and understanding their struggles without judgment.

She glanced between her parents and grandparents, feeling their quiet interest. Without giving away too much of Pete's personal history, she recounted seeing him at the YMCA, the way he interacted with the young men.

"Thinking about those kids makes me realize how lucky I am," she admitted, gesturing to the rows of brown paper bag lunches stacked neatly in the boxes her father had just sealed. "Even now, just something as small as this... it reminds me that I've always had family looking out for me."

Her father's expression softened as he considered her words. "I take it the young men he works with don't have that kind of stability?"

She shook her head. "We didn't get into the specifics, but I'd bet most of them don't."

Grandma Dorothy sighed, her hands resting atop a loaf of bread as she looked wistfully toward the window. "Wouldn't it be nice if everyone had loving mentors, whether they were true family or not?"

"And nice for us old folks to have young people around to keep our spirits high," Grandpa Stan added with a grin, slipping an arm around Angie's shoulders and giving her a squeeze.

The moment settled into something warm, something steady with love woven into every glance, every touch, and every unspoken understanding between them. By the time they finished boxing up the last of the meals, a volunteer van had pulled into the driveway. They all worked together to carry out the boxes, sending the meals off with well-wishes.

Angie hugged her parents and grandparents before stepping back. "I have some housework to tackle today. Grandma, if it's okay, I'll bring over that barbecue for your dinner tonight."

"Oh, that would be lovely, sweetheart."

With parting waves goodbye, Angie turned and headed back down the street to her own house.

The afternoon light filtered through the windows as

she slipped inside, setting her bag by the door. The familiar quiet greeted her, yet her thoughts weren't on the laundry she needed to do or the dishes in the sink. Her gaze kept straying to the sofa.

The very spot where she and Pete had talked last night. Where she had watched him open up just enough to reveal glimpses of the man beneath the badge. And where, in the stillness of that moment, his lips had brushed against hers.

Her breath hitched at the memory, and before she could stop herself, her fingertips ghosted over her mouth. She could still feel the press of his lips, the warmth lingering like an imprint on her skin. A slow, shivery awareness spread through her, curling in the pit of her stomach.

Shaking herself from the thought, she moved toward her dining table and pulled out her satchel, opening her laptop. She skimmed her list of meetings for the week, reviewing the names of the senior residents she planned to check in on. But as she stared at the screen, her grandmother's words whispered through her mind once more.

Wouldn't it be nice if everyone had loving mentors, whether they were true family or not?

She leaned back in her chair, her gaze drifting beyond the screen, beyond the walls of her home. Ideas swirled in her mind like the shifting colors of a kaleidoscope— uncertain at first, blurred and scattered. Then suddenly, they clicked into place, forming something whole and beautiful.

And just like that, a new idea began to take root.

Angie snatched up her phone and fired off a text before she could second-guess herself. **Are you busy?**

The moment she hit send, she cringed, her nose scrunching in regret. *Oh God. It's Saturday. What if he's on a date?* Her stomach twisted at the thought. Ugh. *Fine. If he is, then I don't mind interrupting!* Before she could spiral further, her phone dinged.

No. Just chilling at home. What's up?

She hesitated, chewing on her bottom lip. Should she just say it? Before she could decide, another message popped up.

And if you must know, while I'm chilling at home... I was thinking of you.

A slow, giddy warmth spread through her chest, and before she could stop it, a smile broke free. For a moment, she felt like a teenager again when the cutest guy in school had smiled at her. Not that it happened often, but when it did, it was the best feeling.

She quickly typed out a response. **I had an idea I wanted to talk to you about.**

As soon as she hit send, she winced. That was vague. Too vague. She should've given him more. But before she could fix it, his reply appeared.

Any idea you have, I'd love to hear. Anytime you want to talk, I'm ready.

Her heart skipped. She inhaled, fingers hovering over the screen. **I know we said we'd see each other tomorrow, but is there any chance we could chat this evening?**

Three dots appeared, then his reply filled her screen. **Text? Email? Phone call? Video chat? Visit?**

She laughed, shaking her head as she typed. **I'd love to see you, but I'll take anything.**

His reply came instantly. **Tell me when, and I'll be at your door.**

Her breath caught. The thought of seeing him again had her stomach flipping in excitement. **I'm home for the rest of the day.**

I'm coming now.

Angie shot up from her chair, an uncontrollable grin

taking over as she did a quick, ridiculous happy dance in the middle of her living room. *He's coming now.*

Her phone pinged again. **What do you like on your pizza?**

She paused, brow furrowing as she stared at the screen.

You don't need to bring pizza! You bought dinner last night!

His response was immediate. **What do you like on your pizza?**

She rolled her eyes but couldn't suppress the smile tugging at her lips. **Any kind of meat, no mushrooms.**

I'll call it in, pick it up, and be at your door.

Her fingers trembled slightly as she typed back. **See you soon.**

She bolted upstairs, her mind racing. *Okay, not panicking. Just making myself look... not like I was hanging out in the house.*

She swapped out her lounge clothes for a pair of soft leggings and a bright, off-the-shoulder peasant blouse, something comfortable yet just cute enough. Tugging her hair free from its messy bun, she ran a brush through it, letting the waves fall over her shoulders. A touch of blush. A bit of mascara. And her favorite flavored lip balm.

Throwing open her closet, she grabbed her ballet flats and slipped them on before darting back downstairs.

With a glance at the clock, she headed into the kitchen and pulled out what she had for a salad. Might as well make something fresh to go with the pizza. She chopped crisp lettuce, diced a tomato, and tossed everything together with a light vinaigrette.

Just as she set the bowl aside, a knock sounded at the door.

She sucked in a breath. Then exhaled too fast because her lungs threatened to stop working. Throwing open the door, she found herself face-to-face with Pete. The sight of him nearly knocked the air from her chest again.

Dark jeans. A fitted gray Henley. That easy, almost-shy smile that made her heart trip over itself. And in his hands were two pizza boxes.

"Figured one might not be enough," he said, his voice carrying that low, warm rasp that sent a thrill straight through her.

She stared at him for half a second too long, feeling her heart race, feeling something inside her melt. Then she laughed, stepping aside. "Come in before I just keep staring."

10

Pete still couldn't quite believe that Angie had wanted to spend more time with him again, so soon. And for what? To discuss some ideas she had? He didn't care about the reason. In truth, the details didn't matter. What mattered was that she had thought of him.

The moment she swung the door open, her warm smile lit up her face. "Come on in," she said, stepping aside to let him pass.

His stomach tensed as he carried the pizza inside, hoping he'd chosen right. But the second she flipped open the lids, she let out a delighted squeal.

"Oh, this looks perfect! I made a salad, so we can eat whenever you're ready."

His lips curled into an easy grin. "Up to you, Angie."

"Well, this smells divine. I can't stand the thought of trying to talk while my nose is busy having a party over the pizza."

He chuckled, shaking his head at her choice of words. "Well then, let's make sure your nose and your taste buds get in on the fun."

She grabbed two plates, and they loaded up with generous slices and fresh salad. As Pete settled at the kitchen table, he was struck once again by just how natural it felt to be here with her. Something about Angie's home wrapped around him like a warm, inviting embrace.

"How was your family time?" he asked, watching as she took a seat across from him.

Her whole face brightened. Whatever she was about to say, it clearly meant something to her. "It was great. Actually, that's when I got the idea I wanted to discuss with you." She paused and laughed when he sent her a lifted brow.

"Uh-oh," he teased. "I feel like I'm already lost."

She grinned. "Okay, so my family started this thing we call Easy Breezy Lunches. It helps fill in the gaps where the ESAAA can't always reach. You know, some people don't qualify for Meals on Wheels, but they still struggle to put meals together or don't quite meet the financial threshold for assistance. So twice a month, my family gathers at my mom's house, and we make about a hundred bagged lunches—sandwiches, chips, cookies, fruit. You know... easy breezy."

Pete blinked. "Wow."

"Other volunteers pitch in, so we usually end up with almost two hundred lunches. Then we have a few people who distribute them to those in need. The recipients can eat them that day or refrigerate them for later. It's just... a small way to help."

He leaned back in his chair, nodding. The idea impressed him, but more than that, *she* impressed him. It was clear this wasn't just something she did, but something she cared deeply about.

"So while we were making lunches, my mom and Grandma Dorothy said something that got me thinking."

She took a sip of water before continuing. "I told them about the mentoring you do with the young men. I didn't go into personal details, just that you work with them. I was lucky to have my parents and grandparents growing up. I always had guidance."

"You were lucky," he agreed. "And from the sound of it, they're remarkable people." His voice dropped a little as he added, "They certainly raised an amazing woman."

She laughed softly, shaking her head. "I don't know about amazing, but I learned the importance of helping others. And then my grandmother said something that stuck with me. She said it would be nice if everyone had someone to mentor them, even if they weren't family. And that's when I remembered this program I studied in grad school called Adopt-a-Grandparent."

Pete's brow furrowed. "You're gonna have to explain that one to me."

She set her fork down. "Well, in a way, it's what Frank did for you. He stepped in like a grandfather figure, offering guidance. And I'm guessing you gave something back to him, too."

Pete swallowed. He hadn't thought about it that way, but he remembered the day Frank's wife had told him how much her husband enjoyed spending time with him. "How would this work?"

She leaned in, her enthusiasm growing. "The idea is to pair young people who need mentorship with older adults who want to make a difference. The kids learn responsibility, compassion, and life skills, and the elders get companionship, fresh energy, and a chance to pass down wisdom."

As she spoke, he could see the idea coming to life in her mind, the passion lighting up her eyes. It was contagious, and he found himself nodding along. Before he could say anything, she shoved her purple glasses up onto her head and pressed on.

"I've already identified some challenges," she admitted. "The program I studied had the elders coming to the school for visits, and there were outings with heavy chaperoning. But we'd have to get the kids on board, get parental permission, carefully match each pair, and—"

"I love the idea, Angie." He interrupted, his voice full of conviction.

She hesitated, chewing on her bottom lip. "I'm so glad you do, but the more I think about it, the more I realize how complicated it could be to pull off."

"Then let's work together," he said, reaching across the table to squeeze her hand. "We'll tackle those roadblocks one by one. And if they can't be removed, we'll find another way to make it work."

Her fingers curled around his for a brief, lingering moment before she gave him a soft smile. "You really think we can?"

He held her gaze, his own lips curving. "I *know* we can."

They stood and moved to the sofa in unison. Pete stretched his legs out, sinking deeper into the couch as he studied Angie. Her passion for this idea lit her whole face, her eyes shining with the kind of enthusiasm that was impossible to fake. He could listen to her talk for hours and never tire of it.

"How many kids are you working with now?" she asked, brushing her fingers through her hair as she tucked her legs under herself.

"Richard and I have ten that we meet at the YMCA weekly. Richard's a middle school teacher. He was instrumental in helping pick the kids who could use us the most. But he's also the second adult in the room, for both their protection and ours."

She nodded, absorbing the information. "Ultimately, I'd love for a young person to be able to visit their adopted grandparent in their home. That way, they could see first-hand what challenges an older person faces and actually help in a meaningful way." The second the words left her lips, she hesitated, waving her hands in the air as if trying to erase them. "Wait, that didn't come out right."

Pete tilted his head, amused. "Clarify for me."

She blew out a breath, then brightened. "Okay, did you ever watch that old '80s movie Sixteen Candles?"

"I think that was more of a chick flick," he said with a teasing grin.

She rolled her eyes, waving her fingers at him in mock exasperation. "Whatever! Since you obviously didn't watch it, let me explain. So Molly Ringwald's grandparents were staying over for a wedding, right? And one set of grand-parents brought a foreign exchange student with them. At dinner, they were bragging about how amazing he was, all the ways he helped them—yard work, fixing things, what-ever. But it quickly became obvious that they were basi-cally using him as free labor."

Pete smirked. "Let me guess—this is not the dynamic you're going for?"

"Exactly!" She pointed at him. "I don't want a situation where kids are just running errands or doing chores. But I do think a genuine bond could form. Where both people are learning and giving something valuable to each other."

He studied her for a long moment, then nodded. "I get it now. And I love the idea."

She scrunched her nose. "But…?"

"We'd need to establish clear guidelines before we get too far ahead of ourselves. Then we'd have to gauge inter-est." He paused, tapping his fingers against his knee before his face lit up. "Actually, why don't I bring it up with the kids and Richard on Thursday? No hard details yet… just see if there's an interest."

Her eyes sparked with excitement. "That's a great idea! I'll talk to Belle Simmons at Careway Assisted Living. They have extended their campus to include a building next to the nursing home that has apartments for seniors. Financial need is established to see who can live there. We service most of them for various necessities. I have no doubt I can find older adults who'd love to be part of something like this."

Pete nodded, watching her work through the idea in real-time, the wheels in her mind turning. "Have you thought about how you'll determine who participates?"

"Yes," she said, already ahead of him. "There are plenty of older people in the area with family nearby. While they might benefit, they wouldn't be my first choice. The same goes for people who are already really active in the community—church groups, volunteer programs, things like that. The six who I take to the Y would be perfect."

"Makes sense." He took another sip of his drink, considering her words. "But at the same time, a complete shut-in might not be the best match either."

"Right," she agreed. "Ideally, we'd find people who want a connection but don't have a natural way to get it. Maybe some who can still get around on their own, but who could really use the extra companionship."

She laughed then, and once again, Pete found himself staring, caught up in the sheer joy of her. Angie was beautiful, but it was more than that—it was the way he felt when she was around. Like warmth on a cold day. Like sunlight after a storm.

She leaned back against the couch, scooting a little closer. His arm was already draped along the back cushion, and she fit right up against his side like she belonged there.

"I'm glad you invited me over tonight," he murmured.

She tilted her head, her mouth curving in that way that made his stomach tighten. "Does this mean we're having tomorrow's date today?"

He chuckled as he brushed a lock of hair from her face. "Absolutely not. If you still want to spend time with me tomorrow, then we're keeping our date. And, in case you're wondering, I definitely want more time with you."

Her smile deepened, and her eyes glinted playfully. "Perfect."

Before he could react, she twisted, throwing one leg over his lap and straddling him. The move was effortless, confident, and damn near lethal to his self-control. His hands immediately went to her hips, steadying her even as heat surged through him.

"Is it too forward if I say I really want to kiss you right now?" she asked, her low voice teasing.

One hand slid down to cup the curve of her ass while the other snaked up her spine, holding her close. His eyes locked onto hers, dark with intent. "With me, you can be as forward as you want, Angie."

And then he kissed her. Their mouths met in a slow, smoldering slide of lips and tongues, the kind of kiss that started like a match strike and burned hotter with every second. She melted into him, her fingers tangling in his hair, her body pressing against his. Pete groaned, his grip tightening, needing her closer, needing more.

She whimpered softly into his mouth, rocking slightly in his lap, and the sound nearly undid him. Heat spiraled low in his stomach, his pulse hammering as he deepened the kiss.

A sharp gasp broke between them, and she pulled back just enough to breathe, their foreheads resting together.

Their chests rose and fell in tandem, and hearts pounded against each other.

"Damn," he muttered, his voice rough.

She let out a breathless laugh. "Yeah. Damn."

They groaned in unison, forcing themselves to separate. The moment she slipped off his lap, Pete felt the loss like a cold draft.

She stood, smoothing her hands down her thighs, then grinned. "I should probably walk you to the door before we end up repeating *that* ten more times."

He exhaled a chuckle, running a hand through his hair as he followed her. "You say that like it'd be a bad thing."

When they reached the door, she turned, her expression softer now. "Lunch tomorrow?"

His smile was slow and sure. "Wouldn't miss it."

She leaned up, pressing a quick, lingering kiss to his lips before stepping back. "Good night, Pete."

He hesitated, just for a second, then smiled. "Good night, Angie." And with that, he stepped out into the night, already counting down the hours until he could see her again.

11

Pete and Jeremy sat at their desks, frustration thick in the air between them. The case was going cold, and both men hated that feeling.

"I know it sucks," Jeremy said, rubbing a hand over his jaw. "But they only got two prints off that old meth trailer. One belonged to a guy already sitting in a Norfolk jail."

"And nothing on the other?" Pete asked.

Jeremy shook his head. "No match. Whoever it belongs to isn't in the system."

"I have a call in to the detective who worked the case when the first guy got locked up," Jeremy added. Just as he finished speaking, his phone buzzed in his pocket. When he pulled it out, a slow grin spread across his face.

Pete smirked. That was *not* Jeremy's work grin. "Go on, take your call," Pete said, waving him off. "If the detective calls back, I'll be here."

"Appreciate it, man," Jeremy said, already pushing out of his chair and heading for the hallway. As he answered, Pete heard the warmth in his voice. "Hey, baby."

Pete shook his head with a chuckle. His partner had it

bad. The tough, sharp-witted medical examiner had made Jeremy work for her heart, but Pete knew his friend would guard it like his life depended on it.

Before he could lose himself in his own thoughts, their desk phone rang, jerking him back to reality. He grabbed the receiver. "Detective Pete Bolton."

"Detective Bolton? I'm Detective Marcus Warner from Norfolk PD, gangs division. I believe I spoke to your partner earlier about Terrence Marley."

"Yeah, thanks for calling back. And you can just call me Pete."

"Sounds good. And Marcus will do for me."

Pete pulled out his notepad. "You got anything for us? You already know Marley's prints were in that meth trailer, but there's no telling when he was last there. That place looked like it hadn't been touched in months."

Marcus exhaled. "Yep. We arrested him five months ago for cooking meth in an old house in Norfolk. Took us a while to pin him down—he was slippery. But we had an informant give us his location, and once we got him, that was it. He's been locked up ever since. Sentenced to seven years, but he'll probably serve four."

Pete tapped his pen against his notepad. "So he hasn't been anywhere near that trailer in at least half a year."

"Right. You said there was another print, but no match in the system?"

"Yeah, nothing. You have any idea who Marley was working with over here?"

"No names," Marcus said, "but I can tell you he had ties to the Bloods. That's not their usual MO—they don't cook. They move the product and distribute it. If someone else was in that trailer, it might've been a transporter, maybe someone Marley was trying to recruit."

Pete sighed, rubbing the back of his neck. "We didn't

have much gang activity over here for a long time. It's only just started creeping in these last few years. I've been in the area for about five years, on the task force for three. And it's getting worse."

Marcus let out a dry chuckle. "Yeah, I figured. That highway running straight down the Eastern Shore? It's a gift to these guys. If their drivers stick to the speed limit and don't pull anything stupid, they can get past all the major cities straight into Hampton Roads. And going north, they've got a clear path all the way into Pennsylvania on backroads."

Pete blew out a slow breath. "Yeah, we know that too well." He flipped his notebook closed. "Thanks for calling back, Marcus."

"No problem. Stay safe out there."

"You too." Pete hung up, leaning back in his chair with a sigh. What he really wanted to do was call Angie.

Ever since their time together each day last weekend, he hadn't been able to get her out of his head. Or off his lips. Her kisses were addictive, but hell, so was everything about her. The way she laughed, like sunshine cutting through storm clouds. The way she absently shoved her purple glasses on top of her head when she got animated, only to grab them again a second later and plop them on her nose.

He loved being around her. And damn if that wasn't a little terrifying.

Jeremy strode back in, looking way too pleased with himself. "All okay?" Pete asked, forcing his mind back to the case.

Jeremy nodded. "Yeah. She's got a case that'll keep her tied up till late afternoon." He flopped into his chair. "Anything from your call?"

Pete filled him in on what Marcus had said.

Jeremy muttered a curse. "Bloods. Fucking great."

"Yep. We'll just close the case for now." Pete checked his watch. "You ready to head to the high school?"

Jeremy groaned. "Ready as I'll ever be."

Jeremy and Pete climbed into their unmarked SUV, the late-morning sun glaring against the windshield as Pete pulled out of the lot.

"So," Jeremy said, fastening his seat belt, "you've been in a good mood all week. Got anything to do with a certain purple-glasses-wearing woman?"

Pete smirked. "Maybe."

Jeremy barked a laugh. "Damn, look at you. Can't stop smiling. You're done for."

"Yeah, yeah," Pete said, shaking his head, but he couldn't deny it.

Silence stretched for a few beats before Pete cleared his throat. "Actually... I wanted to tell you something."

Jeremy glanced at him. "Yeah?"

"I, uh... I asked Angie out. For real this time."

Jeremy's grin was immediate. "You finally pulled the trigger."

Pete chuckled. "Yeah."

Jeremy leaned back in his seat, smirking. "When's the first official date?"

"It was last Friday night—"

"Wait, what?" Jeremy said, his head jerking around to glare at his partner.

"We had dinner on Friday night. And then I was back at her house on Saturday evening. And we had lunch out on Sunday—"

"What the fuck, man? I can't believe you didn't tell me!"

Pete shrugged. "I know, but if it had been a bust or she didn't want to see me again, I hated to make a big deal about it."

Jeremy shook his head. "Damn... you and Angie. So I take it you two are dating now?"

"I sure as hell hope so because she came to me with a project." Pete looked over to see Jeremy's confused expression.

Jeremy glanced at him. "What kind of project?"

"It's called Adopt-a-Grandparent. Angie's got a lot of older people in the community who have some independence but don't have family close by. She wants to set up a program that pairs seniors with kids who don't have grandparents in their lives. It's a way to help them build relationships. Kind of like a mentorship program."

Jeremy let out a low whistle. "Damn. That's... actually a great idea."

Pete nodded. "Yeah, I think so too. A lot of these seniors don't have family close by, and a lot of kids in the foster system or single-parent homes don't have that older generation in their lives. Angie got me involved because of the kids I mentor."

Jeremy was quiet for a moment before he said, "That's a hell of a thing, man. You two working on something like that together? Feels like more than just dating."

Pete just shook his head with a grin as they pulled into the high school parking lot. He exhaled, gripping the wheel. "Yeah. It does." And he hoped the words were true.

Two hours later, they were finishing their presentation for teachers in the auditorium and just getting ready for questions. With a visual presentation, they had covered common tattoos and clothing choices for the major gangs that were slowly making their presence known in the area. They showed images of gang graffiti painted on stop signs and the sides of buildings.

"Granted, most of our gang infiltration comes down from Baltimore, but we are on the main transportation line from New York, Philly, and Baltimore, down to Norfolk. The Highway 95 corridor from Florida to New York has long been one of the busiest for drug and gang running. They now include guns and human trafficking. By taking the backroads through the Eastern Shore, they can bypass some of the more policed parts of the highway."

"Is it true that if the police stop a gang member, he has to follow gang code and not deny that he's in the gang? And then he can get arrested for being in a gang as well as for carrying drugs?" one teacher asked.

Pete took the question. "In the past, gang culture emphasized loyalty to the extent that members were forbidden to deny their association. And yes, that did give the district attorneys the option to also charge them with gang activity. The idea was that they could continue to have an influence while in jail or prison. To deny could be punishable by death at the gang's hands. And believe me, a longer prison term for the added charges was preferable to dying at the hands of a gang that now considered the denier to be a traitor."

The moans from the educators could be heard easily.

Jeremy continued the response to the original question. "But now, in some circumstances, especially when dealing with law enforcement or within the judicial system, gang members may deny their gang ties to avoid legal repercussions. This shift is just self-preservation. It's a pragmatic solution that keeps their ranks strong. Especially contrasting with previous stances that strictly opposed any denial of their allegiance."

"I know I've seen some of those drawings on notebooks," another teacher said. "What should I do?"

"Never, and I repeat, never confront any student about those symbols," Pete said with emphasis. "You would need to talk to Deputy Lamont Smith, your resource officer. He's well trained in what needs to be done."

"Don't ignore the signs," Jeremy confirmed. "But take them to the officer here at your school."

As they finished their presentation, they received a round of applause. One of the teachers stood and said, "I've been teaching for twenty-two years. This is the first time I can say that a presentation given on a workday has been so worthwhile!"

Pete and Jeremy grinned, then continued to talk to individual teachers as the assembly slowly dispersed. Along with Deputy Smith, they started a list of students who were of concern to several teachers.

As they were back in the office getting ready to leave, Pete looked over the list. His heart sank as he realized he recognized three of the names. The young men in question lived in the same apartment complex as the kids he mentored. He trusted his kids, but knew gang recruitment was up and particularly harsh. He needed to spend more time talking to them about the dangers of gangs in the area… and prayed it wasn't too late.

1 2

Angie knocked lightly on the open door of Belle Simmons's office, peeking inside with a grin. "Tell me you're not too busy to chat."

Belle looked up from her computer, her dark hair swept into a sleek ponytail, her blue eyes lighting up with a warm smile. "For you? Always. Get in here and sit your butt down."

Angie chuckled, stepping inside and dropping into the chair across from Belle's desk. "I just finished visiting a few of the seniors over at Careway Apartments, and then visited with Grammy Ellen," she said, stretching her legs out with a dramatic sigh. "Now, I'm here to sweet-talk you into letting me use some of your space."

Belle arched a brow, amusement dancing in her expression. "Sweet-talking me, huh? Should I be worried?"

"Not at all," Angie said, pressing a hand to her chest in mock innocence. "I would *never* manipulate a dear friend."

Belle snorted. "Please, you and I both know you're about to ask for something, and I'm probably going to say yes before you even finish."

Angie laughed. "Okay, okay, you got me. But seriously, I was hoping we could use some of the meeting rooms here at Careway for the Adopt-a-Grandparent program. Since the seniors will be from the apartments, I thought it would make sense to host the meetings here. It's familiar to them, and the space is perfect. What do you think?"

Belle's eyes widened with excitement. "I love it. This program of yours... it's exactly what so many of our seniors need. And honestly? It's going to be just as good for the kids. I saw firsthand what Hunter was like before he had a strong male figure in his life."

Angie nodded, touched by the sincerity in Belle's voice. "That's exactly what I was hoping. It's not just about helping the older person, but about connection, you know?"

Belle leaned forward, resting her arms on the desk. "Absolutely. And you've got full access to our meeting rooms. I'll make sure no one double-books you, and if you ever need extra hands, just say the word. I'll rope Hunter into helping if I have to."

Angie grinned. "Oh, I love that idea. Something tells me he'd be great at keeping a group of teenage boys in line."

Belle smirked. "Oh, he'd have them walking the straight and narrow in no time. Plus, he's a sucker for old war stories. Half the guys in the nursing home would have him cornered for hours."

Angie laughed, shaking her head. "Then it's a deal. And Belle... thank you. This means a lot."

Belle waved a hand. "Don't even mention it. I'm just glad you're doing something this amazing." She tilted her head, studying Angie for a second. "But tell me the truth— how are *you* holding up? You take care of everyone else, but are you taking care of yourself?"

Angie opened her mouth to brush it off, but Belle's

arched brow stopped her. With a sigh, she said, "Honestly? I'm exhausted. And my joints have been kicking my ass this week."

Belle's face softened. "Angie..."

"I know, I know. I need to call my rheumatologist," Angie admitted, rubbing at her wrist. "I promise, I'll take care of it."

Belle narrowed her eyes. "You'd better, or I'll drag you there myself."

Angie held up her hands in surrender. "Noted. Now, since I officially have your blessing, I'll let you get back to work."

Belle stood, rounding the desk and pulling her into a quick, fierce hug. "I mean it, Ang. Take care of yourself."

Angie squeezed her back. "I will. Thanks, Belle."

As she stepped out of the office, she felt lighter. She might be tired, but she wasn't alone. And that made all the difference.

Angie led her group of six seniors out of the chair yoga class, the rhythmic sound of sneakers and canes tapping against the polished floors of the YMCA. She had made arrangements ahead of time for Carina to drive them home in the center's van while she stayed behind. Tonight was important. She had already spent two weeks identifying seniors who could benefit from an adoptive grandparent program, not just those who needed companionship but those who had something to offer a young person as a mentor.

She had floated the idea to them gently to gauge interest, and now had a solid list of six single seniors, all living in the Careway Apartments, eager to participate.

Pete had asked for her help in explaining the program to his group of kids. When they'd spoken on the phone earlier, he mentioned that he had already received approval from every parent, guardian, and foster parent involved. The groundwork was set. Now, they just had to bring the two groups together.

As Angie stepped outside with Carina, her gaze immediately found Pete. He stood near the gymnasium men's showers, rounding up his group, effortlessly commanding their attention as he herded them toward the conference room.

"I'll be right back," she mouthed to him. His response was a quick wink. The expression was casual and effortless, but enough to send a warm flutter through her chest. *How is it possible that such a simple expression could make me feel so giddy?*

"He's a good-looking man," Carina noted, amusement dancing in her voice.

"Yeah," Angie sighed, unable to stop the small, knowing smile that curved her lips.

The other seniors chuckled and teased her, but she took it in stride, waving as the van pulled away. The moment they were out of sight, she turned on her heel and hurried back inside, eager to see Pete again.

Inside the conference room, a sudden hush fell over the space as she entered. All ten young faces turned toward her, studying her, and for the first time, nerves prickled along her spine. Speaking in front of adults had never unsettled her. She was confident, well-spoken, and used to commanding attention. But teenagers? That was a different challenge altogether.

She was suddenly aware of her brightly colored blouse, the way her unruly curls framed her face, and even the purple glasses she adored. *What if they think I'm a total dweeb? If they write me off now, I'll lose them before I even begin.*

Before she could dwell on it, Pete crossed the room with his easy stride and reached for her hand, giving it a reassuring squeeze. The warmth of his touch melted away her nerves in an instant.

Turning to the group, he introduced her with a confident, steady voice. "Gentlemen, I'd like you to meet Ms. Angie Brown," he said. "She's here tonight to talk to us about an idea we've been working on together. She's going to sit with us, share her thoughts, and answer any questions you might have."

Following Richard's lead, all ten boys stood in unison and greeted her with a respectful chorus of "Hello, Ms. Brown," before settling back into their seats.

The simple gesture took her by surprise. She stole a glance at Pete, who offered her an encouraging nod. *Alrighty, then*, she thought, taking her seat beside him. *Let's do this.*

Soon, Angie wrapped up her explanation of the program, her voice warm with conviction. She wanted them to truly understand that this wasn't just about them doing things for the seniors.

"As I've said several times," she reiterated, scanning the room, "this isn't about running errands or doing chores for them. It's about building a relationship with someone you might not have otherwise noticed. It's about learning how to help in meaningful ways, and in turn, allowing them to spend time with someone younger, bringing joy into both your lives."

She glanced at Pete, seeking reassurance. He gave her a small nod, his expression steady, encouraging.

Feeling more confident, she smiled and opened the

floor. "Please, ask me questions. Sometimes it's easier to explain when I know exactly what's on your mind."

Pete stepped in smoothly. "And when you ask, repeat your name to help Ms. Brown remember who's who."

A brief silence stretched over the room. The boys glanced at each other, shifting in their seats, hesitant. Then, finally, one of them raised a hand.

"I'm Tony," he said. "So we'd just go out in the community? What kinds of things would we actually do?"

Angie leaned forward, eager to engage them. "Have you ever been to the SuperMart?"

At the mention of the only major national discount chain on the Eastern Shore, grins broke across their faces. A few murmured in agreement, nodding enthusiastically.

"Okay," she continued, "imagine you need to go in and buy some food. Then you remember you need a pad of paper and some pens. Oh, and you also need screws because a doorknob at home is loose. Are those things all in one spot?"

Another boy, frowning in thought, shook his head. "I'm Caleb. My mom always complains about how exhausting it is to go from one end of that huge store to the other. The food's on the left when you walk in. I can't remember where the pens and paper are, but I know school supplies are somewhere in the middle. And I remember housewares being way in the back corner when I was checking out the bikes. So no, nothing's really close together."

Angie nodded with enthusiasm. "Exactly. Now, imagine you're alone, and you just got off the bus because you rely on public transportation. You have a cane or maybe a walker. Just the thought of making that trip would be exhausting, wouldn't it?"

She saw it click for them. Expressions shifted from curiosity to understanding.

"So," she continued, "one outing could be a trip to the SuperMart. You and your adopted grandparent could come up with a shopping list together, and then you'd go along to help them navigate the store."

Interest sparked in their faces. She decided to take it a step further.

"Some of you play sports at the middle school, right?" she asked. "And maybe you don't have someone in the stands cheering for you because your mom or guardian is working. What if we arranged for your adopted grandparent to come to your game? So when you look up in the bleachers, there's someone there for you?"

Another hand shot up. "I'm Darius. What would we even talk about?"

Angie smiled at his honesty. "Are you worried you wouldn't have anything in common?"

He nodded.

"That's one of the best parts of this," she assured him. "You'll get to know someone who has a lifetime of stories to share. Maybe they have old photo albums they need help organizing. They can tell you what life was like when they were your age. And I promise you'll be surprised how much you actually have in common."

"I'm Curly," another boy chimed in. "Where will we meet them?"

"To start, Mr. Bolton and I thought we'd have you come to the Careway Assisted Living, where they have several meeting rooms. I know you guys usually come here on Thursday nights. So for a few weeks, we'd tweak the schedule. After thirty minutes in the gym and then a shower, he and Mr. Pendleton would bring you over to the nursing home. Once we're comfortable, we'll plan outings."

She continued fielding their questions, answering with

patience and enthusiasm. As their session came to a close, she wrapped things up.

"You don't have to decide right now," she assured them. "Think about it, talk it over with your parent or guardian, and let Mr. Bolton or me know—"

"I'm in."

The quiet but firm voice cut through the room. Angie turned toward the speaker, a boy who had been silent throughout the entire meeting. He tilted his head slightly, his expression steady, his words carrying weight.

"I'm Jimmy," he said. He exhaled, as if gathering his thoughts. "I remember my grandpop. I was five when he died. My dad's never been around, so it's just me, my mom, and my little sister. Before he got sick, he lived with us. He read me stories at night. He came to my kindergarten Christmas program when my mom had to work. I remember sitting with him afterward, eating cookies, feeling proud I had someone there for me."

The room fell utterly silent. Angie was certain her heartbeat was the only sound.

Jimmy hesitated for the briefest moment, as if weighing his words, but then he looked around at his friends, unashamed. "If he were still here, he'd be the one telling me stories about the old days. He'd be the one listening when I'm confused, upset, or pissed off. He'd be the one telling me when it's right to fight and when it's right to walk away." His gaze shifted toward Richard before settling on Pete. "You've taken on that role, but I know it's hard. You got a bunch of us to look after, and a tough job to do. It'd be nice to have someone else to call if I needed to."

He turned back to Angie, his deep brown eyes meeting hers with quiet sincerity. She blinked rapidly, forcing the moisture threatening to spill from her eyes to stay put.

"And now," he continued, "you're offering me that. And

if, for all that, I can help them, just like I helped my grand-pop... then yeah. I'm in."

A heartbeat of silence. One by one, the other nine boys echoed their agreement, their faces breaking into smiles.

Angie exhaled, a warmth blooming in her chest. This was it. The first step in something bigger than any of them had realized. At the end, they followed Richard's van, and all the boys were dropped off at their apartment buildings. Pete watched as they each made it to their door.

The ride home was filled with her excitement. She practically buzzed in the passenger seat of Pete's truck, replaying moments from the meeting with an energy that refused to be contained.

"I mean, did you see their faces, Pete?" she gushed, twisting toward him in her seat. "I knew they'd be inter-ested, but I didn't expect them to jump on board so quickly! And Jimmy—oh my God, Jimmy! He completely floored me when he took that chance to answer first."

Pete glanced at her, the corner of his mouth lifting in a quiet smile. "Yeah," he said, his voice low and steady. "That one got to me, too."

Angie exhaled sharply, still riding the high of the moment. "This is going to work, Pete. I can feel it. It's going to be something special."

His fingers flexed on the steering wheel, and he gave a slow nod. "Yeah. I think it is."

Unlike her, he wasn't bursting with words, but there was something in the way he spoke. It was in the way he carried himself that told her he felt it, too. He wasn't just indulging her excitement. He was in this with her.

When they pulled up in front of her house, the truck idled for a moment, both of them lingering.

Pete finally turned to her. "I'll walk you up."

She smiled, stepping out as he rounded the front of the

truck and fell into step beside her. The night air was cool, but she felt warm all over.

They climbed the short steps to her front porch, the soft glow of the porch light casting long shadows across the worn wooden planks. Angie turned to face him, her pulse kicking up as she met his steady gaze.

"So," she murmured, tilting her head, "does this mean you're going to let me celebrate properly?"

Pete arched a brow. "What exactly does 'celebrate properly' mean?"

Her lips curved. "This."

She reached for him, fisting the fabric of his jacket and tugging him forward. He didn't resist. The moment her mouth met his, he was there. Solid, warm, and consuming her in a way that sent heat flashing through every nerve ending.

The kiss wasn't soft or hesitant. It was deep, demanding, and a little reckless. Pete's hands landed on her hips, pulling her flush against him as his lips parted, his tongue sweeping over hers. A small, desperate sound escaped her throat, and he answered with a low growl, angling his head to take more.

Her fingers threaded into his hair, nails scraping against his scalp as he pressed her back against the door. She could feel the strength in his body, the barely leashed control in the way his hands gripped her waist, the way he kissed her like he was fighting not to push further.

When they finally broke apart, both of them breathing hard, Angie let out a shaky laugh. "Well," she whispered, forehead still resting against his, "that was a pretty good celebration."

Pete chuckled, his breath warm against her lips. "Yeah. But if we don't stop now, I'm not going to leave."

Angie bit her lower lip, fighting the urge to tell him *so*

don't. But he was right. They had started something here—something real. And she wasn't about to rush it.

Instead, she exhaled and pulled back slightly. "Saturday," she said. "Come over in the afternoon. We'll talk more about the program. Maybe cook something together."

Pete's gaze stayed locked on hers, intense and unreadable for a moment. Then he nodded. "Saturday."

With one last lingering touch, he brushed his thumb lightly over her lower lip before he took a step back.

"Night, Angie."

She watched as he walked down the steps, climbed into his SUV, and pulled away, her entire body still humming from his touch. With a dreamy sigh, she unlocked her door, stepped inside, and leaned against it. Saturday couldn't come fast enough.

13

Angie pulled into the parking lot of Careway, her fingers gripping the steering wheel a little tighter than usual. Tonight was important, a night when connections would begin—ones that she hoped would provide warmth and stability for both the young men and their adopted grandparents.

She took a deep breath and stepped out of her car, smoothing down the front of her soft knit sweater as she made her way inside. The familiar scent of the facility—clean linen, a faint trace of lavender, and the subtle antiseptic undertone—greeted her as she walked through the automatic doors.

She was usually here to visit her grammy Ellen, but tonight was all about the ones who didn't have family nearby.

Belle had already left for the evening, but the night shift nurse at the front desk spotted her immediately and gave her a warm smile. "Your group is already in the meeting room," she said with a knowing wink.

Angie smiled back, offering a small wave before making

her way down the hall. Excitement and nerves twisted inside her, and she hoped that the older residents hadn't gotten cold feet. They had all been so enthusiastic when she first brought up the idea, but first meetings could be daunting.

Pushing open the door to the large meeting room, her heart lifted. They were all there.

She did a quick head count, pleased to see no one had forgotten. Relief flooded through her, and she moved around the space, greeting each of the older adults with warm hugs and reassuring smiles. Some of them were seated on the room's plush sofas, while others stood near the snack table, their hands clasped, eyes bright with anticipation. The room itself had been set up with several cozy conversation areas, the furniture arranged to encourage easy, intimate discussions.

Footsteps outside the door caught her attention. Angie turned just as the door swung open, and the breath she hadn't realized she'd been holding released in a slow exhale.

Pete.

Her lips curved into a soft smile as she took him in—broad-shouldered, confident, effortlessly commanding the room just by stepping inside. His presence had a way of steadying her, grounding her.

He led the group of young men inside, their faces a mix of curiosity and nervous excitement. Richard, as dependable as ever, brought up the rear, his tall frame and easygoing demeanor offering a sense of stability to the boys.

Angie's gaze flicked to Richard for a moment, knowing how much he had on his plate. His wife was due to give birth any day now, and she knew he would likely be absent from future meetings for a little while. But she appreciated that he was here tonight, offering support where it was needed.

As the boys stepped forward, their movements hesitant but eager, Angie noticed something else… the older adults had risen to their feet. They were smiling, but beneath their expressions, she could see the same nerves mirrored back at them.

She met Pete in the center of the room, their bodies instinctively aligning as they always seemed to. The flicker of connection between them was something she felt in her bones, especially in moments like this.

Pete gave her a small nod, his silent way of saying, *Go ahead. You've got this.*

Taking a deep breath, she turned to the group and spoke, her voice carrying the warmth and reassurance she wanted them all to feel.

"Okay, everyone. I know you're all excited about the possibilities tonight, but with that excitement comes a little nervousness. That's completely natural. So for tonight, there are no expectations—just introductions. I'll pair you up with your adopted grandchild or grandparent, and then you can grab some snacks and a drink, find a place to sit, and just talk. You don't need to learn everything about each other right now. Just a little something to start."

She scanned the room, waiting to see if there were any questions. No one spoke up, so she continued, moving carefully through the pairings.

"And just so you know, our adoptive grandparents said that you can call them by their first name. I like to put the Mr. or Ms. in front, but you can work that out with your partner. Mike, you'll be with Mr. George, along with Rasheem."

Tony, a lanky young man with dark hair and an uncertain expression, took a breath before stepping forward.

George, a retired history teacher, smiled warmly, offering his hand. Angie didn't miss the way Mike squared his shoulders before shaking his hand firmly, just as Pete had coached them. Rasheem followed suit.

"Jalen, you and Darius are with Mr. Bertram. Curly and Mike will be with Ms. Rosetta. Jimmy, you'll be with Mr. Marty…"

One by one, she called out the names, watching each match unfold like a delicate dance—some eager, some a little shy, all of them stepping into something unknown.

When she got to the last pair, she glanced at Pete. He was watching, assessing, his arms crossed over his chest. But when their eyes met, there was something else there, something that made her stomach flip just slightly.

Once everyone had been introduced, she was relieved to see that the older adults immediately encouraged their young partners to grab a plate of food. What surprised her even more was that the young men were quick to help by balancing cups and carrying plates, ensuring their adopted grandparents had what they needed.

Pete's deep voice rumbled beside her. "We've talked to the boys about manners and politeness. It's good to see them actually remembering what we've taught them. This was a chance for them to practice, and they're doing a hell of a job."

Angie smiled, the warmth of pride swelling in her chest. "I think they're doing great."

As she scanned the room, she noticed that some pairs had already settled into easy conversation, their voices drifting through the air like soft, overlapping melodies. Others were still a little stiff, hesitant, unsure how to break the ice.

She turned to Pete, lowering her voice. "I don't want to hover, but after they've had some time to settle, I'd like to ask everyone to share one thing they've learned about their partner. Just something small, something that'll give them a reason to keep talking."

Pete nodded, looking over at Richard, who gave an approving nod of his own. "I think that's a good idea."

Angie exhaled slowly, watching as the young men and their adopted grandparents slowly relaxed into this new experience.

And then, she did something she hadn't even realized she needed to do. She reached out slightly and let her fingers brush against Pete's hand. It was quick, barely conspicuous.

But he noticed. And in response, he turned his hand just enough to let his fingers graze hers.

It was fleeting, but it was there. *I see you*, his touch seemed to say. *I'm right here with you.*

A quiet thrill ran through her, but she forced herself to focus as Pete, Richard, and she began moving around the room, checking in on each pair.

This was only the beginning.

But as she watched the warmth begin to settle in, as laughter replaced uncertainty, and as connections started to form, she knew this was the right thing to do.

The hum of conversation settled into a comfortable rhythm around the room, the initial nervousness having softened into something more natural. Angie took in the sight before her—pairs of young men and their adopted grandparents leaning in toward each other, sharing stories and trading smiles. It was working.

She clapped her hands lightly to get everyone's attention. "Okay," she said, her voice encouraging. "I know it's difficult to get to know someone when you've never met them before. You might be wondering whether you have anything in common or if they'll like you. That's normal."

The adults smiled knowingly, while the boys shifted in their seats, offering shy, almost embarrassed grins.

"In a few minutes, we're going to go around the room, and I'd love for each of you to share just one thing you've learned about your adopted grandparent or grandchild. It doesn't have to be anything big. It can be as simple as their favorite color. But the goal tonight is connection, and I'd love to see that even on this very first night."

She glanced over at Pete, catching the subtle chin lift he gave her, a silent sign of approval. The reassurance she was on the right track settled the last of her nerves.

Giving them a few more minutes, she moved through the room, watching how conversations unfolded. Some of the pairs had already relaxed into easy chatter, while others still hesitated, searching for the right words. "Tony, let's start with you."

Tony cleared his throat, looking a little uncertain, but when he glanced at the older gentleman beside him, his confidence grew. "Mr. George used to be in the Army."

George nodded, then smiled. "And Tony here? He's a hell of a basketball player."

A murmur of approval moved through the room. Angie's heart warmed as she moved on.

"Kyron?"

Kyron glanced at the man beside him before looking at Angie. "Mr. Harold loves sweets. Especially cherry pie."

Harold chuckled. "And guess what? So does Kyron."

The group laughed, a little more at ease now.

Curly and Rosetta discovered a shared love of singing, which led to an enthusiastic discussion about music styles.

Jimmy admitted with a grin that Marty was obsessed with reality TV shows, while Marty revealed that Jimmy had a passion for history.

David's face lit up as he revealed how Hannah loved

gardening and how his mom also loved planting flowers. "We're gonna try working on the Careway garden together," he added, glancing at Hannah, who smiled warmly.

Darius, impressed, shared that Bertram had been in the Navy. Bertram, in turn, found out that Darius had never been on a boat but had always wanted to, and Jalen had always wanted to visit the Baytown Pier.

Mike talked about Rosetta's love for seafood restaurants. "Her favorite food is shrimp."

"And his is hamburgers." Rosetta laughed.

Finally, they'd all shared. Angie pressed a hand to her chest, feeling a lump rise in her throat. In just an hour, young and older strangers had become paired with real, shared moments. She turned, taking in the expressions of the senior adults. They looked happy, engaged... some even a little energized by the conversations. Then she shifted her gaze to the boys, wondering if they felt the same.

Her breath hitched slightly, afraid of what she might find. But instead of boredom, reluctance, or irritation, she saw something else entirely. Smiles. Real smiles.

Her eyes flicked to Pete, who was watching her. She gave him a slight nod, silently asking him to take over.

"I think we can call this a successful start," Pete announced, his deep voice rolling over the room, steady and sure. "We'll meet right here every Thursday. If any of you want to do something outside the group, we'll set up guidelines, and we'll need to obtain parental permission first. But as we move forward, we might be able to plan some things as a group."

His lips twitched, a slow grin forming. "I know we can definitely all go to the Baytown Pier." He glanced at Bertram and Jalen, who both grinned back. "Maybe even charter a boat and watch the sunset. There's also a kitchen here at Careway. If we get permission to use it, maybe we can have a night when we cook or bake together. Just throwing out ideas based on what you all have shared tonight."

Richard stepped up next. "Alright, boys, time to head out. I have the van outside. Say your goodbyes, and let's move." He borrowed a van from his church that would carry all the boys.

Angie smiled as she watched the boys stand, some offering a hand to their adopted grandparents before parting ways. It was a simple gesture, but one that carried weight.

She took a moment to make sure all the leftover food was properly stored before informing the head nurse that anything remaining could be shared with the night staff. By the time she stepped outside, Richard's van was pulling away, the taillights glowing softly in the dark.

She turned back toward the Careway Senior Apartments, walking alongside the older adults, ensuring each of them made it inside safely.

Finally, it was just her and Pete. They stood between their vehicles, the cool evening air wrapping around them, but Angie barely felt it.

Pete stepped in first, wrapping his arms around her. Without hesitation, she melted into him, pressing her face against his solid chest. The steady rhythm of his heartbeat echoed in her ear, grounding her, steadying her.

"This was good," she murmured against him.

"Yeah," he agreed, his voice rumbling through his chest. "The kids will get something real out of this. A deeper appreciation for older people. A chance to talk to someone with age and wisdom but not always the body's ability to do what they want. They'll gain another adult in their world who gives a damn about them."

Angie closed her eyes, breathing him in, absorbing the weight of what he was saying.

"And for the older ones," she added, her voice softer now, "this will be good for them, too. A way to connect, to be around younger energy, to share their music, their stories. To feel... valued."

Pete's hold on her tightened, his lips pressing against the top of her head. "It was a fucking phenomenal idea," he murmured. "And we owe it all to you, Angie."

She swallowed hard, emotion thick in her throat. But exhaustion was settling in, and her body ached in that familiar way that signaled she'd done too much. A hot bath and a good night's sleep would do her wonders. And maybe, if she was lucky, she'd dream of him.

She tilted her head back, meeting Pete's gaze. His eyes were already on her, watching her the way he always did— like he saw everything.

Without thinking, she lifted onto her toes, her arms winding around his neck as she met his lips in a slow, lingering kiss. Pete groaned against her mouth, pulling her flush against him, his hands splaying across her back as he deepened the kiss.

And for that moment—just that moment—nothing else in the world mattered.

14

Angie looked up from behind her desk as Maxine, one of her social workers, strolled in, her sharp gaze filled with curiosity.

"So," Maxine said, settling into the chair across from her. "How's your new Adopt-a-Grandparent program going?"

Angie smiled, leaning back slightly in her chair. "Well, it's only been two weeks, so we've only had two full group meetings, but I think it's going well."

Maxine arched a brow, grinning. "And the kids? No disasters?"

Angie laughed, shaking her head. "The first Thursday night, when Pete, Richard, and I had everybody together for the first time, I honestly thought it was going to be a disaster. The kids looked completely out of their element—awkward, uncertain, and maybe even a little intimidated. And a few of my seniors, who I know could hold a conversation with a brick wall, just sat there looking bewildered."

Maxine chuckled, crossing her legs as she relaxed into her seat. "How did you get things moving?"

Angie leaned forward, resting her forearms on the desk. "Pete and I had spent the weekend before that first meeting going over each youth and each senior, figuring out who might be the best match. Once we got past the introductions that night, we had them sit with their assigned grandparent. That's when things started to shift."

Maxine nodded thoughtfully. "Was it just the group setting that made it so awkward?"

"I think so. But we were careful with our pairings. We didn't put a shy kid with a shy senior. And we looked at physical abilities too. Pete has a few older boys, already thirteen, and two of them are big, strong, athletic types. We paired them with older men who are a little more frail, one of whom was recently diagnosed with early-stage Parkinson's. That way, they could help without making their match feel incapable."

"And what about the couples?"

Angie's eyes warmed. "A few of the kids in Pete's group had never had grandparents in their lives at all. We thought those boys would do well with our senior couples. The women are wonderful cooks, but they're also strong, independent, and very forward-thinking. We figured they'd be great at bringing the kids out of their shells. The men can be excellent role models, as well as Pete and the other mentor, Richard."

"And?" Maxine pressed, leaning in. "Did they actually start talking to each other? Or was it still like pulling teeth?"

Angie grinned. "Oh, it got even better this past week. To get them comfortable, we gave them an assignment. We told them that next week, they'll be taking a trip to the grocery store together. The kids sat down with their seniors to help them create shopping lists, and that's when things really loosened up. The seniors did an amazing job of including the kids, asking them what they would like to get from the store."

Maxine's smile softened. "Sounds like you've got something really special happening here."

Angie exhaled, her heart full. "Yeah," she murmured, a warmth spreading through her chest. "I think we do."

Angie's phone rang just as Maxine stood, tossing her a knowing look and a small wave before slipping out of the office.

"Angie Brown speaking—"

"Angie! It's Sylvia." The voice on the other end was tight with urgency. "I just had one of our Meals on Wheels volunteers try to drop off a meal for Mr. Daniels—Tom Daniels. He lives alone over on Seaport Way."

Immediately, Angie's stomach tightened. "I know Mr. Daniels. What's wrong?"

"No one answered the door," Sylvia said. "She knocked, called his name—nothing. But two days ago, he answered. She's worried, and so am I. I'm stuck at the dentist this morning. Can you check on him?"

Angie's gaze flicked to her planner, where her day was mapped out in a dozen scribbled notes. But this wasn't something to delay.

"I'm on it," she said without hesitation. "I'll call for a deputy to meet me for a wellness check."

"Thank you, Angie. I'll be at the office as soon as I can."

Hanging up, she quickly jotted down Mr. Daniels's phone number on a sticky note, stuffing it into her purse as she grabbed her jacket off the chair. On her way out, she called out to the receptionist, "I'm heading to Seaport Way for a wellness check on Tom Daniels. Push the team meeting back until I return and send out an email to let everyone know."

The drive took nearly twenty minutes, each mile tightening the knot in her stomach. She called the sheriff's office en route, requesting a deputy to meet her there. As she pulled up to the small, aging house, a patrol car arrived right behind her.

A tall, broad-shouldered deputy stepped out, adjusting his belt as he approached. She didn't recognize him.

"I'm Angie Brown with the Eastern Shore Area Agency on Aging," she introduced herself. "Meals on Wheels reported that Mr. Daniels isn't answering the door."

"I'm Deputy Krukowski," he said with a curt nod. "I'll check it out."

They walked together up the short concrete path. The house had the tired look of a home that had stood for decades, its white paint peeling in places, the front stoop slightly uneven. The deputy knocked firmly, calling out, "Mr. Daniels! Sheriff's office! Can you come to the door?"

Silence.

Angie stepped to the side, cupping her hands against the window as she tried to peer in. The lace curtains blocked most of her view, but she saw no movement and no shadow. No sign of life stirred inside.

She pulled out her phone and dialed his number, listening as it rang until finally, voicemail picked up.

"No answer," she murmured, her unease growing.

"Does he have any family we can call?" the deputy asked.

She shook her head. "Not that I know of. Meals on Wheels delivered a meal two days ago, and he was here then."

A voice called from across the street. "What's going on?"

Angie turned as a woman jogged toward them, her blond ponytail swaying.

The deputy intercepted her. "Who are you, ma'am?"

126

"Susan Barnes. I live right across the street."

"Ms. Barnes, have you seen Mr. Daniels today or yesterday?"

"I saw him yesterday," she confirmed. "He came out to get his mail. I'd just picked up my kids from school. We waved at each other."

"But not today?"

She shook her head. "No, not today."

The deputy exchanged a glance with Angie, before turning back to her. "Thank you, ma'am"

"We need to get inside," she said, her voice firm.

"I agree." Krukowski glanced toward the back of the house. "Let me check if there's an open door."

As he disappeared around the corner, Angie wrapped her arms around herself, the chilly day settling deep into her bones. A sick feeling had started in her stomach, one she knew too well.

A minute later, Krukowski returned, shaking his head. "Locked up tight." He turned to his partner, who had just pulled up. The two spoke quietly before Krukowski called out again, then, with a firm kick, he sent the aging wooden door splintering open. The crack of the frame giving way echoed through the air.

Angie followed as the deputy stepped inside, calling out his identification. The house was still, the air thick with the scent of stale coffee and something else—something heavier.

No sign of him in the living room. Not in the kitchen. And then... a sharp inhale escaped Angie's lips as she stepped toward the bedroom and saw him.

Tom Daniels lay sprawled on the floor beside his bed, unmoving. She started toward him, but Krukowski held out an arm, his voice low but firm. "Stay back, ma'am. Don't touch anything."

Angie stopped short, pressing a fist to her chest, her breath shaky. "I'm sorry. I know better. It's just—" She swallowed thickly. "This isn't my first time on a wellness check that turned out like this."

The deputy nodded, his expression grim. "It's always a gut punch."

His partner radioed for an ambulance as Krukowski knelt, pressing his fingers to Tom's neck. A few seconds later, he twisted back, meeting Angie's eyes. Slowly, he shook his head.

She closed her eyes, the ache in her chest growing stronger.

There were so many rewards in her work, but there was always this, too—the moments that shattered her heart a little more each time. She turned and walked back toward the living room, needing space to breathe.

The sound of approaching vehicles signaled the arrival of more responders. She turned as Cora eventually arrived and stepped inside, already suited up in PPE.

"Hey, Angie," Cora greeted gently. "Did you find him?"

She nodded, wrapping her arms around herself. "Meals on Wheels called when he didn't answer the door. The deputy and I went in together."

Cora placed a reassuring hand on her arm. "I'm glad you weren't alone."

Angie nodded, knowing there was nothing more she could do. She slipped outside, rubbing at her temples. The weight of the day pressed down on her—grief, frustration, and exhaustion all wrapped into one unbearable mass.

She gave Krukowski her contact information before making her way back to her car, weaving carefully through the growing number of official vehicles. As she pulled onto the road, she sighed heavily, blinking hard against the sting in her eyes.

By the time she made it back to her office, the fire in her joints was undeniable. The deep, gnawing ache settled into her fingers, her wrists, her hips, even her toes—each movement a reminder that her medication was no longer keeping up.

She rescheduled her work, grateful to avoid any more conversations. The rest of the day passed in a blur of paperwork, reports, and a trip to the county building to drop off documents. Every step sent pain radiating through her body.

By the time she finally drove home, the ache had deepened to a sharp, burning throb. Tears pricked her eyes— not just from the physical pain but from the sheer emotional weight of the day.

The house next door was empty when she arrived since her grandparents were still at their church meeting. She felt a sense of relief because she didn't have the energy to pretend she was fine.

Stripping down, she ran a bath as hot as she could stand, sinking into the water with a sigh, letting the heat ease into her swollen joints. But even as her body relaxed, her mind remained heavy.

She needed to call her rheumatologist in the morning. She needed to have her medication re-evaluated. She needed rest.

After microwaving leftovers and eating straight from the container on her couch, she was startled at the knock on her door. It was too early for her grandparents to be home. She peeked out the security hole. *Pete.*

She threw open the door, not caring that she was in old sweatpants and a worn T-shirt. "Hey," she murmured, finding it hard to speak when all she could think of was how grateful she was that he had decided to surprise her with a visit.

There was a pause, then his deep, steady voice. "Long day?"

A lump formed in her throat. "Yeah." She tilted her head. "Do you know?"

Another pause. He quietly answered, "Cora called Jeremy."

She pressed her lips together, not trusting herself to speak but nodding her understanding.

"You want to talk about it, Angie? I'm here for whatever you need."

And just like that, the tears she had been holding back all day threatened to spill over.

15

Pete didn't hesitate. The moment he stepped inside, he shut the door behind him, wrapped his arms around her, and guided her toward the sofa. Even in loose, slouchy clothes, with tear-bright eyes and the weariness of the day settled in her posture, Angie was still breathtaking.

He sank onto the cushions and gently tugged her into his lap, his hands firm yet tender as he settled her against him. She curled inward instinctively, her arms winding around his neck, her cheek resting on his shoulder as if it were the most natural place for her to be. He held her, saying nothing, just breathing with her, feeling the tremble of her sadness as it passed through her body.

Her sobs quieted faster than he expected, melting into soft sniffles, and then, just silence.

She leaned back slightly, her face tilted up toward his, her expression vulnerable in the dim light. Before she could wipe at her eyes, he beat her to it, the rough pad of his thumb gently brushing away the lingering tears that clung to her cheek.

With a sniff, she reached for the tissues on the end

table, blew her nose, dabbed at her face, and then let out a deep, slow sigh.

"Feel better, or do you need more?" he asked, his voice low and steady, a quiet anchor for her emotions.

She gave a small nod. "I feel better."

"That wasn't a very long cry," he mused.

Her lips twitched. "I didn't need a very long cry."

He studied her, sensing there was more beneath the surface. "Do you want to talk about it?"

She exhaled another slow breath and let her gaze drift over the room before finally settling back on him. "You already know why I love my job," she murmured. "But one of the hardest things is that with the age group I work with, death is inevitable."

Pete didn't rush to fill the silence that followed. He understood the power of quiet. It could pull out confessions, truths, things people didn't even realize they needed to say. And even though Angie was more outgoing than he was, she also appreciated the kind of peace that came from simply being present.

She took another breath before continuing. "Sometimes, death is a release. When someone has been sick or in pain, you know they're not suffering anymore. And if they had family, friends, or even one person who cared, there's a sense of calm in that, even through the grief. But when one of our clients dies alone..." She shook her head. "That's when the sadness is overwhelming. I don't know if they were scared. I don't know if they felt pain. I don't know if they went peacefully, or if their last moments were filled with fear."

She swallowed hard, and he could see the emotion rise in her throat. "He wasn't sick, so hospice wasn't involved. He was just... old. And one day... today... he was gone. I just hate that he was alone."

Pete tightened his hold on her, grounding her in his embrace. "I haven't told you this before, but I'm in awe of what you do, Angie."

She scoffed softly, shaking her head as if dismissing the idea. "You're in awe of me? You put on a badge every day and go after drug dealers. You put yourself in danger to protect people. That's what a hero does."

"There are all kinds of heroes," he said, his voice dropping to a quiet certainty. "Some wear a uniform and carry a weapon. Some stand in front of a classroom full of kids who need someone to believe in them. Some work thankless jobs just to make sure their families are fed. And some, like you, spend their days making sure that older people aren't forgotten. That their dignity isn't stripped away just because they're aging. You make sure they have what they need, that they're seen, that their voices still matter." His gaze locked onto hers, his words laced with conviction. "That's heroism, too."

Their eyes never wavered, the weight of his words thickening the air between them, drawing them closer like an invisible thread winding tight.

"Can you stay tonight?" she asked, her voice barely above a whisper. "Will you stay?"

His arms tightened around her. He leaned in, pressing a soft kiss to the corner of her mouth—just a whisper of contact, just enough to let her feel the tenderness behind it.

"There's nowhere else I'd rather be," he murmured, his lips brushing against her skin as he spoke.

She rested her head back on his shoulder, and he lost track of time, content to hold her, to simply exist in this space with her.

After a while, he spoke, his voice gentle but firm. "Angie, I don't want you to feel like you asked me to stay out of desperation. I'm here for whatever you need, but if at any time you change your mind—"

She lifted her head, a small, knowing smile playing at her lips. "Could you get any better? Because right now, I'm convinced you're perfect."

A chuckle rumbled in his chest. "Far from perfect."

Her fingers traced lightly over the back of his neck, her touch sending warmth through him. "You're perfect to me. Perfect for me." Her gaze softened, filled with something deep and unspoken. "And I haven't changed my mind."

She took a slow breath, then tilted her head, her eyes flickering with something new. "So, really, the only questions I have are, have you eaten tonight, and what time should I set the alarm for in the morning?"

His lips curled into a grin as he pulled her a little closer. "Yes, I've eaten. And don't worry about the alarm—I'll set my own. I can stop by my place in the morning before work."

She shifted off his lap, and he loosened his hold just enough to let her move freely. Without hesitation, she stood and reached for his hand.

He didn't even think before threading his fingers through hers and standing, letting her lead. He wanted her to take the reins. He wanted this to be exactly what she needed, without pressure or expectations.

She led him up the stairs to a hallway with three doors. One was a bathroom. Another looked like a small spare room with half-filled boxes and a yoga mat unfurled on the floor. The third was her bedroom.

She turned to face him once they were inside, her hands still wrapped in his, her expression shifting. A flicker of uncertainty crossed her face, and it nearly undid him. He wanted to erase it, to take away any doubt, any hesitation.

"Angie," he murmured, his thumbs stroking over her knuckles. "I'm here with no expectations."

She exhaled softly, then smiled. "That's good to hear, Pete. In all honesty…" She tipped her head, her smile deepening, a hint of mischief lacing her tone. "I'm here with lots of expectations."

A slow heat rolled through him, settling deep in his gut. He tilted his head, waiting.

Her fingers tightened around his. "Expectations of kisses. Of caresses. Of everything that comes after."

Her words shot straight through him, right to his heart, and lower, to where need pulsed hot and insistent. He willed himself to stay steady, to let her set the pace, even as desire coiled tight in his chest.

And then she stepped closer. The first kiss was soft and tentative, an unspoken promise exchanged between them. But as she leaned in, pressing herself against him, something ignited… a slow, simmering heat turning to fire.

His hands slid up her back, pulling her against him as their lips moved together, deepening, searching, learning. She sighed against his mouth, and the sound undid him. A low groan rumbled in his throat as his grip tightened, his body pressing against hers in a silent plea for more.

By the time they broke apart, they were both breathless, their foreheads touching, their bodies swaying slightly as if they needed to stay connected. And Pete knew this was just the beginning.

Angie stepped back, her chest heaving as she sucked in air. Her hands settled on the bottom of her shirt and she slowly lifted it over her head. Pete now found it hard to breathe as her cream satin bra captured his attention.

He wanted to reach out and drag his finger along the lace at the top of her breasts, but he wasn't sure he could move, terrified that this would be a dream and she would suddenly disappear.

She stepped closer, her hands reaching for his shirt. She slowly drew it upward until she lifted it as high as it would go. He took over and then dropped the shirt to the floor. They stepped closer, and his hands, once again, moved to her waist as hers lifted to his shoulders. Her lips curved slightly, and the gentle smile pierced his soul.

He bent to kiss her again, his tongue dancing over hers. His hands glided along the soft skin of her back and deftly unsnapped her bra. He slowly slid the straps down her arms until the silk material fell at their feet. He pulled her close, and now, with her naked breasts pressed against his bare chest, he felt every inch of her skin branded on him. He cupped her face as he poured every ounce of emotion swirling through him into the kiss. His erection was pressing against the zipper of his jeans, painful and eager.

Now, as they dragged their lips from each other, chest heaving, her thumbs slid into the waistband of her sweatpants.

He unbuttoned his jeans, and as he pulled down the zipper, he felt a sense of relief as his cock had room to swell even more. He toed off his shoes and shoved his pants to the floor. She was still standing with her thumbs in her waistband, her gaze roaming over his chest and down to his cock.

Standing completely naked in front of her, he spied a smile on her face, and he grinned. She wasn't coy and wasn't playing games. She liked what she saw, and he sure as hell liked what he was looking at.

She suddenly blinked as though startled and jerked her sweatpants down. He offered a hand as she stepped out of them, keeping her body steady.

The light of the room was dim, but as his gaze lazily

drifted from her beautiful face down her body, he spied her swollen knee.

"Not now," she raggedly whispered.

His gaze jerked up to hers, uncertain what her words meant.

"Please, please don't ask about my health right now," she begged. "I promise I'll tell you anything you want to know, but just not right now. All I want is to lose myself in you."

So many thoughts swirled through his mind, making it hard to focus. He knew that after the day she'd had, maybe she only wanted sex with him as a comfort. As a way to feel alive after witnessing death. It wasn't unusual... and while he would grant her anything, he would need to hang on to his heart if that was all she wanted from him.

Her hands lifted to squeeze his arms, and she shook her head. "No, Pete, it's not what you're thinking. What I said didn't quite come out right." Her brow had furrowed, and worry creased her face.

"Hey," he said gently. When her eyes landed back on his face, he continued. "I'm here, sweetheart. Whatever you need, I'm here. I'll be your person, whatever that needs to be."

She swallowed deeply and nodded. "When I said I wanted to lose myself in you, I didn't mean that I just wanted sex to feel alive or to erase the day. I meant that I want to be your person, not just a hookup. And yes, I want you to be mine. Whether it's a tough day, or a celebration, or just I'm glad to be with you... it's all of those." She shook her head. "I'm screwing this up, aren't I?"

"Not at all, babe," he said, cupping her face. "Just say what's in your heart, 'cause that's the only way I'll know what's right for me to do."

"It means I want to feel with you. Be with you."

His finger landed on her soft-as-petals lips. "I get it, Angie. And I want to lose myself in you, too."

He bent, and with one hand behind her back and the other behind her knees, he carefully lifted her and carried her to the bed, where he gently set her down. "I'll do anything you want. I just don't want to hurt you."

She smiled and nodded. "My left knee doesn't bend very well right now. But anything else will be perfect."

Wanting to make sure she was as ready as possible, he bent over the bed and placed both palms on either side of her. He kissed first one breast and then the other, circling her nipples with his tongue before sucking deeply. He continued a trail of kisses over her tummy and mound. She opened her legs, and he inhaled her arousal. Like nectar to a bee, he dove in. With the flat of his tongue, he licked her folds.

Her breath hitched, and he loved the little sounds she made. Her hips lifted as though presenting herself to him. His mouth surrounded the bundle of nerves, and he sucked while sliding a finger inside her sex.

"Oh God," she groaned as her fingers wove through his hair, her fingernails lightly scratching his scalp.

The tiny sting only made him suck harder. As her hips undulated, he reached up with one hand and palmed a breast, gently squeezing the nipple until she cried out. Lapping her release, he buried his nose in her trimmed curls, now filled with the scent of only her.

As he kissed his way back up her body, he nuzzled underneath her breasts, then circled each nipple with his tongue before sucking deeply again, trailing kisses over her collarbone, jaw, and then finally settling on her lips.

Another groan came from deep inside her, and he knew she could taste herself from the kiss.

If this had been all she'd wanted, he had given it willingly. He could wait for his own release. She lifted her hands and wrapped her arms around his back, pulling him close until his cock was nestled between her thighs.

"That's all we have to do, sweetheart," he said. "I'll be happy if I can just curl with you in my arms as we sleep."

A smile curved her lips, and he reveled in her beauty with the moonlight barely shining on her face from between the slats and the blinds.

"That was amazing, Pete. But I want more. I want all of you with all of me."

He'd never had anyone say those words to him when they were also his exact thoughts. He wanted all of her with all of him.

16

As Angie slowly drifted back to earth after experiencing the first non-self-induced orgasm she'd had in a while, she opened her eyes to find Pete's face just above her. His gaze was intense. Before he had a chance to say anything else, she pulled him closer with her legs open, hoping he would read her intentions.

His lips curved as his hips settled deep between her thighs, and the tip of his cock nudged the entrance to her sex.

It dawned on her that she didn't have any condoms. Months ago, she threw out the box she had, worried about an expiration date, considering she hadn't had anyone in her bedroom in a long time.

As though reading her mind, he said, "I need to get a condom. I carry one in my wallet, but I don't want you to think it's because I'm always on the prowl."

Thinking of him prowling around looking for a woman to bang had her grinning. In the weeks she came to know him, that wasn't who he was. "When did you put the condom in your wallet?"

"Last week."

Her eyes jerked open. "Really?"

A slight blush rose over his face as he grinned. "I wasn't planning anything, but I was hopeful. Hopeful that at some point, we'd come to the place in our relationship where we wanted this to go further."

"I have to tell you, Pete, I'm at that place now."

He pressed his hips down, and the feel of his heavy erection made her groan. Even though she'd just had an orgasm, she desperately craved the inner friction that she knew he would provide.

He suddenly slid off her body, and she immediately wanted to cry out. But just as quickly, he snagged his pants off the floor, pulled out his wallet, and, as he returned, had a condom between his fingers. He ripped it open and rolled it over his cock, then crawled up her body.

The anticipation had her lifting her hips, but he held his body completely still.

"I want you more than anything, Angie. But you're in control."

She sighed. "To be honest, I'd love to turn control over to you." Seeing his eyes widen and his pupils dilate, she smiled. "But, I know, I'm, um... position limited right now."

She winced, but he placed a gentle kiss on her lips. "I'll take care of you, but I have to know what works for you right now."

"If we're on the bed, being on my back or my side will be the only way my knee won't hurt."

"Babe, you have to know I'll be good. So whichever works best for you, that's what I want."

She chewed on her bottom lip and said, "Are you okay if we're on our sides, with you behind me?" She winced and shook her head, the sudden desire to cry filling her. "God, could I sound any less sexy if I tried?"

He barked out a scoff, and she felt the rumble from his chest to hers.

"There's one thing you've got to understand, Angie. You are the most beautiful woman I've been with and by far, the sexiest. There's nothing unsexy about letting your partner know what works for you. But speaking for myself, anyway that I can have you, even if we're standing on our heads, works for me."

She laughed at the vision. "Maybe we'll save our sexual acrobatics for another time."

"You got it, babe."

She rolled to her side, and he nuzzled her neck as he curled behind her. Her head rested on one of his arms, and his other arm banded around her, his hand cupping her breast. As his fingers danced over her nipple, she lifted her leg as he guided himself into her.

She clutched his hand as he pulled and tweaked each nipple, and she groaned as his tongue danced along her neck until he nibbled on her earlobe and kissed along her jaw. His thrusts were deep, dragging in and out, and she could feel the spring deep inside, coil tighter. Their bodies rocked in tandem, and she twisted her head so that her lips met his. With his cock thrusting in and out, his tongue mimicked the motion. She sucked on his tongue, then dragged hers along the roof of his mouth.

Another deep growl forced its way out of his chest, and she swallowed the sound, wanting to capture everything of his.

The coil kept tightening inside, but she needed more. Sliding her hand down, she pinched her clit, but quickly found her hand nudged out of the way.

Mumbling against her lips, he said, "Mine."

Considering that he began circling the bundle of nerves, she didn't care if he claimed it for himself.

Just as the spring was about to fly loose, his speed increased, and he began to pant, his hot breath now whispering over her cheek. She clutched his arm as her body convulsed, arching her back as the flutters deep inside became stronger. As her release hit, she could swear she saw lights dancing behind her closed eyelids. Desperately hoping he was close, she grinned as his arms banded around her even tighter, and with a final deep thrust, he erupted.

Finally, his body relaxed behind her, and they lay, their sweaty bodies cooling and their heartbeats slowing. When their breathing evened, he slid out, and she rolled carefully until she was facing him.

"Thank you," he said.

"What for?"

"For trusting me with your body. For trusting me to make a bad day a little bit better. For trusting me to carry you when you need help."

Their eyes met, and she smiled. "Can I entice you to take a shower with me?"

"The only enticement I need is the idea of you naked and wet," he said, chuckling.

Her body vibrated with a childlike giggle that burst forth. They rolled out of bed together. He disposed of the condom while she started the shower. They washed each other, and he was obviously being extra gentle with her swollen knee.

After the shower, the steam still lingered in the air, curling around them like the remnants of a dream. Angie stood at the vanity, sliding into a pair of soft cotton panties and a lace-trimmed camisole while Pete pulled on his boxers. The quiet between them wasn't awkward. Instead, it felt like something deeper and richer.

She reached into the drawer and handed him a fresh

toothbrush. Their fingers brushed, a simple touch that sent warmth up her arm.

"Thanks, baby." His voice was husky, his eyes lingering on her before he turned to the sink.

Once they were ready for bed, she flicked off the bathroom light, and they walked toward the bed together. The air shifted, thickening as they stood on opposite sides, gazes locked.

"What side do you sleep on?" His voice was soft, intimate, like a secret meant only for her.

A laugh bubbled up, light and easy. "The side closest to the bathroom."

He chuckled, nodding as if he'd expected that answer. "Good to know."

She slipped onto her side while he moved around the bed, lifting the covers and sliding in beside her. The mattress dipped beneath his weight, and the scent of fresh soap and warmth wrapped around her as he pulled the blankets over them, tucking her close. His arms wound around her, strong and steady, grounding her in a way she hadn't realized she needed.

She shifted slightly, adjusting until she was on her back, her body finding the perfect position against his.

"You want to tell me about your knee now?" His words were gentle, but there was an unmistakable undertone of concern.

A sigh slipped from her lips, followed by a small, rueful chuckle. "Honestly? No. But do I need to? Yes."

Rolling onto her right side, she faced him. A soft glow from the bedside lamp cast golden light over his face, tracing over the angles of his jaw, the curve of his lips, and the depth of his eyes. He was so beautiful that it made her chest ache.

She reached up, her fingers lightly cupping his jaw, her thumb grazing over the roughness of his evening stubble.

His voice dropped to a near whisper. "What are you afraid of, Angie?"

She hesitated, then shook her head, her fingers brushing against his skin. "I think I've been conditioned never to know how someone will react." Her voice was quiet, but there was strength in her honesty. "I have rheumatoid arthritis, Pete. RA for short. I was diagnosed in my early twenties, which is a little unusual. Most people either develop it as kids or much later in life. There's no denying it affects me."

She searched his face, waiting for a shift, waiting for something to tell her this was too much for him. But his expression remained steady, filled with concern, but there was no pity. No revulsion. Just him, listening.

"There are people who don't want to be with someone who has pain. Someone who has bad days, limitations." She scrunched her nose. "I shouldn't say limitations. There are people with RA who run marathons, hike mountains, and do things I probably never will. But if you wanted me to go for a run with you or suggested climbing some insane trail, I'd probably have to say no."

A muscle ticked in his jaw. "Angie, I know so little about it."

She pressed her lips together, then asked, "Do you want to know more?"

"Absolutely."

With his firm voice giving evidence that he really did want to know more, she nodded. "Essentially, it's a chronic autoimmune disease where the body's immune system mistakenly attacks joints, causing inflammation, pain, swelling, and stiffness. There isn't a cure, but various treatments can help manage symptoms and slow the disease's progression. It's systemic and can also affect other organs like the lungs, heart, eyes, skin, and blood vessels. I can't be out in the sun for very long or I start itching because my skin is affected." She shrugged. "I guess that's the gist of the way it affects me. Mostly my joints get stiff and swollen."

His voice was rough, full of emotion. "I hate like hell that you have RA, and hate that you think it would change how I feel about you. Anyone who wouldn't want to be with you because of it is a damn fool. And if you've had that happen before, their loss is absolutely my gain."

A giggle escaped before she pressed her lips together, shaking her head at him.

"The truth is, Pete, it's not just about knowing I might not be able to do some things. Being with me means doctor appointments. It means trying different medications. It means that some days, I might be fine, and others, I might have to cancel plans because my body just won't cooperate. Most of the time, I push through. But sometimes... I just can't."

He shifted closer, his forehead nearly touching hers. His thumb brushed along her cheek, his touch unbearably tender. "Sweetheart, I hope we'll get to the point where I can just look at you and know what you need. But until then, never be afraid to tell me. Never be afraid to say it's not a good day. Never be afraid to tell me how to help. I might not always get it right, but I swear to you, I will always try."

Her throat tightened, emotion swelling too fast, too thick. "I don't expect you to magically know, Pete."

"Then promise me." His voice was fierce, steady. "Promise me you'll talk to me."

A slow, deep breath filled her lungs. She met his gaze,

holding on to the intensity of it, onto the promise he was offering. "I promise."

His fingers sifted through her damp hair, curling around the nape of her neck as he leaned in, his lips brushing against hers in a kiss so soft, so full of unspoken words, it nearly undid her. And then, as he pulled back just enough to hold her gaze, he asked, "What do you think about me? What kind of man do you think I am?"

She hesitated, swallowing around the lump in her throat. When she finally spoke, her voice was barely above a whisper. "I'm afraid to hope."

His hand tightened at her nape. "Angie, we've been seeing each other for weeks now. We work together, we spend time together, we share, we talk, and now we're here —being intimate in every way. So I'll ask again." His voice was quiet but firm. "What kind of man do you think I am?"

She searched his face, her pulse fluttering against her ribs. "I think you're the kind of man who doesn't care if I can't run a marathon."

A slow, knowing smile spread across his face. "That's absolutely right." He shifted, brushing another kiss against her temple. "I don't care if you run marathons, baby. As long as you run to me for whatever you need."

A shuddering breath left her, something breaking loose inside her chest, something she hadn't even realized she'd been holding on to. She didn't think. Didn't hesitate. Her hands fisted in his hair, and she pulled him down, crashing her lips to his.

It wasn't a soft kiss. It wasn't careful. It was deep and consuming, filled with everything she couldn't say, every-thing she wanted, everything she was terrified to believe she could have.

His groan rumbled against her lips as he rolled her beneath him, his weight settling over her, surrounding her.

And as his hands roamed, as his lips claimed her again and again, she knew he wasn't just saying words. He was showing her how much she meant to him.

17

The bright fluorescent lights of SuperMart gleamed down on the wide aisles, reflecting off polished tile floors that had seen countless shopping carts roll over them. The store was packed with towering shelves stacked with everything from cereal to camping gear, and the distant hum of checkout beeps created a background rhythm to the Saturday afternoon chaos.

"No, no. It's not in the baking section. It's going to be where the toothpaste is," Marty said.

"But if it's like a toothpick, it's gonna be with the cake mixes," Jimmy countered. "I know that because I've been with my mom when she got toothpicks." Jimmy's voice held the certainty of someone who had navigated these aisles before.

"It's like a toothpick, but not a toothpick," Marty said, rubbing his chin as if that might help him remember more details.

Jimmy sighed, shifting his weight. "Okay, Mr. Marty, can you just tell me what it looks like?"

"It's blue. Well, sometimes it's green. Or, uh... kind of bluish-green. I think I've even seen 'em in white."

Jimmy's brows drew together. "Okay, let's forget about the color. Is it the shape of a toothpick?"

"Not really. But it does have a sharp point. Only on one end."

Marty squinted, scanning the store. "I tell you what. I think we can find it together if you just help me get to where the toothpaste is."

"You got it, Mr. Marty."

The two set off down the gleaming aisle, weaving through displays of brightly packaged mouthwashes and toothbrush multipacks. After a thorough search, Jimmy finally plucked a bag of floss picks from the shelf, holding them up like a game show prize. "This it?" he asked, his eyebrows arched.

"That's it!" Marty declared triumphantly, a grin splitting his wrinkled face.

Jimmy stared at the package in disbelief, then gave a slow nod. "Well... I'm glad we found 'em."

The pair strolled off, heading toward the next item on the list, leaving Angie watching with a smirk.

From everything she'd seen so far, the kids had more patience than some adults, and the adopted grandparents weren't just shopping for themselves—they were making sure the kids got things they liked too.

Curious, she drifted toward the men's clothing section, where she spotted another unlikely duo deep in a debate.

"I need the large," Harold said, squinting at a package of undershirts.

Caleb, arms crossed, gave him a skeptical once-over. "Mr. Harold, you ain't that big."

Harold frowned. "What do you mean, I ain't that big? I've always bought large."

Caleb flipped the package over and pointed at the sizing chart. "According to this, I think you'd only be a medium."

"But I always wear a large," Harold insisted.

Kryon raised an eyebrow, first looking at Caleb, then back at Harold. "You tryna look like you're from the hood?"

Harold's forehead creased, adding extra depth to the wrinkles already there. "I don't know what that means."

"It's just a look, you know?" Kryon shrugged. "Big over-sized white T-shirts? That's what some guys wear on purpose."

Harold's lips pressed into a thin line as he processed this revelation. With an exaggerated scowl, he shook his head. "I'm not trying to look like anything. I just want my shirts to fit."

Caleb stood next to Harold, still holding the package of undershirts as if he were trying to understand the older man's reasoning. "Can you tell me why?"

Harold frowned and gave a halfhearted shrug. "It's just easier."

"Easier?" Caleb tilted his head. "I don't know what you mean, Mr. Harold."

Harold let out a slow breath, as if deciding how much to say. "My arms and shoulders don't work as good as they used to. If the T-shirt's too tight, it's hard to pull over my head and get my arms through. But if it's a little bigger, I got more room to move, and I can usually get it on by myself."

Caleb stilled, glancing between Harold, Kyron, and the undershirts in his hands. After a beat, he nodded. "Well… okay. I think that makes sense. I never thought about it, but you're right." Without hesitation, he tossed the package of large T-shirts into their shopping cart. Then, with an easy grin, he patted Harold on the shoulder. "What's next?"

Harold gave a small, appreciative smile and nudged the cart forward. "Something on the list about socks, I think."

A few aisles away, Angie had slipped out of sight behind a display of neatly folded jeans, pressing her fingers to her eyes in an effort to keep a tear from falling. She had expected the outing to be productive, maybe even enjoyable. But she hadn't expected moments like this. Moments when her clients weren't just picking out things they needed but also opening up and sharing things they might not have said otherwise.

A warm hand landed on her shoulder, and she jumped, spinning around.

Pete stood there, brows drawn together in concern. "Is something wrong?"

She shook her head quickly. "No, not at all. This is going so much better than I imagined. My clients are opening up. They're telling the kids about things they need or things that bother them. And your kids..." Her voice wavered, but she smiled. "Your kids are amazing."

His frown softened into a grin, and without a word, he cupped her face, brushing his thumb under her eye in a gentle swipe. Then, before she could say anything else, he leaned in and pressed a quick kiss to her lips.

"I'm heading to the food section," he murmured. "Gotta keep an eye on whoever's already there. No tellin' what they'll throw in the cart."

Angie chuckled, shaking her head as he walked off. Out of the corner of her eye, she spotted Curly and Mike standing near the women's clothing section with Ms. Rosetta. Intrigued, she slipped around the next aisle to listen in.

"Why are you getting the dark blue one?" Curly asked, nodding toward the shirt in Ms. Rosetta's hands.

"Because it's nice," she replied, smoothing the fabric between her fingers.

"Yeah, but you looked at the yellow one first." He pointed at the bright, cheerful fabric hanging on the rack. "That one's real pretty. Like a happy color."

Rosetta hesitated. "Yes, but I don't know if it's right for me."

Mike squinted. "You said yellow was your favorite color."

She nodded, then sighed. "I did. But I don't want to look like Big Bird in it."

Mike blinked and looked at Curly before turning his attention back to Rosetta. "Big Bird?"

"From *Sesame Street*. The great big yellow bird."

Curly snorted, shaking his head. "Man, life's too short for you not to get what you want, Ms. Rosetta."

She froze, blinking at the unexpected wisdom in his words. Her gaze flickered between the dark blue shirt and the bright yellow one, a small, thoughtful frown settling on her face.

Angie watched from a distance, biting back a grin. It seemed today wasn't just about shopping. It was about realizing what truly mattered, one aisle at a time.

Curly tilted his head and gave her an expectant look. "Let's ask Mr. George." Without waiting for a response, he cupped his hands around his mouth and called out, "Hey, Mr. George! Which shirt do you think Ms. Rosetta should get?"

Rasheem, who had been helping push George's wheelchair, steered him closer to where Curly, Mike, and Rosetta stood by the racks of women's tops.

George, sharp-eyed despite his years, took one glance at the shirts and grinned. "The yellow one."

Rosetta's lips parted slightly in surprise. "You think so?"

He nodded, his grin widening. "Daffodils are my favorite color, and Ms. Rosetta, you'd look like a beautiful daffodil if you wore that."

The boys shared a look before breaking into identical wide grins, while Ms. Rosetta's cheeks turned a rosy shade of pink.

"Well then," she murmured, reaching out and plucking the yellow shirt from the rack. "I suppose I'll take it."

Curly pumped a fist. "That's what I'm talkin' about!"

Angie watched the scene unfold from a short distance away, her heart swelling. This trip had been about shopping, but more than that, it had been about connections. Moments like this, where a compliment could brighten someone's day or a simple gesture could make all the difference.

As planned, they had saved the grocery section for last. Angie had always intended it that way, but she was pleasantly surprised when Caleb had suggested the same thing the moment they'd entered the store.

She, Pete, and Richard wandered up and down the food aisles, answering questions, offering suggestions, and making sure everything was running smoothly. Truthfully, though, Angie knew she could have left the kids and their adopted grandparents completely alone, and they would have been just fine.

At checkout, the kids quickly took over the bagging, making sure to thank the elders for the little things they had bought for them.

Once the carts were emptied, the bags packed up, and the receipts tucked away, they all made their way outside. The kids helped load everything into the two ESAAA vans, making sure nothing got left behind. Then it was time for goodbyes.

The elders climbed into one large van, chatting among themselves, already making plans for what they'd do with their purchases. The kids piled into the other, still riding the high of a successful shopping trip.

Richard and Pete were tasked with dropping the kids off at their homes before returning to Angie's office, where their personal vehicles were parked.

Angie turned to say goodbye to Pete, but before she could get the words out, she noticed that his attention was locked onto something across the parking lot.

She followed his gaze to the side of the supermarket, where a small group of young men lounged against the brick wall, cigarettes dangling from their fingers. They weren't just hanging out. Dressed in their red and black, they were watching the van full of their kids.

A chill ran down Angie's spine. She stepped closer to Pete and murmured, "Are you okay?"

Pete jerked slightly, as if snapping out of a trance. When he turned to face her, his expression was carefully neutral, but his eyes were dark with something unreadable.

He forced a smile, but it didn't quite reach his eyes. "Yeah, I'm fine. I'll see you back at your office, okay?"

Angie hesitated. Something was off, but she knew pushing him for answers right now wasn't the right move. Instead, she reached out, placing a hand on his arm and squeezing gently.

"Absolutely," she said with a small smile. "I'll be there."

As Pete turned toward the vans, his body tensed with something unspoken. Angie couldn't shake the feeling that the lighthearted joy of the afternoon had just shifted into something far more serious. And whatever it was, Pete knew what it was.

18

The traffic stop should have been routine. A North Heron County Sheriff's Department deputy clocked the car—a sleek, dark sedan with blacked-out windows—barreling down the highway at nearly eighty miles per hour in a fifty-five zone.

But what should have been simple turned into chaos in an instant.

Pete heard the urgency crackle over the radio as multiple deputies joined the pursuit. What started as a single patrol car flashing its lights had escalated into a high-speed chase, sirens wailing.

He and Jeremy had been on their way to meet one of their informants when the call came in. Jeremy, hands steady on the wheel, flicked his gaze to Pete, already tracking the unfolding situation.

"If this idiot keeps heading south, he'll hit the bridge," Pete muttered, eyes scanning the dark highway ahead. "Between us, the CBBT, and Virginia Beach PD, he'll have nowhere to go."

Jeremy huffed a dry laugh, shifting in his seat. "What do you wanna bet he's carrying drugs?"

They listened as the dispatcher's voice cut through the radio again. *Suspect has turned off the main highway. Now traveling at high speeds on rural roads.*

Pete shook his head. "No way he's local. He's got no idea what he's in for. These backroads? Hell, they're more potholes than pavement. He won't be able to keep up that speed for long."

Jeremy keyed his mic. "North Heron, DTF Unit 17, we're standing by near the southern end of the county."

As they monitored the chase, the radio crackled again. The suspect had taken a sharp turn, heading straight for Baytown.

Pete and Jeremy locked eyes. In perfect unison, they growled, "Oh shit."

A high-speed chase was bad enough, but Baytown was another level of danger entirely. No traffic lights, no wide highways. The town was just narrow streets and people out walking or riding bikes or in golf carts. A reckless driver plowing through town at these speeds was a disaster in the making.

Jeremy yanked the wheel to veer off the highway and gunned it toward Baytown.

Through the radio, they caught Baytown's Police Chief Mitch Evans's firm order to deploy the spike strips. A minute later, the radio crackled with an update. *Driver attempted to evade—vehicle's in a ditch. Foot pursuit in progress. One suspect in vehicle.*

A beat of silence. *Suspects in custody.*

Pete exhaled sharply, raking a hand through his hair as Jeremy smirked. Pete grabbed the radio. "DTF Unit 17 en route." Then, turning to Jeremy, he grinned, slow and knowing. "You asked what I'd bet?"

Jeremy raised a brow.

Pete leaned back against the seat, shaking his head. "I'd bet my last paycheck they're carrying. Drugs, guns—something. But he's carrying."

Jeremy pulled the SUV to a stop near the wrecked vehicle, leaving enough space for the emergency responders still arriving on the scene. The flashing red and blue lights painted the ditch in erratic strokes, illuminating the sedan that had skidded off the road and landed on its side in the ravine.

Pete surveyed the wreck, his sharp gaze sweeping over the tilted frame. The car landed on the passenger side, which explained how the driver had managed to bail out and run, leaving his passenger behind.

The driver stood near the back of a deputy's vehicle, handcuffed and mouthing off continuously. The passenger, once pulled from the wreckage, was sitting on the grass nearby as the EMT checked him out. He appeared young, and if his tears were anything to go by, he'd gotten into more than he'd planned.

Pete's attention was diverted as a dog barked. "Good," Pete muttered, spotting the familiar figure of Carly, the K9 handler, and her muscular black shepherd, Nero. "The K9 unit's already here."

Carly turned as they approached, her expression sharp and ready for business. "Took you long enough."

Pete smirked. "I have a feeling Nero's about to make our night a whole lot more interesting."

She chuckled, patting the dog's harness. "He's locked in and ready to go."

Jeremy and Pete followed as she led Nero to the trunk. A deputy popped it open, revealing an empty cargo space.

The suspect, now in cuffs and pinned against a patrol

car, barked out a laugh. "Ain't got no right to be searchin' my shit. Y'all got nothin' on me."

The deputy holding him didn't so much as blink. "Speeding. Evading law enforcement. Resisting arrest. That's plenty."

The man scoffed. "That ain't nothing."

Before Pete could respond, Nero let out a sharp bark and lunged toward the back door of the sedan, his paws scraping against the metal. The energy shifted instantly as every deputy tensed.

Jeremy and Pete moved in, wrenching the door open. A blast of stale air mixed with fast-food grease hit them. The back seat was a mess with discarded soda cans, snack wrappers, and crumpled receipts, but nothing obvious.

Yet Nero wasn't letting up. He sniffed the seat, then abruptly sat on his haunches, ears pricked, muscles taut.

Carly's voice was calm but sure. "He's found something."

Pete took the crowbar from a nearby deputy and wedged it between the seat cushions. With a sharp grunt, he pried them apart. The second he caught a glimpse of the plastic-wrapped bricks crammed inside, he let out a low whistle. He turned to Jeremy, a slow grin stretching across his face. "Bingo."

The energy at the scene shifted again, this time with electric urgency.

"Start bagging it," Jeremy said as the deputies moved in with evidence kits. "And get the forensics team out here."

Carly held Nero back, but the dog was still restless, nose twitching as he pulled against his handler. Pete frowned. "There's more?"

Carly nodded. "Let him work."

She loosened the leash just enough for Nero to guide them. The shepherd sniffed along the floorboards, then suddenly twisted toward the back door and started pawing at the panel.

Jeremy didn't hesitate. He grabbed the crowbar and jammed it into the seam, using brute force to pry it open. A second later, another set of plastic-wrapped bricks tumbled onto the ground.

Pete exhaled. "Son of a bitch."

The team worked efficiently, cataloging each find. Pete jogged back to his SUV and grabbed the field testing kit. He didn't need to test every package—just enough for confirmation. The moment the reagent turned blue, he exchanged a look with Jeremy.

"Cocaine," Pete muttered.

The methodical process of bagging, labeling, and logging began. Photographs were taken, and body cameras recorded every step. No one was taking shortcuts. Pete and Jeremy had seen too many cases fall apart over a sloppy chain of custody.

The tow truck from Baytown rolled up just as the last of the drugs were secured. As the car was lifted from the ditch, they found more hidden compartments—stacks of cash beneath the driver's seat and another stash of drugs crammed behind the dashboard.

They worked alongside Baytown officers, state police, and even a DEA agent out of Virginia Beach for hours, processing what was quickly shaping up to be a major bust.

"The driver keeps swearing he didn't know what was in the car," a deputy said. "Claims he borrowed it from a friend."

Pete snorted. "Yeah, sure. We'll dust for prints."

"What about the kid?" Jeremy asked, his tone shifting slightly.

"Sixteen. A juvenile. Local."

Pete let out a slow breath, rolling his shoulders. "Once everything is processed, we'll question them both."

By this time, the sun was lowering, and Pete and Jeremy also needed to get everything back to the sheriff's department. All the evidence bags were loaded into the back of their SUV in front of witnesses. The DEA agent shook their hands and said he would check in with them tomorrow. The two state police officers did the same. Now, with a convoy of deputy cruisers in front and behind them, they drove to the sheriff's department. Once there, the unloading process was much the same. Everything was cataloged and placed in a secure, locked holding area for potentially dangerous evidence.

The haul was substantial—too damn big for comfort. He barely had time to roll the stiffness from his neck before the ESDTF Captain Terry Bunswick strode into the room, his presence commanding as ever. Right behind him was Colt, the county sheriff, his rugged features etched with the weight of responsibility. The two men, along with the sheriff from Acawmacke County, shared leadership of the Eastern Shore Drug Task Force, and if they were both here in person, Pete knew this bust had already made waves.

"This has already hit the news," Terry announced grimly, his voice edged with frustration.

Pete let out a slow breath and shook his head, glancing at Jeremy, who sat at the desk beside him. "Fucking hell," he muttered, rubbing his temples.

Jeremy barely looked up as he addressed their superiors. "Please tell me you're not going to make us do an interview."

Terry shook his head. "No, not at all. The media relations officer is handling that. But we need a picture of the haul."

Pete exhaled sharply, leaning back in his chair. "Fine. Just don't expect me to be in it."

"Agreed." Terry crossed his arms, his expression darkening. "The Virginia Beach newspaper, as well as the local publication, wanted a full spread—with the drugs laid out and officers standing behind. But I told them no way in hell. I'm not putting my people on display like that. Once this hits national news and the TV stations, I don't want any of you becoming the next target for some cartel looking to make an example."

Pete nodded, a weight lifting from his chest. It wasn't paranoia… it was reality. Drug gangs didn't take kindly to law enforcement seizing their product. "Appreciate that, Captain," he said, offering a grateful chin lift toward Colt. "You too."

Colt gave a firm nod, the silent understanding between them heavy with unspoken truths.

They kept the media away from the evidence room. Instead, the confiscated bags were stacked on a table against a blank wall. Pete and Jeremy moved to the back of the room with other officers, blending into the shadows as the reporters were ushered in. Before cameras flashed, Colt took the lead, setting strict boundaries on what they could and couldn't do.

Pete didn't let his guard down for a second, watching the reporters like a hawk. He didn't trust them. Not because they were the enemy but because information had a way of slipping through cracks, and if the wrong people got their hands on it, someone could end up dead.

Terry answered questions in clipped, practiced tones, offering nothing of real substance. "The investigation is ongoing," he said more than once. That was all the press was getting.

As soon as the reporters left, the tension in the room

eased. Jeremy and Pete stayed behind with the evidence officer, ensuring every last bag was logged and secured before finally heading back to their desks.

The hum of fluorescent lights buzzed overhead as Pete tapped at his keyboard, the familiar monotony of report writing setting in. He hated paperwork. Almost as much as he hated dealing with the press. He thought about the aborted trip to talk to their local informant. "We never even got to talk to Jacko," he murmured, his eyes still on the screen.

Jeremy, leaning back in his chair, cracked his knuckles. "We can still try tomorrow. Talk to him and the two arrested today."

Pete nodded, rubbing a hand over his jaw. "Yeah. Sounds like a plan." He flexed his fingers and took a deep breath. It had been a hell of a day. And something told him tomorrow wouldn't be any easier.

Jeremy nudged him. "You seeing Angie tonight?"

Pete hesitated, then shrugged. "I don't know. Might just give her a call."

Jeremy's grin was unmistakable. "Cora and I are practically living together at this point."

Pete didn't say anything at first. He'd never been the type to rush into things, but the idea of coming home to Angie wasn't something that sent him running. In fact, he couldn't think of anything better.

19

The sterile walls of the interview room seemed to press in, the air thick with unspoken tension. The metal, utilitarian table in the center had witnessed years of similar conversations—some cooperative, some not.

The door swung open, and one of the guards stepped in, leading the scrawny teenager they'd seen earlier that morning. The kid who had been left behind, stuck in the car while the driver took off without a second thought.

No honor among thieves, Pete thought grimly.

Robert Reeves slouched into the chair, his shoulders tense, his knee bouncing under the table. Twitchy, but not the kind of twitchy that came from detox. This was nerves. Fear, maybe.

Pete had seen his file. No priors. Decent school attendance. Yet here he was, sitting across from two detectives, acting like he was about to take on the world. "Okay, Robert. You—"

"Superman," the kid interrupted, lifting his shaky chin in an attempt at bravado.

Pete arched a brow. "If you're trying to say that's your

gang name, I gotta tell you—just because Christopher Reeves played Superman in a movie about forty years before you were born, that don't mean that name works for you."

Robert's mouth twisted into a pout, and his tough act slipped for a second, making him look like a little kid instead of a sixteen-year-old trying to run with the big boys.

Jeremy leaned forward, arms on the table, his voice steady but firm. "Let's cut the shit. This is your first arrest, but it's a doozy. And guess what? They've added new charges. You think you're getting out on charm alone?" He snorted. "Nah. But this *is* your first charge. So tell me you got at least one brain cell rattling around in that head of yours—enough to know that working with us will go a long way with the judge."

Fear raced through Robert's eyes, but he scoffed. "Man, I can't talk to you. I'd be a dead man."

Pete tilted his head, his eyes sharpening. "What makes you think that?"

Robert slouched deeper in his chair, eyes darting toward the door like he wanted to bolt. "I know how this works. In here, I keep my mouth shut and... um... maybe... I... " He swallowed deeply. "I might be protected?" His statement ended up as more of a question.

Pete now knew the kid was in for more than he could handle. He let the silence hang for a beat before repeating, slowly, "Protected?" His voice dripped with incredulity. "You talkin' about by your fellow gang members?"

He caught the slight shift in Robert's posture—the way his chest deflated like the air going out of a balloon.

Pete shook his head, exhaling sharply. "Or... are you talking about your real family?"

Robert's gaze jumped to Pete's.

"Your mom. Maybelline Reeves. Works as a cleaner in the hospital. Steady work, decent money. Long hours, though. Makes it tough to be home when your little brother and sister get off the school bus." Pete leaned in. "That was something you always did, right? You're out of school first, home in time to help out."

Robert's breath froze in his lungs.

"You got a little brother. Ten years old. Richie." Pete's voice was low but relentless. "Does he look up to you? Think you're a big man? What's he gonna say when he hears his big brother got locked up?"

Robert clenched his jaw and dropped his gaze. His hands curled into fists, resting on the table. Pete noted, with some satisfaction, that they weren't tattooed yet.

"And then there's your sister. Sherrie. Eight years old." Pete let the weight of his words settle before he continued. "How's this gonna affect her?"

Robert's shoulders stiffened. "It won't touch her."

"You think?" Pete snapped. "You think when the news says you're in with a known gang member, that won't touch her? That she won't get called names at school? That your mom won't have to answer questions? And your grandfather? If you believe that, you're dumber than you look."

Robert's lips pressed into a tight line, his gaze locked on the table. The silence stretched between them, thick and heavy. Pete and Jeremy didn't rush him. They let him sit with it, let it seep in. Let him feel the weight of it all.

Finally, after what felt like an eternity, Robert let out a slow breath. His voice was quieter now. "Look... I didn't know what he had," he muttered. "I didn't know about all that shit he had stuffed in the car."

Pete exchanged a glance with Jeremy. It wasn't much, but it was a start. And in their line of work, a start was all they needed. Pete folded his arms, his gaze locked on Robert. "So you just get in the car with a stranger you've never met and don't think about what might be in the vehicle?"

Robert let out an irritated huff. "Man, you make me sound like I'm stupid." He leaned back in his chair, trying to play it cool, but his twitchy fingers drummed against the edge of the table, betraying his nerves.

"Explain it to me."

Robert exhaled sharply, shaking his head. "Ciao's been comin' around for a while now. Just talkin', you know? Shootin' the shit. Asking me about school, about my family. Making me feel like I mattered." His voice dropped slightly. "Told me he had a family now. Better than any family he ever had before."

Pete's eyes flicked to Jeremy before settling back on the kid. "Ciao? You mean Lashawn. Another dumbass name."

Robert blinked in confusion.

Pete continued, "And you knew what he meant by family, didn't you?"

Robert lifted his chin, forcing his mind back to the detectives. "Yeah. Saw the tats on his fingers. Bloods." He shrugged, feigning nonchalance, but his knee kept bouncing under the table. "My mom always told me gangs were dirty. Said to stay away from gangs. But I wasn't doing anything. We were just talkin'."

Jeremy leaned forward, elbows on the table. "How long were you two just talkin'?"

Robert squirmed slightly, his bravado slipping for a moment. "I dunno... couple of months, at least."

"Did he come by on a schedule? Same days of the week? Once a week? Twice a week?" Pete pressed.

"Nah, nothin' regular. I get off the bus first, like you

said. I'd be out chillin' with some others. After the first time Ciao came around, I kinda started lookin' for him."

Jeremy's expression darkened. "What about the other kids in your neighborhood? They hang around, too?"

Robert smirked, shaking his head. "Some weren't there 'cause they got after-school shit. Some…" He chuckled, running a hand across his mouth. "Some were scared."

He glanced up, expecting some kind of reaction, but Pete just stared at him, unreadable.

Robert scoffed. "Called 'em pussies."

Pete's eyes narrowed. "I don't know that I'd call them pussies. I think smart might be the word I'm going for."

Robert's gaze dropped. His fingers curled into a fist on the table, but he didn't say anything at first. "I ain't dumb," he muttered after a moment. "It's not like Ciao walked up and said, 'Hey, I'm gonna have a car full of shit, wanna come for a ride?'"

"Okay," Pete said evenly. "So what did he say?"

Robert licked his lips, eyes darting toward the mirrored window before settling back on Pete. "Just said he was gonna grab somethin' to eat. Asked if I wanted to roll with him."

Pete tilted his head. "Was your mom home?"

Robert shook his head. "Nah."

"So who was gonna get your brother and sister off the bus?"

Robert flinched, his fingers tightening in his lap. "Look, I ain't there every day. If I'm not waitin' on them, they go to one of the neighbors. They let 'em hang out till Mom gets home."

Pete gave a slow nod, then continued. "Alright. So you get in the car with him. He decides to go for a little ride. You ever get something to eat? Did you ever stop?"

Robert scoffed, shaking his head. "Didn't get the damn

chance. He was goin' too fuckin' fast, and then the deputy got on his ass."

Jeremy folded his arms. "What were you doing during all this?"

Robert dropped his gaze, his hands clenched together, knuckles white. His voice was quieter now, stripped of the false bravado. "I told him to slow down." He exhaled, shaking his head. "Then when they started chasin' us, I told him to stop."

Pete waited a beat. "And he didn't."

Robert let out a bitter laugh, but there was no humor in it. His jaw tightened as he lifted his gaze, eyes filled with something sharp and exhausted. "I think you already know the answer to that," he bit out.

Pete leaned in slightly, his voice even but unrelenting. "Right. So he didn't slow down, didn't stop. What was going through your mind then?"

Robert sucked in his bottom lip, biting down hard, like he was trying to keep something painful from spilling out. His knee bounced under the table again, but this time, it wasn't cockiness—it was something raw. "I was scared, okay?" he finally burst out, voice sharp with frustration. "Is that what you wanna hear?"

Jeremy tilted his head, his expression unreadable. "Well, hearing that you were scared tells me you still got a brain cell left," he said. "If you hadn't been scared, I'd be thinking you were a lost cause."

Robert's shoulders slumped. Some of the fight drained out of him, and for a second, he just stared at the table, jaw tight, hands clenched into fists.

Pete pressed on. "When all hell broke loose with sirens, cops everywhere... and then Lashawn lost control of the car, I wanna know what went through your head when he climbed out and took off."

Robert's gaze snapped up to Pete's, his chest rising and falling with a deep breath. He let it out slowly, but his eyes didn't waver.

"He got his door open," he said quietly. "Stepped on the damn steering wheel while I was still trying to get the airbag out of my face. Since we were up on our side, he climbed out first." Robert swallowed hard, like the words physically hurt to say. "I was still stuck in my seat belt. I called for him to help me."

His throat bobbed, and his voice cracked slightly as he said, "He left. He fucking ran away."

Neither Pete nor Jeremy said a word. They let the silence settle over the room, let Robert sit with the weight of his own words.

Pete gave a slow nod, like he was acknowledging the truth of it without needing to say I told you so. After a long beat, he finally spoke. "And when we found the drugs hidden in the car?"

Robert flinched. His face twisted for a second, like he wanted to deny everything, but then his shoulders slumped again. "I was… surprised," he admitted, voice quieter now. "And then I wasn't sure why I was surprised. And then I just thought… I was fucked."

He exhaled sharply. "I don't even know why he needed me to come with him. I don't know if he really was gonna get food or if that was just—" He shook his head. "I don't know. I still don't know."

Pete didn't glance at Jeremy. He didn't need to. They were in sync, reading the situation the same way. Robert was cracking, piece by piece.

"We can't tell you what Lashawn was really planning," Pete said evenly. "We'll talk to him later. But if I had to guess?" He leaned back in his chair, arms crossed. "He probably was gonna get food. That'd be an easy way to keep talking to you without anyone else around. Keep working on you. Keep making you feel like he was your boy, like you belonged."

Robert was staring at the table, but Pete could tell he was listening.

"That's how they do it," Pete continued. "They make you want it. Make you feel like you need them. They don't come right out and say, 'Hey, wanna sling drugs for us?' Nah. They take their time. Get you thinking they're family. That you owe them something. And then, before you know it? You're running drugs. Selling. Getting caught up in something you can't walk away from."

Robert pressed his lips together, his breathing shallow.

Pete let the words sink in before he finished, "And you? You were an easy target."

Robert's head jerked up, eyes flashing. "What's that supposed to mean?"

Pete didn't flinch. "It means you looked like you wanted someone to pay attention to you. And they saw that. They saw you wanted in, and they started reeling you closer. And you were going along with it."

Robert swallowed hard. His fists clenched again, this time tighter. "That'd kill my mama and my grandpa," he murmured, voice barely above a whisper.

Jeremy nodded. "Yeah. It probably would."

Robert dropped his chin to his chest. His breath hitched slightly, and then, before he could stop it, a tear slipped down his cheek. He wiped it away fast, but they saw it.

"I knew," he mumbled. "The second he stepped on the gas instead of slowing down... I knew everything was gonna go to hell."

"Pretty much," Jeremy agreed. He let a moment pass before adding, "But this is your first arrest. You weren't driving. No alcohol, no drugs in your system. That's gonna go a long way with the DA."

Robert didn't answer. He just sat there, staring at the table, his body rigid.

Pete exchanged a look with Jeremy. They had him now. Now they just had to figure out what came next.

Robert's leg bounced under the table again, his fingers drumming an uneven rhythm against the metal surface. His eyes darted to the door, like he was already planning his escape from this conversation.

"But if I talk about anything that happened," he muttered, his voice tight, "they'll come after me, won't they?"

Pete didn't answer right away. Instead, he leaned back, keeping his tone casual—like he wasn't asking for the most dangerous thing Robert had probably ever been asked to do. "Have you seen Lashawn talk to any other kids in your apartment complex?"

Robert hesitated, then shrugged. "Some," he admitted. "I mean, it's not like I'm the only one he talks to. He drives up in his car, all big talk and flashy. There are usually a few who hang around."

Pete nodded like he expected that. "Can you remember who they are?"

Robert's face twisted, and just like that, the wall slammed back into place. He leaned forward, shaking his head. "Nah. I ain't saying nothin' else." His voice had an edge of panic to it now, covered up by forced defiance. "I'm sixteen. They might not send me to Norfolk for juvie. Right now, they're keeping me here, but I'm separate from the adults. That's the only thing keepin' me safe." His voice dipped lower, his throat working as he swallowed. "But I ain't stupid. If I start answering more of your questions, it's gonna get back to them. I know it will."

Pete didn't argue. Didn't push. He just sat there, waiting.

Robert sucked in a shaky breath, his hands gripping the edge of the table like he needed something solid to hold on to. "I wouldn't put it past Ciao to kill me himself," he admitted, voice barely above a whisper. "That's why he got the name, you know. Anybody crosses him, and it's goodbye."

Neither Pete nor Jeremy spoke right away. They let the weight of those words settle, let Robert sit with them.

Finally, Pete nodded and rapped on the door. The guard stepped in, waiting for instructions.

"We're done for now," Pete said. But before Robert could be led out, he added, "You can get ahold of us anytime you want to talk. Doesn't matter when. You let the guards know, and they'll call us."

Robert didn't respond, just stared at the table. But Pete saw the flicker of hesitation in his expression, like maybe he wasn't ready to be thrown back into this mess alone.

The guard led Robert out, and as the heavy door clicked shut behind them, Pete let out a slow breath.

Jeremy glanced over as they made their way down the hall. "What are you thinking?"

Pete ran a hand through his hair, exhaling sharply. "I want to go talk to some of my kids. They live in that apartment complex. I'd like to make sure none of them are looking in the wrong direction."

Jeremy nodded. "All right. Tell me when and where, and I'll come with you."

Pete gave him a grateful nod. He was glad for the backup. But at the same time, he hated that this was even something they had to do. Because deep down, he knew Lashawn wasn't just looking at Robert. And Pete prayed that none of his kids were getting caught in the same web.

20

He finished his paperwork, then sent a message to Angie. **Long day. Just heading home.**

Unfortunately, her short but simple reply didn't tell him anything. **I'm sorry. Talk to you later.**

Pete stared at his phone, rereading her text for the third time. *Talk to you later?*

That was it. There was no... *I'll see you soon,* or *I can't wait to see you,* or *do you need anything?* He wasn't sure why he wanted more, but for some indescribable reason, he did. Yet his own text had been just as brief.

His fingers drummed absently against the steering wheel as he debated stopping by her place on his way home. Angie's house sat between the station and his, a natural detour that wouldn't take him more than five minutes. But her message hadn't exactly been an invitation. If she'd wanted him to drop by, wouldn't she have said so?

He sighed heavily, rolling his shoulders to loosen the tension gripping them. He'd never been the kind of guy to second-guess himself, but somehow, Angie had him over-thinking every damn thing. In the end, he kept driving, pushing aside the urge to turn down her street.

By the time he pulled onto his own driveway, his mind was tangled in a mess of thoughts. Relationships were complicated—at least, the real ones were. The ones that mattered. And maybe that was what scared him a little. He and Angie had been easy from the start. Good chemistry, incredible sex, and an effortless way of working together on their project. She listened to him without judgment, never tried to change him, and made him feel like who he was, even flaws and all, was enough.

But it had only been a few weeks. Was that just the so-called honeymoon phase? And what the hell did he even know about a honeymoon phase? He hadn't exactly been the poster boy for long-term relationships.

His grip on the steering wheel tightened... then immediately loosened when his gaze landed on the car parked in his driveway. His breath caught at the sight. *Angie.*

A slow smile tugged at his lips as he shoved the truck into park. Before he could even get the door fully open, she was stepping out of her car, bending over the passenger seat to grab something. He barely registered the cool night air as he crossed the distance between them. By the time she stood with a large paper bag in her arms, he was there.

She looked up at him, nerves flickering in her eyes... or maybe it was uncertainty. Her gaze mirrored his, and he didn't like it. When it came to him, he wanted her to feel nothing but confident.

"I brought some dinner," she said, her voice soft. "I knew it was a bad day. Cora called me and told me what was happening."

Pete huffed out a chuckle, reaching for the bag. "Looks like our medical examiner has decided to play matchmaker."

Cora Wadsworth was as dedicated as they came, but like Pete, she wasn't exactly an open book. The fact that she'd gone out of her way to make sure Angie knew what kind of day he'd had? That said a lot. And maybe it meant Cora thought Angie was sticking around.

He wasn't sure why that thought hit him square in the chest, but it did. Love changes all of us. The thought came unbidden, making him jolt inside. Love? No, not yet. It was too soon. But falling... maybe that was happening. *Shit...*

"Pete?"

Angie's voice pulled him back, her forehead creased in concern.

He shook himself. "Sorry. My brain's running in too many directions."

She let out a breath, shifting her purse onto her shoulder. "I just thought maybe you hadn't eaten since breakfast, so I wanted to make sure you had something. I'm not inviting myself in," she added quickly, the nerves he'd seen earlier flashing again. "I just wanted to see you. Even for a minute."

Dammit. He'd made her feel like she wasn't welcome, and that was the last thing he wanted. He took a step closer, bent as he lowered his voice, and said, "Angie, I'm glad you're here. And there's no way I'm letting you go anywhere else tonight."

Before she could reply, he leaned in and brushed his lips against hers. A soft, fleeting kiss—just enough to feel the warmth of her mouth before he pulled back. With his free hand, he wrapped an arm around her shoulders and guided her toward the house.

Inside, he set the bag on the kitchen counter, glancing around. He wasn't worried about any messes since he kept his place neat. But compared to hers, it lacked personality. No cozy touches, no small details that made it feel like home. Just a place to sleep, eat, and go back to work.

"It's small," he admitted. "But it works for me."

Angie smiled, looking around. "The house is adorable. And the yard... I'm guessing the landlord takes care of that?"

He shook his head. "I do it. Maintenance, too. Keeps my rent from going up."

"I like it." She turned to face him fully. "It fits you."

He nodded. "I don't need a lot of space. I don't have a lot of... stuff."

She tilted her head. "Because you don't like clutter? Or because you don't let yourself settle?"

He stilled. He could tell she wasn't asking to pry, but because she really wanted to know him better.

Before he could answer, she gestured toward the counter. "Let me heat this up."

He hesitated. "Would you mind if I took a shower first? I smell like a long day in heavy gear."

She laughed, rising on her toes to rest her hands on his shoulders. "I wasn't going to say anything, but..."

He groaned as she leaned in, pressing her lips to his. Her tongue darted out in a quick, teasing lick before she stepped back. *Christ.* His cock twitched in response, a slow throb of heat pooling low in his stomach.

She knew exactly what she was doing. "Go on," she urged, her grin downright wicked.

With a muttered curse, he kissed her forehead and headed down the hall. In his bedroom, he secured his weapon, stripped off his uniform, and grabbed clean boxers, sweats, and a T-shirt. Then he stepped into the bathroom, turned on the water, and let it run until steam curled into the air.

The moment he stepped under the spray, tension began

to unwind from his muscles. He braced his hands against the tiled wall, letting the massaging showerhead do its job. This was one of the few things he'd upgraded in the rental —no soft rainwater nonsense for him. He needed pressure and force to dig into his muscles and strip away the day. He exhaled, tilting his head back—

The sound of the shower door sliding snapped his eyes open. Cool air hit his back as he shifted. He turned, and his heart slammed against his ribs.

And then she was there. Completely, stunningly naked. A slow, knowing smile curved her lips as she stepped carefully into the shower. "I thought maybe I could make a long day even better than just bringing dinner."

Pete swallowed hard, heat roaring through his blood. He reached for her, his voice rough with need. "Angie, sweetheart, just seeing you makes any day better. Knowing you brought food warms my heart. And seeing you now, like this? You're rocking my world."

Her smile widened, a spark of mischief in her eyes. And just like that, the rest of the day faded into the background.

Steam curled in thick tendrils around them, the heat from the shower matching the heat simmering between their bodies. Pete stood under the spray, watching as rivulets of water cascaded over Angie's bare skin, glistening against her curves. Every inch of her was breathtaking.

She reached for him first, her soft fingers trailing over his chest, her nails scraping lightly as she moved downward. The simple touch sent a tremor of desire racing through his veins. "Let me take care of you," she murmured, pressing her lips against his collarbone before moving lower.

Pete caught her chin, tilting her face up to his. "You already are," he rasped before claiming her mouth with his.

He took his time kissing her, slow and deep, pouring everything he felt into the press of his lips. His hands explored, tracing the elegant lines of her back, the curve of her waist, the swell of her hips. When his fingers brushed against her slightly swollen knee, he paused, brows pulling together.

"Does it hurt?" he asked, voice rough with concern.

She shook her head. "It's just a little stiff."

He dropped to one knee, ignoring his own desire for a moment as he took her leg in his hands, rubbing slow, firm circles over her knee. "Let me help."

Her lips parted on a breathy sigh. "That feels good," she admitted.

He continued massaging the sore joint, his hands gentle. He'd seen the way she favored her knee earlier, and he didn't like it. If she was in pain, he wanted to ease it, to take the burden off her however he could.

Her fingers threaded through his damp hair, tugging lightly until he looked up at her. "You're amazing, you know that?"

He grinned, pressing a kiss to the inside of her thigh before rising to his feet. "I know," he teased, sliding his arms around her waist and pulling her flush against him. "But keep saying it. I like hearing it."

She laughed, the sound vibrating against his chest, but her amusement faded the second he dipped his head and took a peaked nipple between his lips. He flicked his tongue against it, savoring the way she gasped and arched against him.

Moving between her breasts, he feasted on her soft skin, nipping and sucking until she panted with need. Her fingers dug into his shoulders, and he groaned, loving the feel of her nails biting into his skin.

Pete lifted her easily, bracing her against the shower

wall as she wrapped her legs around his waist. The warmth of her body and the slick heat of her core pressing against him had him nearly losing his mind.

"Wait," she whispered, breathless.

His body tensed, and every muscle coiled tight. "What's wrong?"

She cupped his face. "Nothing. Just… do we have a condom?"

Pete froze. He hadn't even thought about it. "Shit. I don't have one in here."

Angie bit her lip, then shook her head. "I've been on the pill for a while, and I'm clean. Are you…?"

"Yeah." His grip on her tightened. "I'm clean. Tested for work."

Relief and need flickered in her eyes. "Then I want this," she whispered, brushing her lips over his. "I want you."

A growl rumbled in his chest, and he didn't hesitate. His gaze locked onto hers, asking for permission one last time. She nodded, her pupils blown wide with desire. With one swift thrust, he buried himself inside her.

A strangled cry escaped her lips as she clung to him, her body stretching to accommodate him.

Pete went still, gripping her thighs, his forehead pressing against hers as he struggled to hold himself together. She felt like heaven—hot, tight, perfect.

"Jesus, Angie," he groaned.

She wiggled, a teasing smile curving her lips. "Pete, please. Do something."

A deep chuckle rumbled in his throat. "Oh, sweetheart, you don't have to ask me twice."

Bracing her against the tile, he began moving, slow at first, savoring every glide, every sensation. Her moans filled the steamy air, and he swallowed them with a kiss, his tongue mimicking the rhythm of his thrusts.

He moved faster, deeper, gripping her hips as he lost himself in the feel of her. His self-control hung by a thread, but he held back, determined to make her come first. Sliding a hand between their bodies, he found the taut bundle of nerves and circled it with his thumb.

Angie's breath hitched, her body tensing.

"That's it," he murmured against her lips. "Come for me, baby."

She shattered. Her head fell back against the shower wall, her back arching as she cried out his name. The sight of her parted lips, eyes squeezed shut, and body trembling in release was enough to send him over the edge.

A guttural groan ripped from his chest as his own climax slammed into him. He held her tight, his muscles locking as he spilled deep inside her, his entire body trembling from the force of it. For a long moment, neither of them moved, both caught in the aftershocks. Pete then slowly eased her down, keeping his arms around her so she wouldn't slip.

She rested her forehead against his chest, breathing hard. "Well," she finally said, her voice drowsy and sated. "That was... incredible."

Pete huffed a laugh, pressing a kiss to her damp hair. "Yeah. I'm keeping you."

She tilted her head, giving him a teasing smirk. "Oh? That a fact?"

"Damn right." He kissed her again, slower this time, pouring all his emotions into it.

They stayed under the spray a little longer, letting the warmth wash over them, before finally stepping out. Pete grabbed a towel, wrapping it around her first before taking another for himself.

They dressed in comfortable clothes—he in sweats and

a T-shirt, and she in one of his old shirts that swallowed her frame—and made their way back to the kitchen.

The scent of the food she'd brought still lingered in the air, but Pete barely cared about eating anymore.

Angie moved to heat their dinner, and he stepped behind her, wrapping his arms around her waist and pressing a kiss to the side of her neck. She hummed in contentment, leaning into him.

"Thank you," he murmured.

"For what?"

"For being here. For taking care of me. For…" He hesitated, then finally admitted, "For making me feel like I'm not in this alone."

She turned in his arms, resting a hand against his cheek. "You're not."

Something shifted between them at that moment. Something deeper than lust, more profound than just desire. Pete wasn't sure if it was love yet. But he was sure of one thing. Whatever this was between them, it was real. And he wasn't letting go.

21

ROBERT

Robert's hands trembled as he picked up the old-fashioned phone receiver, his grip unsteady. He hadn't called anyone when they'd first booked him... hadn't wanted to. He'd tried to act tough by wearing the kind of expression that said he didn't give a damn. Maybe if he looked mean enough, they'd leave him alone. That was what he'd told himself. But the reality of sitting in a drab cell, the weight of his choices pressing against his chest, had him feeling anything but tough.

All those rumors about jail that made grown men piss themselves had been swirling in his mind ever since they'd locked the door behind him. He thought he could fake his way through it, but after the detectives finished questioning him, it hit him like a freight train. He wasn't just going to walk out of here. Not when he'd been in a car packed with things he didn't even know were there. Not when he was tied to a guy like that.

He closed his eyes, but the memories played in his mind like a horror movie on repeat. He shook his head. The name had sounded slick like something out of a movie. But now, it felt cheap. Fake. The detective had said his real name was Lashawn. And just like that, the illusion cracked wide open.

It had all seemed so easy at the time. Like playing pretend when he was a kid.

A tough guy rolled up in a nice car, the kind that turned heads. Robert had rarely seen anything that flashy near their apartment complex. So when Lashawn stepped out, Robert couldn't look away. The dude wasn't even that scary, not really. Yeah, he had tattoos, but nothing crazy. It was the way he carried himself. The way he moved, like he had the whole world in his back pocket. Like he didn't give a shit about anyone's rules. That was what Robert wanted —to be the kind of guy people noticed, the kind they respected.

And the best part? Lashawn actually talked to him. Treated him like he was someone. Didn't brush him off like some annoying kid. He asked questions and listened. Made Robert feel important. And when he came around again, he acted like he was happy to see him. Like Robert mattered.

God, I wanted that so bad.

Lashawn had fed him stories about moving and starting fresh. That kind of freedom sounded impossible. People in Robert's town didn't leave. They were born on the Shore, lived on the Shore, and died on the Shore. The idea of getting in a car and just going? That was the dream.

Then Lashawn talked about his people, his family, his friends. He never said the word Bloods, but Robert wasn't stupid. The red and black clothes and the inked letters across his knuckles made it obvious. But instead of scaring him, it made Lashawn look even cooler. Even tougher. A whole lot more than the nobodies Robert was surrounded by every day.

So when Lashawn asked him to go for a drive and grab

something to eat, Robert didn't hesitate. He wanted that moment of rolling up to a diner, stepping out of a car like that, feeling like he belonged to something bigger. More than just another kid going nowhere fast.

But reality had a way of slamming back hard.

His stomach twisted as the memory crashed over him. The way the air had been sucked out of his lungs when he barely had time to buckle before Lashawn floored it. The tires shrieked against the pavement as they fishtailed out of the parking lot.

"You gotta take it easy, man," Robert had warned, his voice uneven. "Cops patrol here all the time."

Lashawn had just laughed, leaning back in the driver's seat, one hand loose on the wheel. Then he pressed the gas harder. Robert's pulse had spiked with fear and then something dangerously close to exhilaration. This. This was what being cool felt like. Untouchable. Unbothered by society's bullshit rules.

But the thrill didn't last. A few minutes later, the sharp wail of sirens cut through the air. The moment Robert saw the flashing red and blue lights in the mirror, a new kind of fear hit him. Not the adrenaline rush of speeding. Not the shallow worry of getting caught doing something dumb.

This was different. This was the kind of fear that settled deep in his bones. The kind that whispered, "Oh shit, we're in real trouble."

And no matter how much he told himself he hadn't been the one driving, that he hadn't known what was in the car, none of it mattered. Because after sitting in this cell, and now, gripping a phone with hands that wouldn't stop shaking, he knew one thing for sure... he wasn't walking away from this. Not without a fight.

Lashawn hadn't stopped. If anything, he slammed his foot harder against the gas pedal. Robert's fingers had dug into the armrest, his knuckles going white, stomach twisting into knots.

"Slow down, man!" he'd begged, his voice barely holding steady.

Lashawn had turned to him, eyes gleaming with something dark and manic, lips curling into a sneer. "Shut the fuck up, kid."

And that was when Robert knew—this wasn't a joyride. This wasn't some harmless stunt. Every nerve in his body was screaming as adrenaline coursed through his veins like fire.

More sirens joined the first, their shrieks slicing through the air. Lashawn didn't even flinch. Instead, he jerked the wheel, swerving off the main road. Robert's gut clenched. He knew these roads. God knows he'd spent years bouncing along them on the school bus. The dips and bumps weren't made for high-speed chases. But Lashawn only laughed, gripping the wheel tighter as the car went airborne, tires slamming back down with brutal force.

With every jarring thump, Robert felt his stomach lurch, his heart hammering so hard it hurt. Another sharp turn. Then another. The realization dawned, cold and brutal. They were heading straight into Baytown. A town. A place with people. Families. Kids.

Robert's breath hitched. His mind flashed with images of a speeding car barreling through crosswalks, slamming into bikes, and tearing through lives like it was nothing. "Stop! You gotta stop! This isn't the right way!" he screamed.

Lashawn had both hands on the wheel now, but with a snarl, he lashed out, slamming his fist into Robert's chest. "I said shut the fuck up."

Ahead, the flash of police lights illuminated a line of officers throwing something onto the road.

"Fuck!" Lashawn roared, jerking the wheel hard. But he miscalculated. The car veered toward the ditch, hit the culvert, and flipped onto Robert's side.

Robert's head bounced back as the airbag detonated, slamming into his face and chest. He gasped, then coughed, sputtering and clawing at the bag. His hands shook as he fumbled for the seat belt.

Lashawn was already moving. Unbuckling, then climbing onto the console, he pushed open the driver's door that was now above them.

"Help me!" Robert cried, his voice breaking.

Lashawn didn't even glance back. He just launched himself off the wrecked car and ran, leaving Robert trapped.

Deputies swarmed, weapons drawn, shouting commands that Robert barely processed. *"Hands up. Stay still."* And at that moment, lying in the wreckage, guns pointed at him, the weight of everything came crashing down.

He wasn't a badass. He was just a scared kid in a ditch, caught in something way bigger than himself.

They pulled him out of the wreckage and placed him on the ground. The harsh glare of a flashlight cut through the terror, blinding him as a rescue worker leaned in close, checking his eyes.

"You hurt anywhere?" the man asked, his voice steady but sharp.

Robert shook his head. His body ached, but nothing felt broken. His head throbbed, but when the medic checked his pupils, his brain wasn't rattling too badly. No concussion. Just a lucky idiot sitting in the dirt, hands shaking, trying to catch his breath.

But luck only stretched so far. Because a second later, cold metal cuffs snapped around his wrists, and a deputy hauled him to his feet. He didn't fight. Didn't argue. Didn't even ask questions. He just let them shove him into the back of the police car, his heart pounding so hard it echoed in his skull.

He'd stared out the window as the cruiser pulled away, the flashing lights reflecting against the glass. He thought about his family. His mom was at work. His grandpa was probably waiting for the kids to get off the bus, unaware that his grandson was now locked in the back of a cop car, heading straight for a cell.

But what about later? Would his mom come home to find a message from the police? Would his grandpa answer the phone and hear that Robert had officially thrown his life into the gutter?

Would they still look at him the same? The thought made his stomach twist so hard he thought he might throw up.

By the time they booked him and took him to a lone cell, the fake toughness he'd been clinging to had shattered into a million pieces. The reality was cold, brutal, and staring him right in the face. He'd tried to act tough when the detectives interviewed him, but that act quickly fell apart.

"Make your fuckin' call, asshole!"

The shout from behind jolted him, snapping him back to the present. Robert swallowed hard, gripping the phone tighter. His hands were still shaking. He forced himself to punch in the number, his fingers trembling over the keys.

It rang once. Twice. Then his grandfather's voice, gruff and sharp, came through the line. "Hello?"

"Grandpa?"

"Where are you, boy? I almost didn't pick up, then saw the sheriff's department on the ID."

Robert's throat tightened. He forced the words out. "Grandpa, it's Robert—I messed up. I messed up real bad."

Silence. Then a slow inhale, the kind that told Robert his grandfather was already bracing for the worst. "Oh, boy," his grandpa murmured, his voice low with disappointment. "The deputies came to talk to your mom, but I want to hear it from you. What have you done?"

Robert's chest ached. "I got in a car with someone I shouldn't have. They wrecked, and then they had..." He squeezed his eyes shut, unable to say it.

His grandfather's sharp intake of breath cut through the line. "I can't believe that was you!" His voice had risen now, almost a shout. "Some gangbanger drug dealer tearing through town, wrecking his car with some teenager with him."

Robert swallowed hard, his throat thick, his eyes stinging. "I didn't know, Grandpa." His voice cracked, the weight of it all pressing down on him. "I mean, I knew he was some badass, but I didn't know he had drugs in the car. He just asked if I wanted to go for a ride."

His grandfather let out a long, slow breath. It wasn't relief. It was something worse. "Boy, you've done it now," he muttered. "That was the dumbest thing you could've done."

"I know," Robert whispered. His fingers curled around the receiver, his knuckles white. "I know."

He let the silence stretch, barely able to breathe past the lump in his throat. "I'm in jail," he finally said. "And you're the one call I'm making."

Another beat of silence. "Then why the hell didn't you call your mother?"

Robert flinched.

"She was worried sick leavin' for her shift tonight without hearing from you," his grandfather added, his voice heavy with something Robert wasn't sure he could handle hearing.

"I knew she was working." He sucked in a shaky breath. "I knew she couldn't come. I knew you'd be okay for one night, but Grandpa, you gotta call someone. Someone to help you." His voice cracked again, and he hated himself for it. "I'm not gonna be there for you."

His grandpa was quiet for a long time. Then his voice dropped lower, rougher. "Oh, boy." A sigh, low and broken. "You done broke my heart."

Robert squeezed his eyes shut, but it didn't help. The tear slipped out anyway, trailing hot and fast down his cheek. He wiped it away with his shoulder, jaw clenched tight. "I know, Grandpa," he whispered. "I know."

Another breath of silence. "I'll talk to the detectives tomorrow," he admitted, his stomach twisting. "But I'm scared. I never joined a gang, Grandpa. But what if it gets back to someone that I talked?"

His grandpa didn't answer right away. The pause stretched, the quiet pressing in on Robert from all sides. Finally, his grandpa sighed again. That quiet, weary sound that cut deeper than any words. "I don't know, Robert," he murmured.

The whisper of air over the phone sent another tear sliding down Robert's face. His hands tightened on the receiver. "I'm sorry," he whispered.

His grandpa didn't say anything for a moment, then asked, "Are you gonna be okay?"

Robert's throat burned. "I don't know." And for the first time since this nightmare started, he let himself admit the truth. He wasn't sure he ever would be. "Yeah," Robert finally murmured, rubbing his palm over his face. "They've got me separate from the adults. I gotta wait and see if they're sending me to juvie. The deputy who brought me in said I might get off easy."

His grandpa let out a slow breath. "What do you need from me, Robert?"

The question caught him off guard.

"You may have made a big mistake," his grandfather continued, voice firm but steady. "But you're my grandson. I love you, no matter what. You know that, don't you?"

Robert's throat tightened. Another tear slipped down his cheek, and this time, he didn't bother wiping it away. He didn't care who saw. "I know, Grandpa." His voice broke. "I love you, too."

His grandpa sniffed. "I'll call someone to check in on me, so don't you worry about that, boy."

Robert exhaled, his shoulders slumping. "That's good, Grandpa. You tell Mom that I'll talk to her soon." He swallowed hard. "You're the person I thought of calling first. I just… I needed to make sure you were okay."

Silence stretched for a beat. "That. That right there." His grandfather's voice hitched. "That's what tells me you're not beyond redemption."

Robert squeezed his eyes shut.

"I've noticed you, boy," his grandpa went on, softer now. "Hanging around outside more, looking for something. Thinking those men had it all together. Thinking they got things you want. But listen to me"—his voice sharpened, that steel-threaded wisdom cutting straight to Robert's chest—"you go back to who you are. Not who you were trying to be. You go back to being the grandson I know. You'll be fine."

Robert sniffed and nodded even though his grandpa couldn't see it. "Okay," he murmured. "Tell Mom everything. I'll talk to her soon."

His grandpa hesitated, then said, "Take care of yourself, boy."

Robert heard the way his grandpa's voice wavered. The soft, barely-there sniffle on the other end of the line. It cut through him like a blade. Swallowing hard, he forced out, "You too, Grandpa." Then, before he lost the courage, he hung up.

Behind him, another juvenile grabbed the receiver without hesitation. Robert barely noticed. His feet moved on autopilot, following the guard back to his cell.

The moment he sat on the thin mattress, his hands curled into fists, and his head dropped. He inhaled deeply, then let out a long, shaky breath. He wasn't sure if it was exhaustion, regret, or something else entirely pressing down on him, but damn if it didn't feel heavier than anything he'd ever carried before.

Later, when the guard stopped by and asked if he needed anything, Robert lifted his gaze. "Will I be able to talk to the detectives tomorrow?" he asked. "If not... can you tell them I'd like to?"

The guard studied him for a second, then gave a small chin lift. "You got it, kid."

Yesterday, being called "kid" would have pissed him off. But now? Now, he knew the truth. He had a hell of a lot more growing up to do if he wanted to be the man his grandpa believed he could be.

22

Pete navigated his car down the narrow alley behind a run-down strip mall. The place had seen better days, its parking lot pockmarked with cracks and oil stains. A dollar store, a tool shop, and a pawn shop were the only stores still open, with the other storefronts now empty. At the far end, the convenience store and gas pumps stood.

Pete rolled the car to a stop beside a dumpster in the back lot of the store. Jeremy sat in the passenger seat, his posture easy, but his eyes scanning.

A minute later, the back door to the store creaked open. A man stepped out, hauling two black garbage bags. He moved like he had all the time in the world, tossing the bags in the dumpster before glancing around. The shift of his shoulders, the way his gaze lingered on corners, told of a habit of looking for threats.

Jeremy stepped out, his boots crunching against the gravel, and without a word, he slid into the back seat. The man hesitated only a second before approaching, pulling open the passenger door, and folding himself into the seat beside Pete.

"Man, I thought I caught a break when you ain't showed yesterday," Jacko muttered, dragging a hand over his scruffy jaw.

Pete twisted slightly, his eyes locking onto Jacko's, the air in the car thick with an unspoken warning. "Let's not forget who's keeping your pockets from running dry, Jacko."

Jacko had been playing both sides for two years now, skating just above trouble while others around him fell. His luck ran out when he got popped moving a small bag of dope too close to the high school. A plea deal kept him out of a cell, but it chained him to Pete and the Eastern Shore Drug Task Force instead.

Pete didn't trust him and never would, but he knew Jacko had roots here, raised by a mother, aunt, and grandmother who had done their best to keep him straight. At some point, their lessons must've sunk in because Jacko had made it clear he wasn't looking to end up a name on a toe tag.

They didn't use him often, just when Pete needed ears on the ground. "What did you hear?"

Jacko snorted, a low, humorless chuckle. "Y'all serious? Shit's all over the news, bro. Some dumbass got jammed up runnin' weight through the Shore. Word is, a Blood got caught sittin' on a trunk full of dope, lookin' like a damn piñata waitin' to get cracked open." He smirked, flashing gold in his teeth. "Lemme guess—y'all were the ones that made that play?"

"We just happened to be nearby. Now we need to know everything we can before we sit down with him. Blood ink on his knuckles and shoulder, set tags all up his neck and arm."

Jacko shook his head, clicking his tongue. "Stupid motherfucker. Walkin' round flagged up like he got an S on his chest." He reached into his pocket, pulling out a pack of cigarettes. "Mind if I light up?"

"Yeah, I mind," Pete snapped. "I don't want my car smelling like that shit."

"I'll roll down the window," Jacko tried to bargain.

"Then we'll smell like smoke and garbage."

Jacko huffed but didn't argue. "Fine, fine. Hit me with the questions so I can get back inside before my boss starts thinkin' I ran off with the cash drawer."

Pete pulled a photo from his jacket of Lashawn, handing it over. "You seen him before?"

Jacko barely glanced at it before shaking his head. "Nah, but remember, I got me a legit job now. Not cruisin' for you."

Pete slid another picture in front of him. Jacko let out a sharp laugh. "Now this dumbass kid? Yeah, I seen him round. Think he lives over at them apartments, runnin' with the wrong ones. Ain't tight with nobody real. Just a kid with thoughts of living grand. He's nuthin' but a crash dummy."

"You ever see the Bloods sniffing around him?"

Jacko exhaled through his nose, his expression tightening. "Not heavy, but yeah, I seen a few come through. Ain't like they floodin' the place, but I peep a ride pull up, homie hop out, post up with someone for a minute. Ain't no hand-to-hands, though. Just talkin'."

"Recruiting?" Pete asked.

Jacko shrugged. "What else? They ain't in the charity business. Either they tryin' to stack soldiers or gettin' they money up some other way—dope, tricks, whatever. The block too dry for 'em to be out here for fun."

Pete leaned forward slightly, his voice steady. "Keep your eyes open. I want names, times, plates. If they so much as sneeze near those apartments, I wanna know."

Jacko smirked. "You askin' a lot. Might have to bump up my hazard pay." He let out a rough chuckle, only to break into a coughing fit.

Pete waited until the coughing eased. "Make it worth our while, and we'll talk."

Jacko nodded, then slid out of the car, stretching his arms over his head. He glanced back once. "One last thing —some of them boys comin' through? PA tags. My guess... Philly mostly."

"So now we gotta worry about them," Jeremy muttered under his breath.

Jacko nodded. "Few locals, some Maryland, but a bunch of them whips rockin' Pennsylvania plates. Philly's a grimy-ass city, man. Ain't no surprise they lookin' for softer ground." He snickered, then wheezed, the laugh rattling in his chest.

Pete narrowed his eyes. "Stay safe, Jacko. And that includes getting yourself a nicotine patch."

Jacko shot him a lazy salute before heading back toward the store, disappearing inside without another word.

Jeremy shifted into the front seat, shutting the door. Pete started the car, pulling back onto the road. The air between them was thick with unspoken thoughts, but they both knew one thing—this wasn't over.

Later that morning, Pete and Jeremy found themselves sitting at a table across from Lashawn Jeffries. Pete's gaze moved to the tattoos on his fingers that read Blood when his knuckles were visible, which Pete noticed was all the time. Elaborate tattoo lettering on his neck said Ciao.

"Ciao?" he said.

"Yeah, man. Ciao. That's my name."

"I'll stick to Lashawn."

"Whatever. You wastin' your time, man. My time, too.

Didn't say nuthin' to the others. Not gonna say nuthin' to you."

True to his threat, the prisoner said nothing. He sat, his gaze hard and his eyes staring at a spot on the wall behind Pete's shoulder. Closing the folder, Pete and Jeremy stood. Lashawn looked over and grinned. "Givin' up so soon?" he taunted. "Man, I'll sit in jail and rule. Be like a king."

"Not wasting our time with you," Pete said.

Lashawn narrowed his eyes. "You wanna know why I go by Ciao?"

Pete looked at him, a bored expression on his face.

"'Cause when you meet me, it's goodbye. I go where I want." He chuckled while staring at the detectives.

Pete and Jeremy shared a look. "That's fucking lame," Jeremy said, walking out the door.

"Fuck you!" Lashawn shouted.

Pete refused to give the gang member any more attention, not even looking at him as they walked out of the jail and over to the DTF offices. They ran into their captain.

"Any luck?" Terry asked.

"Not from him. He's too hopped up on his own self-importance. But what we do know is he's Lashawn Jeffries. Twenty-four. From Philadelphia. Juvie file, then as an adult, he's had four arrests, three on drug charges and one on stealing a car. He's had gang tattoos since his first arrest when he was thirteen."

"He's in for a long time with the charges from yesterday," Jeremy said.

"We're waiting to talk to the juvenile again. Just need to get a call that we can see him—" Pete halted as his phone vibrated. He looked down at the message, then lifted his head and grinned. "Just got the word. We'll catch him after we visit the middle school."

23

Pete and Jeremy stepped into the middle school. The front desk secretary barely glanced up before motioning them toward the principal's office, her expression a mix of curiosity and suspicion—cops in schools were never a good sign.

Mr. Morrison, a solidly built man in his late fifties with thinning hair and a tie that looked like it had been yanked loose too many times, stood as they entered. "Detectives." His handshake was firm but quick. "What can I do for you?"

"We appreciate you seeing us on such short notice," Jeremy said, as he and Pete settled into the chairs.

"It's not a problem," Mr. Morrison replied. "Is there an issue?"

Pete nodded. "We need to talk to five of your students. I could have caught them at home, but they all live in the same apartment complex, and we'd rather not be seen talking to them in uniform."

Jeremy added, "They're not in trouble or anything. We just want to make sure they stay safe. We know for a fact that at least one Bloods gang member is hanging around the complex."

Mr. Morrison's expression darkened. "That's concerning." He folded his hands on the desk, nodding. "We can call them out of class—"

"Is there a way to do it discreetly?" Pete interrupted. "The last thing we need is them being labeled as snitches."

The principal considered that, then reached for his phone. "Yeah, I think we can handle that." He pressed a button and waited. "Ms. Lipton? Can you come to my office, please?"

A moment later, the door opened, and a tall woman with sharp eyes and an easy smile walked in. Ms. Lipton, the director of counseling, radiated the kind of warmth that made kids feel safe, something Pete immediately appreciated.

Mr. Morrison turned to her. "The detectives need to speak with a few students, but we don't want to pull them in a way that makes it look like they're in trouble."

Ms. Lipton's brow lifted slightly, but she nodded without hesitation. "I'll take care of it. I'll say I need to check in with them about their grades or an upcoming school event. I'll have them meet you in the conference room."

Pete exhaled, grateful. "Perfect."

Ten minutes later, the door to the conference room swung open, and five middle school boys shuffled in. Their expressions ranged from wary to downright anxious, their sneakers scuffing the tile floor as they took in Pete and Jeremy.

"What's going on?" Tony asked, his voice cracking slightly.

"Why are you here?" Caleb muttered, glancing to the side.

"All of us at once? That's gotta be bad," Jimmy added, shoving his hands in his hoodie pocket.

Pete held up his hands in a calming gesture. "Relax. No one's in trouble." He gestured to Jeremy. "This is Detective Pickett. He's with me on this."

Jeremy nodded, his expression easygoing. "We just need to talk. Take a seat."

Reluctantly, the boys sat, their gazes darting between one another. Pete leaned forward, his voice dropping slightly. "Here's the deal. I'm only talking to you oldest ones for now. We just found out a Pennsylvania Bloods gang member has been hanging around your apartment building."

A collective silence fell over the group. Wide eyes. Shoulders stiffening. A few exchanged glances, the weight of what Pete said settling in.

"Are you serious?" Jalen asked, brows furrowing.

"No way," David muttered.

"I need you guys to be smart," Pete continued. "Stay away from anyone suspicious. Don't get involved. Keep yourselves safe."

Tony hesitated, then spoke up. "Does this have anything to do with that car chase and arrest yesterday? Everyone's been talking about it."

Pete nodded. "Yeah, it does. That gang member picked someone up from your complex, said they were going to grab some food. Next thing you know, it turned into a high-speed chase, a crash, and a major drug bust."

"Damn," the boys muttered in unison.

David crossed his arms. "Someone said it was Robert."

Pete's gaze sharpened. "Is Robert someone you hang out with?"

Tony and David immediately shook their heads.

"I don't," Jalen said. "He's older."

"I live at the far end of the complex," Jimmy added. "I never see him. But I think his brother and sister ride the elementary bus."

Caleb nudged Tony. "His apartment isn't far from ours. You see him sometimes, right?"

Tony shrugged, looking uncomfortable. "Yeah, but I never saw him with anyone I thought was a gang member."

Jalen let out a low whistle. "They teach us about the signs in school. The tats, the colors. My mama would beat my ass if she even thought I was talking to someone in a gang."

Caleb nodded. "Honestly, Mr. Pete, I go home, help my mom with dinner, Kyron and I do our homework, then we go to bed. Sometimes I hang out, but it's with kids I know. The ones I trust."

Pete gave him an approving nod. "Smart."

Jeremy leaned forward, resting his elbows on his knees. "That's exactly what you should do. Keep your friends close. Know who's worth trusting."

Jimmy hesitated, licking his bottom lip before finally asking, "You want us to watch out for you? Let you know if we see something?"

Pete's expression hardened instantly. "Absolutely not." His voice was firm, leaving no room for argument. "Listen to me, all of you. These gangs? They're dangerous. The man we arrested yesterday? Bloods. That's serious. If someone threatens you, I want to know. If you see something that doesn't sit right, get somewhere safe, then call me. But don't go looking for trouble. Don't ask questions. That's how people get hurt."

He held each boy's gaze, one by one, making sure they understood. "Say it back to me."

All five echoed at once. "I get it."

Pete exhaled. "Good. Now, I'll see you guys later. And have a good time with the grandparents later this week."

Jeremy stood, heading to the door. Ms. Lipton was already there, waiting. She handed each boy a pass and shot Pete and Jeremy a reassuring smile. "Thank you, Detectives."

As they walked out of the school and back to their cruiser, Pete glanced at Jeremy. "I'm following up with the detectives in Philly. I want to know what the hell Lashawn is doing down here. Running drugs through our area is one thing, but recruiting? That's a whole different problem."

Jeremy nodded grimly. "We already have Bloods here. We don't need them expanding."

Pete agreed, but as they drove off, he wondered if that was possible.

24

Angie glanced up from her desk as the ESAAA receptionist called out, "Angie, you've got a call on line four."

"Okay, thanks." She pushed her reading glasses up onto her head and pressed the button on her phone. "This is Angie Brown. How may I help you?"

"Ms. Brown?"

The voice on the other end belonged to an older man. His tone was steady but carried a faint tremor, an edge of worry that sent a prickle of unease through her.

"Yes, this is Ms. Brown. Who is this, please?"

"This is Jed. Jed Reeves, ma'am."

Recognition settled over her. Mr. Reeves was a familiar name, one of the clients who occasionally needed transportation when his daughter worked late shifts. He also received Meals on Wheels twice a week. Angie sat up straighter, her instincts sharpening.

"Mr. Reeves, what can I do for you? Is everything okay?"

"Not really, Ms. Brown. I... I'm sorry to have to call. I

don't want to be a burden, but things aren't so good right now."

His hesitance deepened her concern. She softened her voice. "Can you tell me what's going on? Are you safe? Are you hurt or injured?"

"No, ma'am, nothing like that. It's my grandson. Robert. When he gets off the bus, he helps with his brother and sister until his mom gets home—if she's working during the day. But... but he's been arrested."

Angie inhaled sharply. "Arrested?"

She tried to recall what she knew about Robert. Teenager. Responsible. At least, that was her impression. But teenage boys could make mistakes, and whatever had happened, Mr. Reeves was clearly shaken.

"Do you need help at home? Someone to step in while your grandson can't?"

"Yes, ma'am. Our neighbor's real sweet—she watches the younger kids when she can. But my daughter's upset, and she doesn't know what to do. She switches between day and evening shifts and takes double shifts when she can for extra money. I just... I just don't know how to help her."

His voice wavered, and Angie's heart clenched. "Are you at home alone right now?"

"Yes, ma'am."

"Why don't I come over? We can sit down, have some tea, and figure out a plan together."

A small pause, then a breath of relief. "Oh my goodness, Ms. Brown. You're an answer to my prayers."

"Don't worry about it. I'll also notify Karen, our home visiting nurse. I know she checks in on you every other week. I'll let her know I'm coming out and fill her in."

"That's real nice of you, ma'am."

"Give me about twenty minutes, and I'll be there."

After disconnecting, Angie glanced at her schedule. With a few adjustments, she could still get everything done. As the head of ESAAA, her job was largely administrative, but she loved getting out into the community when she could. The adoptive grandparents' program gave her a sense of purpose, and if she could ease Mr. Reeves's worries, she'd gladly make the time.

She dialed Karen and quickly explained the situation. "If I get there and he seems distressed, I'll call one of the nurses to check on him."

"That sounds good," Karen agreed. "Let me know if I need to move him up in my schedule."

Angie ended the call, fired off a few emails, and grabbed her satchel. Slipping it over her shoulder, she strode out the door, pausing just long enough to inform the receptionist where she was headed.

As she slid into her car, another thought nagged at her. Her rheumatologist appointment was later that afternoon, and she really didn't want to miss it. The swelling in her knee hadn't gone down, and she knew Pete was worried. He'd already told her how much he hated seeing her in pain.

She exhaled as she started her car. If she handled things efficiently with Mr. Reeves, she'd still make it to her appointment. At least, she hoped so. With one last glance at her watch, she pulled out onto the road, determination settling deep in her chest.

Soon, she was climbing the worn steps of the apartment building. The structure had seen better days—its once-white paint had faded to a dull gray, and rust clung to the metal railings. A few people lingered at one end of the building, their voices low, their gazes watchful. For the most part, it seemed like a decent place to live, but unease coiled in her stomach. She had no idea why Robert had been arrested, but she prayed it wasn't linked to drugs or gangs preying on this neighborhood. She hated to think of the boys in their group, or any children, being exposed to that danger.

She knocked on Mr. Reeves's door, hearing the soft shuffle of movement inside before the locks clicked. The door creaked open, and he peered out, his lined face weary but warm.

"Oh, I'm so glad to see you using your walker. The last time I visited, you were still in your wheelchair."

"I'm glad, too, Ms. Brown. Come on in."

She stepped inside as he moved aside, closing the door behind her. The apartment was modest but tidy, with a few well-worn armchairs and a recliner arranged in front of a television.

"You have a seat, and I'll heat some water for tea."

"That sounds mighty fine, Ms. Brown, but I'm not sure what my daughter has."

Angie grinned and reached into her satchel, pulling out two tea bags. "I come prepared!"

He chuckled, shaking his head, but the sadness rolling off him in waves was impossible to miss. She busied herself in the small kitchen, filling the kettle and setting it to boil. In minutes, the tea was steeping, and she even tossed an ice cube into his cup to cool it faster. Carrying both mugs over, she placed one on the coffee table for herself and handed the other to him in his recliner.

"Okay, Mr. Reeves, tell me what's happening, and let's figure out how to make this easier for you."

For the next several minutes, she listened as he explained the changes he'd seen in his grandson, then he told her about the phone call he'd received from Robert. Her heart ached for the young man who'd made such a grievous error in judgment, but she was heartened to know that he was not involved in drugs. She even decided to bring the situation up to Pete, but said nothing to Mr. Reeves about that plan.

She didn't offer false hope and knew they needed to plan for the worst possibility. "I know you'd like your daughter to continue working her regular shifts so her pay isn't compromised."

He nodded. "She works changing shifts, either seven in the morning to three thirty. Or she works three in the afternoon to eleven thirty at night. Sometimes, if overtime becomes available, she'll take it for the extra pay. Robert gets the little ones up when she has to leave early in the morning. Our neighbor helps them get on the bus with her kids. When my daughter works afternoons, Robert gets home first and gets the kids off the bus."

He rubbed his whiskered chin. "Between her, me, and Robert, we managed to get the younger ones up and on or off the bus, whichever is needed. I can do it by myself, but it's gonna be a lot harder."

Angie's mind raced with the possibilities they could work out to assist. "I know you are on Meals on Wheels twice a week. Let's move that to four days a week during this time. Technically, if someone is coming to assist you, their job is not to babysit children."

"Oh, I totally understand, Ms Brown. The kids are so good. They come in and have a snack and do their home-work or watch TV. I can handle that, but if Robert's not here to help out with me, it's not so easy for me to move around easily."

"I'll need to have your daughter's work schedule, so I'll know when we might need someone to assist. I can't promise that we can have somebody here every day, but I'll try to get someone here to assist in the afternoons or mornings."

He nodded, his face more wrinkled than she'd ever seen it, and his shoulders slumped as though the world's weight pressed upon him. "I still have hope, Ms Brown. Robert's a good kid who made a dumb decision. But he wasn't using any drugs, and he was in the passenger seat. I'm hoping he'll end up okay and can come home soon, and we won't even need this help."

"I hope for the same thing, too, Mr. Reeves." They finished their tea, and he seemed more relaxed as they chatted. She washed the empty tea cups and left them on the drying rack. Grabbing her purse, she bent to offer him a heartfelt hug. "I can let myself out, but I know you want to lock the door."

He pushed himself up, gripping his walker. "You're a real angel, Ms. Brown."

She opened her mouth to object, but he shook his head. "Nope, it's true. At least to me."

Smiling, she stepped outside, hearing the latch click behind her. As she descended the steps, her gaze flickered toward the group of young men still gathered at the far end of the building. A chill ran down her spine, but she kept walking, slipping into her car and pulling away.

She never noticed the dark car with tinted windows parked nearby. Nor the hidden driver watching her. And the slow, knowing smile that spread across his face, his gold tooth sparkling.

Angie settled into the chair across from Dr. Ketz, shifting slightly to ease the stiffness in her knee. The sterile scent of antiseptic mixed with the faintest hint of floral from the air freshener plugged into the wall. A soft hum filled the room as the doctor typed something into her computer, her gaze flicking up with a warm, knowing smile.

"How have you been feeling?"

Angie scrunched her nose, already feeling the familiar internal debate. "I'm programmed to say that I feel fine, but I'm trying to remind myself that this is where I need to be honest."

Dr. Ketz chuckled, leaning back slightly in her chair. "Think of your older clients, Angie. When you ask them what they need..."

Angie sighed, then grinned. "I need them to be honest, or I can't help them properly."

Dr. Ketz nodded approvingly. "Exactly."

Angie inhaled deeply, steadying herself. "My joints hurt —especially my hands. When I try to grip something too tightly, it's like they rebel against me. At night, my hips and knees are the worst. And, of course, my left knee is still inflamed and swollen."

Dr. Ketz listened intently, her fingers flying across the keyboard, documenting everything. Then she lifted her gaze and gave Angie an encouraging nod. "I appreciate your honesty. It seems like I either have patients who tell me everything hurts but can't be specific, or patients who put on a brave face and refuse to be honest, which isn't helpful for diagnosis or treatment."

Angie let out a dry laugh. "It's just hard to have a condition where I look the same as always, except for my knee. But on the inside, I feel different. Sleep is hard. Moving in the morning is hard. Fatigue is my constant companion... one I'd really like to break up with."

Dr. Ketz smiled at her description but didn't downplay the reality. "I can imagine. Given how your symptoms are progressing, I'd like to start you on one of the injectable medications. If that doesn't work, we may need to consider moving to infusions."

Angie exhaled slowly, shaking her head. "I know both of those options are expensive. The injections are cheaper since I can do them at home, but I can't imagine going to the hospital every month for a four-hour infusion."

Dr. Ketz's expression softened. "I understand. It does sound daunting, and yes, intrusive. But our goal is to prevent as much damage to your joints as possible."

Angie nodded, understanding the necessity, even though she resented the reality. She hated the idea of relying on medication just to function.

"You also need to ensure you're getting enough rest, eating well, and trying to reduce stress."

Angie snorted before she could stop herself, then blushed. "I'm sorry, Dr. Ketz. But I'm not sure reducing stress is an option for any of us. And I'm not just talking about me. It seems like everyone is under stress."

Dr. Ketz laughed, nodding in agreement. "I know. I have the same conversation with all of my patients. There's no way we can live completely stress-free lives."

"I doubt even if we moved to a mountaintop in Tibet and lived with peaceful monks that we'd be able to do that."

Dr. Ketz's shoulders shook with laughter. "You might be right. But sleep is important—it allows your body to heal as much as possible."

They continued talking for several more minutes before Angie climbed onto the examination table. Dr. Ketz carefully examined her joints, taking extra care with her left knee, manipulating it gently but thoroughly. After more consultation, Angie met with the nurse practitioner, who placed the order for her injectable medication.

"Many of our patients prefer injecting into their thigh,"

the nurse explained. "But some prefer the stomach since there's a little more fat under the skin, making it less painful."

Angie wrinkled her nose, then sighed. "Okay, let's try the stomach."

She lifted her shirt slightly, and the nurse pinched her lower abdomen, then pressed the injector firmly. Angie braced herself, but the sting was minor—nothing compared to the deep aches she lived with daily. The nurse counted to ten before pulling the device away, leaving only a tiny red mark on Angie's skin.

"Whew," Angie breathed, inspecting the spot. "Not too bad. I can do that."

"This particular medication is only administered every other week. Once you receive it in the mail, keep it refrigerated until you're ready to use it."

Angie nodded, absorbing the information as she finished up at the office. When she finally stepped outside, the sun was shining, the sky a brilliant blue, but she couldn't shake the lingering unease. Even the warmth on her skin couldn't dissolve the uncertainty gnawing at her.

She sucked in a deep breath, walking toward her car, giving herself a pep talk. *A lot of people have it worse than this. You can do it. One little shot every other week. Stop acting like a wimp—*

"Do you always talk to yourself when you leave the doctor's office?"

She jumped, her heart stuttering in her chest. Lifting her gaze, she spotted an SUV parked beside her car. Leaning casually against it, arms crossed, was Pete. The day suddenly felt a little brighter.

"Hey!" she said, her lips curving into a surprised smile. "What are you doing here?"

He shrugged, pushing away from the car. "You

mentioned you had a doctor's appointment today. I thought I'd stop by and see how you were."

Reaching out, he caught her hand, his fingers warm and steady as they intertwined with hers. Without resistance, she let him pull her closer, his strength grounding her. When she leaned into him, he wrapped his arms around her, and she melted against his chest, closing her eyes.

The world still spun with uncertainties, but at this moment, she felt calm. Stronger. Whole.

25

Pete relished the feeling of Angie in his arms. She was a woman who carried herself with confidence, her laughter bright and full of life. But seeing her step out of the doctor's office, shoulders weighed down by frustration, her usual spark dimmed—it gutted him.

As she neared, he almost smiled, catching the way she seemed to be giving herself a pep talk under her breath. But there was no humor in it for him. He didn't want her to feel like she had to pick herself up. He wanted to be the one to hold her steady. To remind her she wasn't alone.

Wrapping his arms around her, he pulled her in tight. She hesitated for just a second, then melted into his embrace, her warmth pressing against him. And when she finally looked up at him with a small smile, something in his chest eased.

That smile meant everything. "Looks like you've had a crappy day," he said, keeping his voice light, though he still felt the tension in her body. "How about I take you out for dinner?"

Before she could answer, the muffled chime of her phone sounded from her purse. She sighed and reached in, pulling it out. As soon as she glanced at the screen, her expression softened. "Oh, it's my mom."

"Take the call, sweetheart," Pete said easily. He didn't want her to ignore her family just because she was with him.

Her face brightened as she answered. "Hey, Mom."

There was a brief pause, and then she continued, "It was okay. She's going to try me on a new medication, and we'll see how it goes. No, I won't have to have it at the hospital. I just have to give myself injections every other week."

Pete's jaw tensed slightly at that. He hadn't known that was even an option. Hearing her say it so casually made something tighten in his chest, but he forced himself to stay quiet and listen.

"Well, Pete is here with me—"

Another pause, and then she laughed, the sound light and easy. "Okay, I'll ask him and let you know."

She muted the call and tilted her head up at him. "Mom wants us to come to dinner. My grandparents will be there."

Pete hesitated, rubbing his thumb along the side of her arm. "I don't want to take time away from your family." He hated the idea of not seeing her tonight, but he also understood how important family was to her. The last thing he wanted was to intrude.

Her lips curved into a soft smile, her eyes warm as she shook her head. "You won't be taking time away from my family," she murmured, her voice gentle yet sure. "Because you're coming with me."

He chuckled, tilting his head. "That sounded more like a declaration than an invitation."

"Take it however you want," she teased, stepping closer, her palms flattening against his chest.

Pete's breath hitched at the warmth of her touch, the way she looked up at him with something unguarded in her eyes.

"Pete, you mean something to me," she admitted, her voice soft but steady. She nibbled on her bottom lip as if choosing her next words carefully. "I know we've only been dating a few weeks, but I'd really love for you to spend time with my family. If that doesn't feel right to you, or if it seems rushed, or—"

"I'd love to," he interrupted.

She blinked, her head jerking back slightly, surprise flickering across her face.

"Okay, now that sounds like a declaration," she said, laughing.

"Take it however you want to," he echoed with a grin, reaching up to tuck a stray piece of hair behind her ear.

Still smiling, she glanced back down at her phone and pressed a button. "Mom, we're on our way. Do you want us to pick up Grammy Ellen?" Another short pause. "Great. See you soon."

As she ended the call, Pete felt something settle deep inside him—something steady, something sure. Tonight, he wasn't just spending time with Angie. He was stepping into her world.

As Angie ended the call, she scrunched her nose in thought before pushing her glasses up onto her face. "I need to stop by Careway and pick up my Grammy Ellen."

"I'll follow you there," Pete said, slipping his hands into his pockets. "That way, I can make sure everything goes okay. Then I'll follow you to your parents' place."

Her lips curled into a smile. "Perfect."

Before she could move, he bent down and brushed a light kiss against her lips. "Yeah, you are. Perfect."

She let out a soft laugh, rolling her eyes in that way she always did when he caught her off guard with something sweet, but he didn't miss the way her smile lingered.

He pulled open her car door, and once she was settled inside, he jogged around to his truck, falling in behind her as they made their way to Careway Assisted Living.

Once they arrived, Pete hesitated in the parking lot, unsure if he should follow her inside or wait in his vehicle. He knew Angie came here often, but this was different—this was family. He didn't want to intrude.

Before he could second-guess further, Angie turned, caught his gaze, and waved him over with a small motion of her hand.

He climbed out and joined her as they walked through the entrance. The facility was warm and welcoming, the air carrying the faint scent of fresh flowers from a nearby arrangement. Of course, he'd been here when they met with the adoptive grandparents and the kids, but this was the first time he'd ventured deeper into the halls. The rest of the facility was just as inviting as the entrance, the walls adorned with framed paintings and the occasional bulletin board displaying upcoming activities.

At the end of the hall, they stopped at a door that was propped open. Angie knocked lightly against the frame. "Grammy Ellen? It's Angie."

A warm voice floated from inside. "Oh, how are you, sweetheart?"

Pete watched as an older woman slowly maneuvered her walker forward, her smile widening the second she spotted Angie. The love in her expression was unmistakable, and he understood the emotion behind it. After all, every time he saw Angie, he wanted to smile, too.

Angie stepped forward, bending to hug her grand-mother before shifting to the side. "Grammy Ellen, I'd like you to meet a friend of mine. This is Peter Bolton."

The older woman's eyes widened slightly, a hint of amusement sparkling in their depths. Keeping one hand steady on her walker, she lifted the other in greeting. "Mr. Bolton! How lovely to meet you."

Pete stepped forward, gently taking her hand in his and giving it a careful squeeze. "You can call me Pete, ma'am."

"And you can call me Grammy Ellen," she corrected with a firm nod. Then, with a playful glint in her eyes, she added, "And just so you know, I'm a hugger."

She shifted her weight slightly, arms lifting, and he didn't hesitate—carefully wrapping his arms around her, more for balance at first, but then realizing how firm and full of warmth her embrace was.

"We're here to take you to dinner, Grammy Ellen," Angie said, her tone light.

The older woman nodded. "Your mother called. Said you were coming with your young man." She arched a knowing brow, shifting her gaze back to Pete. "You intro-duced him as a friend."

Angie let out a nervous laugh, a slight blush creeping into her cheeks. "Well, I didn't want to—"

"I am dating your granddaughter," Pete said without hesitation, his voice steady.

Grammy Ellen's face broke into a delighted smile, and she clapped her hands together. "Lovely!"

Gripping the handles of her walker, she straightened. "Lead on. I'm ready."

Pete met Angie's gaze, catching the way her lips curved in quiet amusement as they turned to escort Grammy Ellen out the door.

They walked out of Grammy Ellen's room, Angie

pausing just long enough to pull the door shut behind them. The slow shuffle of their steps echoed lightly down the carpeted hallway as they made their way toward the front desk. The scent of fresh-baked cookies from the common area mingled with the soft sound of distant chatter, the atmosphere warm and familiar.

At the front desk, Angie signed her grandmother out as Pete stood by, watching the easy way she navigated this part of her life—caring for her family, making sure everyone was accounted for, looking out for the people she loved.

The trio stepped outside, the warm evening air wrapping around them as they entered the parking lot. Angie glanced toward the far side of the lot. "I'll drive around, Grammy Ellen," she said before darting away toward her car.

Pete remained at Ellen's side, shifting slightly on his feet as she turned to look up at him. Her bright eyes, filled with both kindness and quiet assessment, locked onto his.

"Are you taking good care of my Angie?"

The weight of the question wasn't lost on him. There was no hostility in her voice, no harsh judgment—only deep, unwavering love for her granddaughter. This wasn't a casual inquiry… it was a grandmother's way of making sure the man standing beside her understood exactly what was at stake.

He held her gaze, his voice steady when he answered, "Yes, ma'am. I'm caring for her as best I can."

Her lips stretched into another warm smile, her lined face crinkling with satisfaction. "Lovely," she proclaimed again, her voice full of approval.

Pete exhaled slightly, relaxing just a fraction.

Angie pulled to a stop beside them a moment later, then she climbed out to help. Together, they assisted Grammy

Ellen into the front seat, then Pete quickly folded the walker, his hands steady and sure as he tucked it into the back seat.

"I'll follow you," he told Angie, his voice low but sure.

She met his gaze and smiled, her expression warm and full of trust. A few moments later, they were back on the road.

Pete drove a few car lengths behind Angie, his fingers gripping the wheel tighter than usual. His thoughts drifted as he followed the familiar curves of the road, but this wasn't just another drive.

What the hell am I doing? Family dinners weren't something he'd ever had growing up. Grandparents weren't a part of his childhood. Holiday gatherings usually consisted of him and Sally sitting at a rickety kitchen table, their drunk parents shouting in the background. There had never been warmth. Never been easy conversation or shared laughter over a meal.

Now, he was heading straight into something he didn't quite understand. Something foreign. He shifted uncomfortably in his seat, his jaw tightening. But he knew deep down that Angie was offering him more than just a meal with her family tonight.

She was offering him a piece of her world. A glimpse into what family was supposed to look like. And if he was going to move forward with her and build something real, then this wouldn't be the last family gathering.

It would be the first of many. His chest tightened, uncertainty gnawing at him. He just hoped to hell he didn't screw it up.

As they drove through the neighborhood, Pete glanced to the side as they passed Angie's duplex. She had mentioned that her parents lived just down the street, and she hadn't been exaggerating. They barely passed two houses before Angie turned into a driveway.

He parked behind her, but before his nerves had a chance to settle, instinct took over. He jumped out of his truck, moving quickly to retrieve Ellen's walker and offer her a steadying hand as she maneuvered out of the passenger seat.

Grammy Ellen beamed up at him, her eyes crinkling with warmth as she patted his hand. "I love a man who doesn't mind assisting an old lady."

Pete glanced around, his expression playful as he feigned confusion. "I'm sorry, Grammy Ellen, but I don't see an old lady anywhere."

Her laughter was rich and so much like Angie's that it made something settle inside him.

"Are you flirting with my grandmother?" Angie asked, appearing beside him. Her arms were crossed, but her smile gave her away.

"Maybe," he teased, shooting her a playful glance.

They bypassed the front door, instead making their way to a side entrance with a wheelchair ramp. The door was already open, and a beautiful woman stepped out, her smile wide and welcoming. Pete didn't need an introduction to know who she was. She was an older version of Angie.

Her thick blond hair, streaked with strands of silver that blended seamlessly like natural highlights, fell past her shoulders. Bright red glasses perched on her nose, giving her an air of vibrant energy.

"Come in, come in!" she called out, her voice carrying the same warmth that radiated from her expression.

She immediately hugged Ellen first, whispering, "Love you, Mom," before turning to Angie and wrapping her arms around her. "Love you, baby girl."

Then she turned toward Pete, her smile never faltering. And just like Grammy Ellen, she was clearly a hugger. Without hesitation, she threw her arms around him. "I'm Roseann, Angie's mom. It's so lovely to meet you, Pete!"

Normally, this would be the part where Pete felt awkward. Social situations outside of work weren't always his strong suit. As a detective, he was in control. At the American Legion, he was surrounded by friends. And when he mentored the kids, he naturally fell into the role of leader.

But walking into someone's home and meeting their family was different. Except the discomfort never came. The warmth in Roseann's hug, the laughter in Grammy Ellen's voice, the easy way Angie fit into the embrace of her family—it was all so effortless. And for the first time in a long time, Pete didn't feel like an outsider looking in.

He hugged Roseann in return, then stepped aside, allowing the women to enter first. He followed, taking in the house as he stepped inside.

The kitchen wasn't large, but the open floor plan gave the home an inviting, communal feel. The scent of something warm and comforting filled the air, and the soft hum of greetings and conversation wrapped around him.

As Ellen pushed her walker to the side with Roseann assisting, another older couple stepped forward.

"Pete, I'd like you to meet my grandparents," Angie said, her voice filled with warmth. "This is Grandpa Stan and Grandma Dorothy."

Pete extended his hand to shake Stan's, the older man's grip firm and steady. Then he turned toward Dorothy, who bypassed the handshake entirely and pulled him into yet another hug.

Pete chuckled, returning the embrace as Angie spoke up behind him. "They've been dying to meet you because they've seen your truck parked outside and know we're dating."

Pete met Angie's gaze over her grandmother's shoulder, catching the slight blush on her cheeks. There was no doubt about it—he wasn't just meeting the family. He was becoming a part of it.

26

As the rest of the family moved toward the living room, Pete noticed a man stepping forward, his gaze sharp but friendly. He exuded the quiet authority of a man who had spent his life providing for and protecting his family.

"Pete, welcome to our home. I'm Bob, Angie's dad."

Pete immediately straightened, sensing the weight of this introduction. The way a father welcomed a man into his home spoke volumes. But Bob's expression, assessing yet warm, eased some of the tension curling in Pete's gut.

Angie hurried back after finishing her hugs with her grandparents, a slight flush on her cheeks. "I'm sorry, I didn't even get to introduce you."

Bob chuckled, wrapping an arm around his daughter's shoulders and pressing a kiss to the top of her head before releasing her. The action was effortless, full of love, and Pete couldn't help but notice how easily Angie fit into the embrace, as if she'd been tucked into moments like that her entire life.

She stepped back toward Pete, looping her arm around

his waist, and he automatically settled a hand at her lower back. The simple touch grounded him.

"Pete? Can I get you a beer?" Bob asked, stepping toward the fridge.

"I'll have whatever you're having, sir," Pete replied.

Bob dipped his chin in approval, retrieving two beers and handing one to Pete. "Stan and I are having one, so you're welcome to join us. And please, call me Bob."

Before Pete could respond, Roseann shooed them both toward the living room with a wave of her hands. "Now, I need to get you men out of the kitchen!"

Bob grinned, pressing a quick kiss to his wife's cheek before waving for Pete to follow. "When it's just me and Roseann, we do a lot of cooking together. But when the whole family is over, she likes her women in the kitchen so they can gossip." His voice dropped conspiratorially. "After the meal, we men will clean up, and then we can gossip too."

Pete chuckled, following him into the living room, where Grandpa Stan was already reclining comfortably in his chair.

The house was small, but it felt lived in—loved. The open floor plan made everything feel connected, giving an easy flow to the space. The furniture was warm and inviting, with neutral tones, but splashes of color in the pillows and decor reminded Pete of Angie's style. Family pictures covered the walls, interspersed with framed paintings, their vibrant swirls of color catching his eye.

"I see you're looking at the paintings," Bob said, setting his beer down. "That's Roseann's work. She doesn't paint as much these days, but she used to."

Pete took another glance at the art before nodding. "They're really nice, Bob. I don't pretend to know much about art, but I know what I like."

Grandpa Stan let out a gruff chuckle. "That's what I always said. When Bob first brought Roseann around and told me she was an artist, I worried it'd be that weird modern stuff. But then I saw the way her colors blended, I liked it."

Bob shook his head, amused. "Dad, just admit it... you liked everything about Roseann from the moment you met her."

Stan smirked, not even bothering to deny it. "That's true. My son picked out a lovely woman." He looked toward Pete with a sharp but approving nod. "And that seems to be a trait you share. My granddaughter Angie is as sweet as they come."

Pete met his gaze, his answer coming without hesitation. "I'd have to agree with you, Stan."

Before Stan could respond, Bob leaned back, arms crossed over his chest. "She tells me you're a detective—"

"Stop interrogating him!" Roseann's voice rang out from the kitchen.

Bob chuckled, raising his voice in response. "Well, dear, you shooed us out of the kitchen!"

"Yes, but if you ask him all the questions now, then we won't hear the answers, and we'll just have to ask them again during dinner," Roseann shot back. "And then he'll have to repeat himself."

Angie appeared in the doorway, fighting back a grin. But her amusement won, and she let out a soft laugh. She met Pete's gaze, her expression full of quiet amusement as she mouthed, *"You okay?"*

The idea of being interrogated by her family should have terrified him. But instead, something settled in his chest. These people forming this loud, affectionate, involved, loving family were important to Angie. And if he wanted to be in her life, that meant they would become important to him too.

He smiled, nodding once. "I'm okay."

Roseann rushed in, wiping her hands on a dish towel. "Well, we can sit down to dinner, and then we can all find out about Pete."

"Mom!" Angie huffed. "I don't want to scare him off!"

Roseann pressed her lips together, fixing her daughter with an innocent look before turning to Pete. "I promise I won't scare you off!"

Pete chuckled. "I think I can handle it."

The men stood and followed the women into the dining room. The table was already set in a way that said family. It wasn't about impressing anyone. It was about being together.

Angie guided him to a seat beside her, and as he settled in, he leaned in closer. "I wish I'd stopped to get flowers."

She shook her head. "No. This is just us. They wouldn't want you to feel like you had to do anything for them." Her grin widened. "They just want me happy."

Pete let his fingers brush against hers under the table, giving them a gentle squeeze. "And do I make you happy?"

Her gaze softened, her voice barely above a whisper. "Absolutely."

The moment stretched between them, quiet but full. Then the sounds of plates clinking and food being passed around brought them back to the present.

As Pete took in the warmth of the family gathered around the table, he noticed something. Both Angie and Roseann had pushed their glasses to the tops of their heads in the same absent-minded way. The action made him grin.

The casualness of the meal... the simple dishes, the lack

of fancy wineglasses or expensive serving platters, felt like an invitation rather than an expectation.

"I hope you don't mind homestyle," Roseann said as she handed him a plate. "We're just family here."

Pete accepted it, his voice steady when he answered.

"For me, this is a special treat."

The others smiled, likely assuming he was just referring to the fact that he was a bachelor. But as Pete caught Angie's gaze, he knew she understood the truth. He'd never had this growing up. He'd never sat at a table where laughter flowed easily and where the conversation was light and teasing instead of harsh and cutting. This wasn't just dinner. This was home.

By the time dessert had been served, Pete felt more at ease than he'd expected. The easy conversation flowed around him, blending playful banter with more thoughtful discussions. The meal had been simple, nothing extravagant, but it was warm, satisfying, and real.

And no one had pushed him into an interrogation.

Not until Bob, who had been listening quietly, set down his fork and turned toward him with a thoughtful expression.

"We know you work with Angie on the Adopt-a-Grandparent program," he said. "I believe she mentioned that you were already mentoring young people before that. That's very admirable, Pete. Can I ask how you got into it?"

Pete hesitated, his mind racing for the right response. He could have kept it vague by offering a standard, polished reply that wouldn't reveal too much. That was what he usually did. It was easier that way. But then his gaze flicked to Angie.

She was watching him, her head tilting ever so slightly. And though her smile was soft, she gave the smallest shake of her head, sending a silent message. *You don't have to say anything you don't want to.*

But looking around the table at her family—their open, expectant faces, not judging, just waiting—he realized something. He wanted to tell them.

Because if he and Angie were going to move forward, if they were going to keep building something real, they deserved to know the truth about him. And he wasn't going to pretend that one day, he'd be bringing her home to his family for a meal like this. That would never happen.

Clearing his throat, he finally spoke. "My family wasn't like yours," he admitted, his voice steady but low. "We didn't have pleasant meals where everyone talked about their day or debated interesting topics. We didn't have *this.*" He gestured vaguely around the table, at the warmth, the easy camaraderie, the love that practically radiated from every interaction.

A quiet hush fell over the room.

"My parents were both alcoholics," he continued. "And I'm not sure they ever cared for each other very much."

Roseann let out a soft gasp, her face crumpling slightly in sympathy. "Oh, Pete," she murmured. "Please don't feel like you have to explain anything to us."

He glanced around the table, bracing himself for the usual shift—the pity, the discomfort. But what he saw instead was acceptance. No one looked at him like he was damaged. No one averted their eyes as if embarrassed for him. Instead, there was quiet understanding. Empathy.

He exhaled slowly, feeling a bit lighter. "I don't feel like I have to," he said finally, looking at Roseann. Then he shifted his gaze to Angie, the warmth in her expression settling something deep in his chest. "But I care about your daughter a great deal. And if she and I continue the way I hope we are, I don't see a reason to hide anything."

Angie reached for his hand, threading her fingers through his. She shifted just enough that her body pressed against his, solid and reassuring.

He squeezed her hand once before continuing. "I'll be honest—I got into some trouble when I was younger. Early teens. I was headed down a bad path, and I could've easily ended up in juvie, or worse." He exhaled sharply, rubbing a thumb along the back of Angie's hand. "But I was lucky. A store owner and a local police officer gave me a second chance."

Bob leaned forward slightly, his expression unreadable.

Pete glanced at him before continuing. "They didn't have to, but instead of getting me locked up, they let me work off what I'd done. The store owner gave me a job, and the cop... he became a mentor. Probably the first real male role model I ever had." His throat tightened for a moment, but he pushed forward. "Because of them, I stayed out of trouble. I graduated, joined the military, and eventually became a detective. Now, I work with the Drug Task Force because it's what I'm passionate about."

A small squeeze from Angie's hand made him look toward her. Her eyes were shining, filled with something deep and unwavering. He didn't know if it was admiration or understanding—or maybe both—but it calmed the last bit of nervous energy in his chest.

When he glanced back at her parents and grandparents, he saw nothing but quiet approval.

"I never had a grand plan to mentor young people," he admitted. "But one day, I saw some kids... and I recognized them. They were like me at that age... angry, reckless, looking for something, anything to hold on to. With the help of one of the teachers at the middle school, we put together a program. We work with ten young men. We meet at the YMCA. Sometimes just to let them work out, other times to go over homework. But mostly, we just talk. About life. About the things no one else might be telling them." He shrugged. "It's nothing formal. But I figure… maybe it'll make a difference."

A beat of silence passed.

Roseann smiled, her voice warm when she finally spoke. "I think that sounds amazing."

Pete glanced back at Angie, and the pride in her expression made something tighten in his chest.

He smirked slightly. "Well, I think what your daughter does is amazing, too. That Adopt-a-Grandparent program fills such a need for the kids."

Roseann's smile widened. "It does. But so does your work, Pete. And we're grateful for people like you who take the time to see those kids."

Pete nodded, his throat feeling oddly tight. He wasn't used to people genuinely caring about the things he did. But maybe, just maybe… he could get used to it.

Angie gave his hand another squeeze, and when he turned to look at her, she was already smiling. And that made everything feel a little bit lighter.

The conversation continued to flow easily, shifting from one topic to another, but Pete still felt the weight of Angie's gaze on him. He looked down, finding her watching him, her smile steady but not quite masking the concern in her eyes.

He gave a small shake of his head, reassuring her as he leaned in closer, his voice meant only for her. "It's good. It's all good."

Her shoulders loosened, the tension melting away as she exhaled softly. And damn if that didn't make him smile. It hadn't felt strange to talk about his past with her family. It had been a relief.

There were no awkward silences, no pitying looks that

made his skin crawl—just understanding and quiet acceptance. And that? That was something he'd never expected but found himself deeply grateful for.

Across the table, Roseann's gaze flicked to Angie. "So now, tell us what Dr. Ketz said."

Pete immediately turned his full attention to her.

Angie gave a small shrug, clearly trying to downplay it. "Not much difference, except she wants to step up my medication. With my knee inflammation, she's putting me on a course of cortisone for a couple of weeks, and I'm starting a new medication." She hesitated, then added, "I had an injection, and they already ordered the next shipment. Every other week, I'll give myself an injection, and we'll see how it goes."

She made it sound so simple, so matter-of-fact, but Pete didn't miss the way her family's expressions shifted. There was no dramatic reaction, no one pressing for details, but the concern was there, flickering in their eyes, heavy in the momentary silence that followed.

Angie noticed, too. She looked almost relieved when no one pushed further, when the subject naturally drifted back to other things. Pete knew she didn't want to be fussed over and didn't want her health to become the centerpiece of every conversation. So he filed it away in the back of his mind, knowing he'd check in on her later.

By the time the meal was finished, the dishes were cleared, and the kitchen was being cleaned, Pete found himself elbow-deep in warm water, scrubbing plates alongside Bob and Stan.

To his relief, there was no gossiping—just the occasional chuckle as Bob and Stan exchanged old family stories, while Pete quietly took in the easy rhythm of it all.

A normal family. A family where cleaning up together wasn't a punishment but just something you did. More like the continuation of the meal and the time spent together. And for the first time in his life, Pete found himself wanting to be part of it.

When it was finally time to leave, Roseann stepped forward, looping her arm through Ellen's. "I'll take Mom back to Careway."

That simple statement set off a chain reaction—one that Pete had quickly learned was mandatory in this family. The round of hugs began again. This time, he didn't hesitate.

Dorothy, warm and soft, pressed a kiss to his cheek before stepping back. Ellen squeezed his hands tightly before pulling him into a surprisingly strong hug. And Roseann had hugged him once and clearly had no intention of stopping now.

And then there were the handshakes. Stan's grip was firm, accompanied by a nod that carried an unspoken approval. Bob clapped him on the shoulder before shaking his hand, his expression unreadable for half a second until a slow smile spread across his face.

"You did good tonight, Pete," Bob said, his voice gruff but genuine.

Pete nodded, something settling deep in his chest. "I appreciate that, Bob."

He wasn't sure what he had expected coming here tonight, but whatever it was, it wasn't this overwhelming sense of belonging. As they stepped outside into the crisp evening air, Pete inhaled deeply, letting the coolness clear his head. The stars were bright above them, and the night carried a stillness that felt oddly peaceful.

Angie's voice pulled him from his thoughts. She looked up at him, something playful but undeniably hopeful in her eyes. "You want to come to my place?"

He grinned before sliding an arm around her shoulders,

pulling her close, letting his lips graze the top of her head. "You better believe it."

And just like that, he knew he'd follow her anywhere. But tonight, spending time with her in the quiet intimacy of her home? That felt like he'd just hit the jackpot.

27

Pete and Jeremy sat across from Robert in the same room where they had met before. The harsh fluorescent light overhead cast stark shadows on the boy's face, highlighting the tension in his features. Gone was the cocky bravado and the ridiculous demand to be called Superman. Now, Robert sat small in his chair. His shoulders curled inward as if he could make himself disappear. His fingers were clenched together so tightly on the metal table that his knuckles had gone white.

Pete tested him, his tone even. "State your name for the record."

He didn't hesitate. "Robert Reeves."

Pete nodded, choosing not to comment. "We were surprised to hear from you so soon," he said, his voice gentle but firm. "What changed?"

Robert grimaced, his Adam's apple bobbing as he swallowed hard. "I-I'm sorry."

The unexpected apology gave Pete pause. He flicked his gaze to Jeremy, who remained silent, waiting. Neither of them wanted to interrupt whatever was unfolding in the boy's mind.

Robert exhaled shakily. "I'm sorry I wasted your time before." His voice hitched slightly, but he powered through. "I talked to my granddad." He stopped again, swallowing against the thickness in his throat. "He-he's disappointed in me." His eyes darted to Pete's, then away. "And I don't wanna be that. I don't wanna be someone he's ashamed of."

Pete's jaw tightened, his chest pulling with something unexpected. He had a hunch that Robert's grandfather was the kind of man who meant every word he said, and that kind of belief—the unwavering kind—had the power to change a boy's path.

Robert squared his shoulders, his fingers still locked together. "But he also said he believes in me. He said I can fix this. And that's why I wanted to talk to you again."

Jeremy, ever the patient one, leaned forward slightly. "Alright. So talk to us."

Robert nodded, his breath shaky but determined. "What I told you before was the truth. I was just hanging out, you know? And then Lashawn rolled up, and he acted like he wanted to talk to me. I felt like—I don't know, like I was someone. Like I mattered." His lips pressed together as if the admission left a bitter taste in his mouth. "So yeah, I got in the car with him. I thought we were just going to grab something to eat. I had no idea he had drugs. No idea he had that much cash. And definitely no idea he'd drive like a lunatic or try to outrun the cops."

Pete nodded, his expression unreadable. He leaned forward, mirroring Robert's posture, forearms braced on the table. "We believe you," he said, voice steady. "But is there anything else you remember? Anything at all?"

Robert hesitated, his jaw working. He shook his head once, but Pete could see it—the hesitation, the flicker of something in his expression. Hope curled in Pete's chest, cautious but real.

Finally, Robert exhaled sharply, his voice dropping. "He always came by himself. Recently, I mean." He winced, rubbing a hand over his face. "But the first time I ever saw him? He wasn't alone."

Jeremy leaned in. "Who was with him?"

Robert's fingers flexed, and for a moment, he stared at his hands like they might hold the answer. "He pulled up in a black sedan. The windows were dark, and the car looked new. Like, really new. And he wasn't alone." He licked his lips, shifting his gaze between Pete and Jeremy. "The other guy—he was smaller than Lashawn. Not small-small, but stockier. He had sunglasses on. The kind that… uh… are kinda like a mirror."

"Reflector lenses?" Pete supplied.

Robert snapped his fingers. "Yeah! The kind where you can see yourself when you look at him."

Jeremy took a slow breath. "Anything else?"

Robert nodded quickly, his energy shifting. "He was wearing this red Nike tracksuit. The kind that looks expensive, you know? And black high-tops. But he never talked, or at least not that I remember." He shrugged, looking younger than his sixteen years. "I thought maybe he was just a tagalong. You know, Lashawn was the main guy, and this dude was just… there."

Pete's senses sharpened. "Did he have any distinguishing features? Tattoos?"

Robert's brows pulled together. "He wore long sleeves and pants, so I didn't see much, but—" He stopped suddenly, his eyes widening. "His hands. His knuckles. He had tattoos across them. They spelled 'BLOOD.' And he had a gold tooth, right here." Robert pointed at one of his incisors.

Jeremy's expression remained carefully neutral, but Pete could see the shift in his posture, the quiet intensity in his eyes.

Robert winced. "I know what they were. But they didn't seem so bad. I didn't know why they'd want to hang around our apartment building."

"You ever see any gang members hanging around your building?"

"No. I mean, there are some guys that don't work. I don't know what they do." He snorted. "Probably nothing. Some of them work farmwork, so it's kind of seasonal. But mostly, it's families just getting by, you know?"

"Yeah, I know," Pete said, understanding more than he let on.

"But when Lashawn started coming around, it wasn't the adults he hung with. It was me and a few other teens." He swallowed deeply. "I was being used, wasn't I? He was recruiting for the Bloods, and like you said yesterday, I was just there, ready for anything."

"But not now," Jeremy reminded him. "Today, you're thinking more clearly. You're showing us that you have integrity, just like your grandfather knows."

Robert blew out a long breath. "You were asking about the guy who showed up with Lashawn. He had a tattoo on his neck. Some kind of star." He lifted a hand, fingers hovering near his own throat as if tracing the memory.

The room went still for a moment. Then Pete gave a slow nod. "That's good, Robert. That's real good."

Robert sagged back in his chair, the tension in his shoulders easing just slightly. He had done something right —maybe for the first time in a long time. And for the first time, Pete saw a kid who wasn't trying to be Superman. He was just trying to be better. And that was something worth believing in.

Pete studied Robert carefully, his pen poised over his notebook. "Did you see him more than once?"

Robert hesitated, his fingers tapping nervously against the tabletop. "The first time I ever saw him was the first time I met Lashawn. I saw him maybe twice after that. Then it was just Lashawn coming around."

Jeremy leaned in slightly. "Did you ask Lashawn about it?"

Robert nodded. "Yeah. I asked if his friend was coming back, and he just laughed. Said his friend told him he could 'have the area.'"

Pete's brow furrowed. "'Have the area'? Did he explain what that meant?"

Robert shook his head and gave a small, defeated shrug. "He didn't explain, and I didn't ask." His eyes flicked up toward them, and for a moment, Pete was struck by how young he looked. Just a kid. But there was something haunted in his gaze, something that hinted at knowledge no sixteen-year-old should carry. "I was never scared of Lashawn," Robert admitted, his voice quieter now, "but he didn't seem like the kind of guy you wanted to keep pushing for answers."

Pete nodded, jotting down the information in his notebook, the scratch of his pen filling the silence. "And you never saw this other guy again?"

"No. Never." Robert let out a long, weary sigh. "I know it's not much, but I swear, I'm trying. I'm trying to give you everything I can think of."

Pete set his pen down and met Robert's gaze. "We appreciate this, Robert. We really do." He gave the boy a reassuring nod before continuing. "We know you were drug-free and in the passenger seat. We also pulled your school records. Your attendance is solid, and your grades are decent. That tells us you weren't out skipping school to run with some gangbanger."

For the first time, hope flickered in Robert's expression. "Will you tell the judge that?"

Pete leaned back slightly, exchanging a glance with Jeremy before answering. "Right now, you don't have to worry about a judge."

Robert blinked, confusion evident in his widened eyes. "I don't understand."

Jeremy spoke this time, his voice steady but reassuring. "The way this works is the district attorney reviews our evidence and decides whether you'll be prosecuted for a crime. Everything you've told us, your drug test results, your school records, the fact that you weren't driving that car—all of it is taken into account. And what you're doing right now, helping us? That goes a long way in your favor."

Robert swallowed hard, his lips pressing together as tears welled up in his eyes. He nodded, unable to speak as the emotions overwhelmed him. A single tear slipped down his cheek, and he swiped at it hastily, as if embarrassed. "I'm grateful for anything you do."

Pete and Jeremy stood, prepared to leave, but just as they turned toward the door, Robert's head jerked up suddenly.

"A mole!"

Both detectives stopped in their tracks, swinging their heads back toward him. "What?" Pete asked, eyes sharp with interest.

Robert lifted a shaky hand and pointed to the side of his nose. "That other guy—the one who was with Lashawn. He had a mole. Right here." His fingers hovered just to the side of his nose. "It was kinda big, but I didn't want to stare, so I can't tell you much more."

Pete exchanged a look with Jeremy, a spark of something passing between them. This was new. This was something. "Good job, Robert," Pete said, his voice filled with approval.

As they stepped out of the room, Jeremy signaled to the guard to escort Robert back to his cell. He exhaled, running a hand down his face before turning to Pete. "I want to check with the Philadelphia DTF, see if they can ID this guy and what they've got on Lashawn. Then we'll talk to the DA."

With a firm nod, Pete clapped Jeremy on the back. "Let's get to work."

Pete sat at his desk, flipping through the file in front of him, his fingers skimming over pages of mugshots, arrest reports, and surveillance notes. Lashawn Tate. Twenty-four years old. A history that read like a road map of bad decisions—multiple drug arrests, suspected in at least two gang-related assaults, and a two-year stint in prison that clearly hadn't done much to straighten him out.

Jeremy leaned against the desk, arms crossed, listening as Pete hit the speakerphone button and dialed a number from the file. It rang twice before a gruff voice answered.

"Philly DTF, Detective Russo."

"Russo, it's Pete Bolton, Eastern Shore DTF. Got a minute to talk about Lashawn Tate?"

A brief pause, then the sound of heavy fingers on a keyboard met their ears. "Yeah, I know him. Bloods. Small-time player with a big-time mouth. Always had more ambition than sense."

"Looks like he's still trying to play big shot. He got himself tangled up in a bad situation here. Transporting cocaine. About fifty grand in tens and twenties. Speeding. Evading police. You get the picture. And he's sitting in jail right now."

"Well, well… good you got him down there. He won't have quite the same group as he had up here."

"We've got a witness putting him in a black sedan with an unknown male—Blood tattoos, shorter and stockier than Lashawn. A gold incisor. The guy has a mole on the side of his nose. Ring any bells?"

Russo let out a slow exhale. "Lashawn, I know. The guy with the mole? Not off the top of my head. But I can ask around, see if it shakes anything loose. You got anything else on this mystery man?"

Pete glanced at Jeremy, who shook his head. "Not much. Penchant for reflector glasses, last seen in a red Nike tracksuit. Could be nothing, or he could be the real shot-caller."

"Could be. If he's rolling with Lashawn, he's either using him as a front or keeping him on a short leash."

Pete's jaw tightened. That was his thought too, and it didn't sit well. "You got anything fresh on Lashawn? Last known associates, recent heat?"

Russo grunted. "Last we had him pinned, he was running deals for a mid-level supplier. Name came up on a couple of wiretaps, but nothing solid enough to charge him. We know he's still moving product, but he's gotten cautious. Keeps his circle tight."

"Anyone in his crew we should be looking at?"

"Couple of names, but none that match your guy. Still, I'll run it through my informants, see if anyone's seen this mole-faced mystery man. Might take a day or two."

Pete tapped his pen against the desk. "Appreciate it, Russo. Keep me posted."

"Yeah, yeah. And Bolton—" Russo's tone dropped, all humor gone. "Watch your back. If Lashawn's pushing into new territory, it means someone bigger is letting him.

That's the guy you need to worry about. My guess is that he's recruiting down there."

Pete met Jeremy's gaze, the weight of Russo's words settling between them. "Noted. Thanks."

The line went dead, and Pete leaned back, exhaling slowly. Jeremy pushed off the desk, his expression unreadable. "So we wait?"

Pete nodded, closing the file with a snap. "For now. But I hate the idea of someone down here."

"I wonder if it's the guy Robert saw?"

"If so, we need to make sure no trail leads back to him."

"When do you want to talk to the DA?" Jeremy asked. "'Cause I'm ready now."

Pete grinned. "Same here."

28

The Commonwealth Attorney's office occupied the top floor of the courthouse. Cedric McCalister sat behind his imposing desk, his silver hair perfectly styled despite the late hour. Jeremy and Pete sat in the leather chairs facing him, their expressions neutral but alert.

A knock on the door preceded a woman entering the room. Pete recognized Sandra O'Neill, one of the attorneys from the Legal Aid office.

"Sandra, good of you to come on such short notice." Cedric's voice carried the authority of three decades in prosecution, though his tone remained cordial. "I believe you know Detectives Pickett and Bolton."

Pete nodded toward her as she settled into the remaining chair.

"The Reeves boy," Cedric continued, his weathered hands steepled before him. "You had called me saying you knew his mother."

Sandra nodded. "Yes, she works part-time as a cleaner for our offices, and I've had the opportunity to get to know her, and on occasion, Robert, as well.

Cedric looked down at the file in front of him. "Sixteen years old, found in a vehicle containing enough narcotics to suggest distribution."

Sandra straightened her back. "Mr. McCalister, with respect, from what I've been told by his mother, Robert Reeves was a passenger in that vehicle. He had no knowledge of the drugs, no involvement in their distribution, and no criminal history whatsoever."

Pete leaned forward, his frustration evident. "Yes. Clean record. Wrong place, wrong time. Yeah, he got into the car with the wrong person, but he's cooperating. Giving us real information on Lashawn Tate, who is a Blood and is running through the Shore."

"The initial report had him in the vehicle at the scene of a crash," Cedric countered, his tone measured but firm. "Narcotics in the vehicle. That's more than 'wrong place, wrong time.'"

"He wasn't driving," Pete said. "He wasn't carrying. He wasn't high. The blood work came back completely clean. We've had time to dig, and there's no evidence he knew what was in that damn car. He's just a kid, Cedric. And we know he's not the kind you make an example of."

"Legally, I could argue he was in possession by proximity," Cedric replied, though his voice lacked its usual conviction.

"Legally, you could argue a lot of shit that doesn't make sense," Pete retorted.

"Constructive possession requires knowledge and intent," Sandra said, her gaze on Cedric. "Two things the Commonwealth cannot prove because they don't exist. This boy got a ride home from school with someone he thought was a friend. He had no idea what was in the trunk of that car."

Pete offered her a smile, approval in his chest. She leaned forward, her brown eyes meeting Cedric's steady gaze. "This isn't someone who belongs in the juvenile justice system. Prosecuting him doesn't serve justice. It destroys a promising young life for the sake of statistics."

Cedric was quiet for a long moment, his fingers drumming against the leather-inlaid desk blotter. "You three are really pushing for this kid."

"Because it's the right call," Pete added.

Cedric's weathered face remained impassive, but Pete caught the slight softening around his eyes. "Fine. No charges. But I want updates, and if he puts one toe out of line, I expect to be the first to know."

Jeremy nodded and said, "Appreciate it."

Sandra let out a breath she'd been holding, and added, "His mother will implement stricter rules about his social activities, and he can work with her cleaning the Legal Aid offices two afternoons a week."

"Community service," Cedric mused aloud. "Something visible, something that shows the community we're taking this seriously."

Pete felt the tension drain from his shoulders, replaced by the familiar surge of satisfaction that came with victory. "Thank you, Mr. McCalister. You won't regret this decision."

Walking out, he felt like he could breathe again. As he and Jeremy left the DA's office and started the trek back to their building, he said, "Robert should be released within the hour."

"You going by to see him again?" Jeremy asked.

"Not sure. I'd like to check in with him later. For now, though, let's head back and see if there are any updates to work on."

"Jesus, I hate paperwork," Jeremy complained.

Pete agreed but simply nodded. Two hours later, Pete and Jeremy sat at their desks, the fluorescent lights overhead giving him a headache. The office hummed with the quiet sounds of typing, the occasional shuffle of paper, and the muted chatter of deputies passing through the bullpen.

Both men were lost in the familiar rhythm of wrapping up case files—some neatly closed, others frustratingly inconclusive.

Across from them, Cybil, a determined young deputy studying for her detective exam, sifted through a stack of reports, eyes scanning details with the same intensity that had earned her a place working alongside them. She'd proven herself sharp, eager, and capable. All the qualities they respected.

Pete broke the silence first. "We never got anything back from the lab on that old meth trailer we processed a couple of weeks ago," he said, rubbing his jaw as he stared at the incomplete report in front of him. "No hits on prints or any of the old supplies."

Jeremy let out a low whistle and shook his head. "Typical," he muttered. "Thing's gotta be disposed of properly before it turns into a toxic death trap. I mean, you let that crap sit too long, and you're asking for a hazardous materials disaster. Not to mention, we don't want some idiot cooking up a new batch out there."

"How is it disposed of?" Cybil asked.

"You wouldn't believe the steps," Jeremy moaned. "It involves DEA, the local government, HAZMAT, environmental agencies, and then, when everyone is satisfied, a certified meth lab removal contractor comes in to evaluate and destroy."

"Good grief!" Cybil shook her head. "And who pays for all that?"

"Usually the land owner. But I have no idea what they'll do with this one," Jeremy replied.

Pete nodded in agreement, already reaching for the closure form. "For now, I'm going to file it and close out the report."

Jeremy exhaled, drumming his fingers against the desk. "Sounds good. Always hate to have things left hanging, but all we can do is our best."

Just then, Terry walked in, his boots scuffing against the floor as he pulled up a chair near them. He carried the weight of experience in the faint lines of his face and the casual yet purposeful way he moved.

"I got a call from my counterpart up in Philly," Terry said, stretching out his legs. "He knew we had a Lashawn Tate down here and that you've spoken to Detective Russo."

Pete sat up a little straighter. "Yeah, that's right, Captain. Did he have anything else to add?"

Terry's expression darkened slightly. "He said they've run into some gang members who claim affiliation just for protection, but Lashawn? He was the real deal. Active member. I told him that Lashawn would be spending a good chunk of his life in our prison system. That seemed to make him happy."

Jeremy smirked. "Bet it did."

As Terry stood to leave, Jeremy shot him a knowing look. "Oh, by the way, we talked to Cedric about Robert. He agreed there was no reason to charge him, so he's being released. And, Sandra O'Neill was there."

Terry paused, his expression carefully neutral, only giving a small dip of his chin in acknowledgment. "Yeah, I heard."

He turned slightly, prepared to walk away, when Jeremy added, "Pretty lady."

Pete knew that tone. Knew that grin, too. Terry's face remained impassive, but his grunt of agreement made Jeremy laugh outright. Pete, unable to help himself, kicked Jeremy's shin under the desk.

"You fucker." Pete chuckled as Terry walked away without another word.

"Better you than me getting on the Captain's bad side. Although, as your partner, if you piss him off, he's likely to take it out on me, too."

Before Jeremy could respond, Cybil glanced up from her file, brows furrowed. "What is the G-Shine?"

Pete leaned back in his chair, rubbing his temple. "They're part of the Bloods. Started in prison behind bars, but now they operate both inside and on the streets."

Jeremy added, "G-Shine stands for Gangster Killer Bloods."

Cybil stared at them like she was waiting for a punchline. "Jesus. What a stupid name."

Pete let out a dry chuckle. "Yeah, well, they're part of the United Blood Nation. Used to go by GKB—same meaning, just more aggressive. At some point, they rebranded to G-Shine, supposedly to distance themselves from the early reputation."

"Didn't change much," Jeremy muttered. "They're still deep in drug trafficking, robbery, extortion... and they sure as hell haven't moved past violent crime."

Cybil shook her head, exhaling slowly. "People like that always think they're untouchable."

Jeremy nodded. "Until they aren't."

Cybil tilted her head, her expression thoughtful. "Interesting that some claim affiliation mainly for protection. Do you think that's younger members who are just afraid?"

Pete leaned back in his chair, rubbing the tension in his

forehead. "I honestly don't know," he admitted, his voice tinged with frustration. "But I'd hate to see that happen here in our area. I don't want any part of it touching our kids."

Jeremy nodded, his mouth tightening. "Yeah, and the problem is, once a kid gets in, it's damn near impossible to get out. Even if they aren't real players, just tagging along for protection, it only takes one bad situation before they're in too deep."

Cybil absorbed that, her brows knitting together. "Are all the Bloods working together?"

Jeremy let out a short laugh, though there was no humor in it. "Believe it or not, some of them are working against each other. It's not all one happy family. Especially with the drug pipelines coming from New York, Philly, Baltimore, and DC. We're right in the middle of it—ripe for a damn turf war."

A heavy silence settled between them as they returned to their work. The weight of the conversation pressed on them, an unspoken understanding that their quiet little county was always just one bad shipment, one new recruit, one stupid decision away from chaos.

The office had settled again when Pete noticed a new email pop up on his screen. He clicked it open, scanning the details before speaking. "Looks like we got fingerprints back from Lashawn's vehicle. As you can imagine, there are Lashawn's and Robert's. Some are smudged, but they pulled up three others."

Jeremy leaned forward, his interest piqued. "Anything we can sink our teeth into?"

Pete's eyes flicked across the report. "Two are from the Philly area. Both served time. Both are tied to the Bloods. I'll send their pictures around. But the third one…" His fingers stilled on the keyboard as he read further. "The third one is Tamarcus Waters. He's not from Philly—his record's out of Norfolk."

Jeremy's brows lifted. "Norfolk? I wonder if he's the one Robert saw around here."

Pete's fingers moved over the keyboard, pulling up the police database. "Getting an image of his mug shot now."

Jeremy and Cybil abandoned their chairs, moving around to look over Pete's shoulder. The moment the grainy booking photo loaded, Pete let out a low whistle.

"Well, I'll be damned," he muttered.

Jeremy exhaled sharply, shaking his head. "Looks like Tamarcus Waters might be the guy Robert saw with Lashawn Tate." His eyes zeroed in on the distinct features in the image. "Tattoo of a star on his throat, mole right on the side of his nose—same description Robert gave."

Pete didn't hesitate. He grabbed his desk phone and dialed the DTF office in Norfolk. After a few rings, a woman's voice answered.

"NPD, how can I direct your call?"

"This is Detective Pete Bolton from Eastern Shore DTF. I need to speak to someone about Tamarcus Waters. Looks like his last arresting officer was Detective Paul Munfries."

"One moment."

After a few minutes of hold music, a gruff voice picked up. "Munfries."

"Detective Munfries, this is Pete Bolton, Eastern Shore DTF. We're looking into Tamarcus Waters. We think he may have been up here with a Lashawn Tate, a Blood from the G-Shine out of Philly. Goes by Ciao."

There was a low growl of irritation from the other end of the line. "Fucking gang bangers and their names," Munfries muttered. "That little prick, Tamarcus? Goes by *Flame*. Supposedly because he wears red. Hell, they all wear fucking red."

Pete couldn't help but smirk at the detective's mini-rant. "You have anything on him recently? I saw he got out of jail about two years ago."

"Nothing solid. He's been lying low around here. But if that motherfucker's been seen in your area, he's up to something. Down here, he runs with the OGB—Outlaw Gangster Bloods."

Pete exchanged a glance with Jeremy. "Are they working with or against the G-Shine?"

Munfries snorted. "Who the fuck knows? I don't even think they know."

Pete chuckled, shaking his head. They talked for a few more minutes, but Munfries didn't have any fresh intel. Pete thanked him and hung up, staring at the computer screen in thought.

Jeremy stretched, rolling his shoulders as he glanced at the clock. "What's next?"

Pete reached for his phone again. "I'm gonna check on Robert." He dialed the jail, his jaw tightening as he waited for someone to pick up. When the deputy on duty finally answered, Pete asked about Robert's status.

"His mother picked him up about an hour ago," the deputy replied.

Pete nodded to himself. "Thanks."

Hanging up, he looked over at Jeremy. "It's almost the end of the day. I'm going to run by Robert's apartment to make sure he got home okay and see if he can confirm that Tamarcus Waters is the guy he saw with Lashawn. I'll show him the picture, leave him my card, and let him know he's got someone looking out for him."

Jeremy gave a nod of approval. "Sounds good."

The two men grabbed their things and headed out together. Once outside, Pete made his way to his vehicle and, before getting in, pulled off his protective vest. He kept his weapon holstered but tugged on a jacket to conceal it. He didn't want to walk into Robert's place with his outfit screaming DTF, but at the same time, this was professional, even if he was also checking in personally.

Sliding into the driver's seat, he exhaled, gripping the wheel for a moment before starting the engine. The day wasn't over yet.

29

Angie sat with Marty in his apartment, assisting him with the online forms he needed to complete for the hearing aid he hoped to qualify for.

"I don't understand why I have to do this with a computer," he grumbled. "I can't see the little print good enough."

"I know, and I'm so sorry. There are a lot of changes that make it more difficult for some people to get the services they need, but that's why I'm helping today. I printed off the forms for you, and we can do them together." She looked at the form, focusing on the next of kin. "I didn't realize you had a relative nearby."

"Oh, I don't. I put that down because it looked bad to leave it blank. That's my great-nephew. He don't come around much. In fact, I just met him. But he now drops by occasionally. Lives in Norfolk."

Angie nodded. "Okay. Um… is he someone you trust with your medical information?"

Marty's brows drooped. "I reckon. I don't have any secrets. Lord knows, when I kick the bucket, there won't be any money to give to anyone, so he can't be visiting for that reason."

"Okay, well, we'll leave it then."

A sudden knock on the door startled both of them. Angie glanced up from the stack of forms she and Marty had been working on, her brows drawing together.

"I'll see who it is," she said, pushing back her chair.

She moved to the door and peeked through the security hole, blinking in surprise. "It's Jimmy! How did he get here?"

Marty chuckled, setting his pen down. "He rides his bike over sometimes. I forgot he said he'd be coming by today. Go ahead, let him in."

Angie unlocked the door and swung it open, revealing a slightly startled but grinning Jimmy.

"Ms. Angie! I didn't expect to see you here!" he said as he stepped inside, his energy filling the space.

Angie laughed, motioning for him to come in. "Funny, I was just saying the same thing to Mr. Marty. He told me you ride your bike over to visit."

Jimmy nodded enthusiastically. "Yeah! Me and a couple of the guys come over after school now and then."

Angie folded her arms, tilting her head at him. "I hope you're being careful."

"Oh, we are," he assured her quickly. "It's a little farther, but if we take Weyburn Road from our apartment building and circle onto Parsley, we don't have to get out on the highway."

She nodded, considering the route. "You know, you're right. Since I drove down the highway, I never thought about going that way."

"It's only about a mile," Jimmy added. "On our bikes, that doesn't take too long."

As she closed the door behind him, it suddenly dawned on her to ask, "Did anyone else come with you today?"

"Usually Caleb or Jalen would, but they had homework and a test to study for, so it's just me."

"Well, Mr. Marty and I are just finishing up some forms. Then I'm going to check on Gerald. If you want to visit with Mr. Marty for a bit, I'll go see Mr. Gerald. After that, if you're ready, we can load your bike in the back of the van, and I'll give you a ride home."

Jimmy's face lit up with gratitude. "That'd be nice, Ms. Angie."

She smiled and gave a small wave to Marty before heading down the walk to the next apartment. She found Gerald in his living room, where she helped him navigate the same website he'd struggled with before. Once he was squared away, she made her way toward the parking lot and spotted Jimmy waiting near the van.

"All set?" she asked as she pulled open the back door.

"Yeah, no problem." He quickly lifted his bicycle and maneuvered it into the back.

Angie slid into the driver's seat, following the route Jimmy had suggested. He was right—it was only about a mile, and they completely avoided the highway. The drive was short, easy, and surprisingly peaceful.

As she pulled into the apartment complex parking lot, Jimmy suddenly pointed out the window. "Look! Isn't that Mr. Pete?"

Angie's heart gave its familiar, foolish lurch at the sound of his name. She turned her head, and sure enough, there he was—stepping out of his SUV with the unassuming swagger of a man who was confident but didn't have to prove it. Sunlight hit his profile just right, casting sharp shadows over his strong jaw, his stance solid and sure.

"You're right," she murmured, barely aware she was speaking.

Jimmy wasted no time jumping out of the van, waving enthusiastically. "Hey, Mr. Pete!"

Pete turned at the sound of his name, his expression briefly surprised before his gaze settled on Angie. The boys from the complex were already gathering, surrounding him like he was some sort of local hero. He greeted them all, but there was no mistaking the way his attention shifted entirely to her as he closed the distance between them.

Angie tilted her chin up, a slow, teasing smile curling her lips. "Fancy meeting you here," she said, adding a playful wink for good measure.

Pete's lips twitched in response, his eyes warm as they met hers. "Yeah, what are the odds?"

For a moment, everything else faded—the boys talking, the sounds of the parking lot, even Jimmy securing his bike. It was just the two of them, caught in that electric pull she was starting to recognize all too well.

Pete's eyes twinkled with amusement as he looked at Jimmy. "Where'd you pick up your hitchhiker?" he asked, a slow grin spreading across his face.

Jimmy, clearly unfazed, puffed up slightly. "I rode my bike to visit Mr. Marty."

Before Angie could add anything, a couple of the other boys chimed in, nodding eagerly.

"Yeah! Sometimes we ride over to visit our adopted grandparents, too," one of them said. "We see them on Thursdays, but we go by after school sometimes, too."

Pete shifted his gaze to Angie, one brow lifting in mild curiosity.

She shook her head, offering a small smile. "I didn't know until today."

Pete's expression softened, but his voice carried the weight of authority as he addressed the boys. "As long as your parents or guardians know," he cautioned.

"They do," one of the boys quickly assured him. "And we always check with our adopted grandparents first to make sure they're home."

Pete seemed satisfied with that, nodding before one of the boys piped up, tilting his head. "What are you doing here, Mr. Pete?"

He hesitated for half a beat, the shift in his demeanor so subtle most wouldn't notice. But Angie did. Realizing it must be official business, she jumped in smoothly. "He has to make visits, just like I do."

The explanation seemed good enough for the kids, and after a few more goodbyes, they scattered, waving as they headed back toward their apartments.

As soon as they were alone, Pete turned to her, his lips quirking as he slid his arm around her waist in a quick but familiar gesture. "Thanks for that," he murmured, voice low enough that only she could hear.

Angie glanced up at him, her heart doing the ridiculous little skip it always did when he touched her. "I had a feeling you must be here for something official."

"Sort of," he admitted, his voice turning serious. "I'm going to check on Robert Reeves. I just wanted to make sure he had my card in case he ever needs to call me."

She arched a brow. "Well, that's a coincidence because I was heading to see Jed Reeves, his grandfather."

Pete nodded.

"Then I take it Robert's back at home?"

"Yes," he confirmed. "The DA agreed there was no reason to charge him."

A deep, relieved sigh escaped her lips. "That's good. For him, but also for the family."

He nodded, his gaze steady, and without another word, they fell into step together, making their way toward the Reeves's apartment.

When Robert's mother opened the door, her expression instantly brightened at the sight of Angie, but as her gaze shifted, her eyes went wide at seeing Pete standing just beside her.

Pete, ever aware, was quick to ease any tension. He held his hands up slightly, his voice calm and reassuring. "I'm just here to make sure Robert got home safely and that everything's okay. I also wanted to give him my card in case he ever wants to reach out."

Mrs. Reeves visibly relaxed, her shoulders easing as she stepped back, motioning them inside. "Of course, come on in."

Inside, Angie's attention was immediately drawn to Jed Reeves, the older man sitting near the kitchen table. She smiled, greeting him first, then turned to the two younger children sitting at the table, their book bags leaning against their chairs. They eyed the visitors curiously but didn't stop what they were doing.

Her gaze then landed on a lanky teenage boy sitting near Jed, his posture slightly hunched, as if he wasn't quite sure how to carry himself in the room. His movements were hesitant, guarded.

She could see the uncertainty in his eyes, the way they darted between her and Pete. He looked wary but not defiant—just a kid who'd been through something big and wasn't sure what to make of it all yet.

Angie softened her smile and walked toward him. "Mr. Reeves," she said, looking at Jed first. "I see good things happened for the family today."

"Oh, Ms. Angie," Jed exhaled, his relief palpable. "They

decided my grandson could come home. No charges, nothing."

Her heart warmed at the joy in his voice, but she didn't miss the way Robert was subtly glancing at her, unsure of what to expect.

Without hesitation, she stepped closer and thrust out her hand. "Hello, Robert. I'm Angie Brown—I work with some of the older persons in the county. I'm so glad you're home."

For a moment, he hesitated, his fingers twitching slightly before he ducked his head and reached out, shaking her hand. "Thank you, Ms. Brown," he said, his voice quiet but sincere.

Then his eyes shifted toward Pete, and like his mother before him, they widened slightly.

Pete didn't waste a second. He moved forward smoothly, extending his own hand, his presence steady but not imposing.

"Robert," Pete said with an easy nod. "It's good to see you at home. I only stopped by to make sure you got back safe and sound. And I wanted to give you my card." He held it out. "I wasn't sure if you were able to keep the one I gave you before, but you have this now. It has my work number, and it also has my cell number."

Robert's gaze flickered between Pete's face and the card, a trace of something unreadable passing through his expression. Slowly, he reached out, taking the card carefully, his fingers gripping it like it was more than just a piece of paper.

Angie watched the interaction closely, something in her chest tightening at the unspoken connection happening in front of her. Pete wasn't just doing his job—he was making sure this kid knew he wasn't alone.

Robert turned the card over in his fingers, studying it

for a moment. There was hesitation in his posture, a wariness that Angie recognized as the natural instinct of a kid who wasn't sure who to trust. But then, something in Pete's steady expression must have reassured him, because Robert gave a small nod.

Pete met his gaze directly, his voice calm but firm. "You don't have to use it, but I want you to know it's there if you ever need it. No pressure. No expectations. Just an option."

"Thanks," he said, his voice still subdued but carrying a note of something deeper—maybe relief mixed with gratitude. "You talked to the attorney lady, right? You're the reason I got to come home."

Pete shook his head slightly, keeping his voice even. "I just made sure she had all the information to make the right decision."

Angie swore she saw Robert swallow hard, but he gave another small nod before tucking the card into his pocket.

Mrs. Reeves, still standing nearby, let out a quiet breath, as if she hadn't realized she'd been holding it. She wiped her hands on a dish towel and offered a genuine smile. "I really appreciate you stopping by, Detective Bolton. This has been... a lot, for all of us."

Pete inclined his head. "I can only imagine."

"Yeah, thank you," Robert echoed quickly, his gaze still locked on Pete. Then his brows furrowed slightly, a flicker of realization passing over his face. "Wait—you're the officer who talks to some of the kids around here, right?"

Pete nodded. "That's right. I run a mentorship program for a few middle schoolers who don't have someone in their life to give them a helping hand."

Robert's eyes flickered toward his grandfather, something unspoken passing between them. "I'm lucky," he said after a moment. "I got Mom and Granddad."

Pete's smile was warm and understanding. "Yes, you

are. You've got your granddad as a good role model." He paused, then added, "But if you ever want to make some new friends, I know they're in middle school, but the boys I work with are really good kids. A couple are fourteen, pretty close to your age. Some will be in high school next year."

Robert considered that, nodding slightly. "Thanks," he murmured, and this time, when he pocketed the card, it wasn't with hesitation.

Angie could feel the tension in the room beginning to ease, the atmosphere shifting from apprehensive to something lighter. She turned back to Jed, her voice warm. "And how are you, Mr. Reeves?"

While Pete and Robert chatted briefly, Angie took a seat next to Jed, lowering her voice as she leaned in. "I take it with Robert home, you won't be needing anyone extra in the house right now?"

Jed let out a chuckle, shaking his head. "That's right, Ms. Angie. And now I feel like a damn fool for having you give up your time and energy trying to figure out what to do, only for Robert to come home the very next day."

Angie reached out, covering his weathered hand with her own. "Never feel bad about that," she said, her voice gentle but firm. "That's what we're here for. I'm just glad things turned out the way they did."

Jed gave her a grateful look, patting her hand in return.

After speaking briefly with Mrs. Reeves, Angie and Pete made their way toward the door. Before Pete could step away, he reached into his jacket pocket and pulled out his phone. "Robert, before I go, I need you to take a look at something."

Robert's posture stiffened slightly, but he nodded. Pete swiped across the screen and pulled up a mug shot. The image of a man with sharp features, a distinct mole near his nose, and a tattooed star on his throat filled the screen.

Robert's eyes widened. "Yeah... yeah, that's him." He exhaled sharply, shifting his weight. "That's the guy who came with Lashawn the first time he talked to me."

Pete's expression didn't change, but Angie saw the flicker of confirmation in his eyes. "You sure?" Pete pressed, his voice calm but firm.

Robert nodded again. "Positive. But... I haven't seen him in a couple of months. Not after he stopped coming with Lashawn."

Angie leaned in, studying the photo herself. Her stomach tightened at the sight of the man's cold stare.

Pete locked his phone and slid it back into his pocket. "Alright, good to know. Thanks, Robert. If you do see him again, or hear anything about him, let me know."

Robert's fingers twitched at his side, but after a beat, he nodded. "Yeah. I will."

Pete clapped him lightly on the shoulder in reassurance. Then, without another word, he and Angie stepped away, exchanging a glance. As they walked outside, the cool evening air greeted them, carrying the distant sounds of kids playing and neighbors chatting on their balconies.

Angie felt a warmth spread through her chest as she turned her attention back to Pete. His hand rested lightly on her back as they made their way down the stairs toward their vehicles. The air between them had shifted —quieter, heavier with something unspoken yet deeply felt.

Once they reached her van, Pete leaned against the driver's side and exhaled, rubbing the back of his neck. "That could've gone worse."

Angie glanced at him, amused. "That was your takeaway?"

He smirked. "What? Did you expect me to say something profound?"

She rolled her eyes but smiled. "I just think it's nice to see a little proof that the system doesn't always fail. That a kid who got caught up in the wrong place at the wrong time actually got to go home."

Pete looked at her for a long moment, something unreadable in his expression. Then, without warning, he reached out and brushed his knuckles lightly over her arm. It was a fleeting touch, but enough to make her skin tingle.

"You've got a good heart, Angie."

She swallowed, her breath catching slightly at the way he was looking at her. The easy charm in his expression had faded, replaced by something deeper, something that made her pulse jump.

"You have to return the van?"

"Yeah," she said, resting her hand on the door handle. "I'll drop it off, then head home."

He nodded, considering something before pushing off the vehicle. "How about I grab some dinner from the Italian place down the road and bring it to you?"

She tilted her head, smiling as she took a step closer. Without hesitation, she slid her arms around his waist, feeling the steady warmth of him beneath her fingertips.

"That sounds perfect," she murmured, looking up at him. Then, softer, more certain, she asked, "Will you be able to stay?"

Pete's hand skimmed up her back, his touch deliberate and reassuring. His lips quirked into a slow, knowing grin.

"For you?" His voice dropped slightly, sending a delicious shiver down her spine. "Always."

And just like that, the weight of the day melted away, replaced by something infinitely better. It felt like falling with someone who would always catch her.

30

Pete had already spoken with Richard earlier in the day, outlining his plan for tonight's discussion with the boys. Richard wouldn't be joining them since his wife had just given birth, but he fully supported what Pete had in mind.

Now, as the boys pushed through the double doors of the YMCA, their usual energy was dampened by curiosity when Pete met them just inside, his expression serious.

"We're skipping gym tonight," Pete told them, motioning toward the hallway. "Conference room first."

Jalen frowned. "What's up, Mr. Pete?"

"Aren't we meeting our adopted grandparents tonight?" Darius asked, his brow furrowing.

"This is weird," Mike mumbled as he fell in line behind the others.

Pete didn't answer right away, leading them down the familiar corridor. The fluorescent lights buzzed faintly overhead, casting a cool glow against the scuffed linoleum floor. He could feel their unease growing, the shift in routine making them restless.

When they stepped into the conference room where they usually worked through homework, talked about life, and built their bond, Pete motioned for them to take a seat. The laughter and chatter were missing now, replaced by the quiet scrape of chairs against the floor as the boys settled around the table. Their expressions shifted from mild curiosity to concern.

Pete rested his hands on the table and met their eyes. "I talked to some of you at school the other day... the older ones. Now, I want to talk to all of you together."

He had their rapt attention, so he continued. "You all know that one of the biggest things Mr. Richard and I talk about is making good choices. And I know most of you have heard about what happened recently—the high school kid who got into the wrong car, with the wrong person, at the worst possible time."

The boys nodded, wide-eyed.

"I heard the car flipped ten times before stopping," Rasheem said, his voice edged with awe.

Curly scoffed. "Man, I heard drugs went flying out the windows, like a movie or something."

"They said it was one of the high school kids from our building," Mike added.

"Somebody on my bus said he escaped," Darius said.

Kyron rolled his eyes. "If he escaped, how'd they catch him, then?"

The older boys sat in silence as the younger ones slowly grew quiet. Pete raised his hands. "Alright, enough. First lesson, don't believe everything you hear." He swept his gaze across the table, making sure they were listening. "Here's what actually happened. The car ended up on its side, not flipping down the road like some action scene. No one was hurt, and no, drugs weren't flying everywhere. I know because I was there."

Silence settled over them as the weight of his words sank in.

"The second lesson? Don't make situations worse by spreading rumors. Gossip isn't just harmless talk—it can hurt people. It can ruin lives. It's one thing to share facts to help someone, but it's another to spread stories just to sound like you know something."

Heads bobbed in understanding, their previous excitement tempered by Pete's serious tone.

"And third," Pete continued, leaning forward slightly, "we're not going to talk about the kid who made the bad decision. That's not what tonight is about. What I want— what I need—is for you to think about your own choices."

Tony scrunched his nose. "But what kind of choices, Mr. Pete?"

Pete exhaled, his voice softer now. "The older you get, the harder it'll be to choose the right friends. The more pressure you'll feel to go along with things that don't sit right with you. And sometimes, stepping away from danger is going to feel like turning your back on people you care about." His gaze moved around the table, making sure each of them heard him. "That's why you need each other. This group… it's more than a program. It's a family. You don't need a gang to have a brotherhood. You have this. You have your teachers. Mr. Richard. Me. And now, you've got your adopted grandparents. You're surrounded by people who care."

For a long moment, no one spoke. The only sound was the faint hum of the air-conditioning kicking on.

Then Caleb broke the silence, his voice quieter than usual. "This was hard for you, wasn't it, Mr. Pete?"

The unexpected question caught Pete off guard. He met Caleb's gaze, then glanced around at the other boys. Their faces weren't just filled with curiosity anymore. Their eyes were filled with something deeper.

Pete nodded slowly. "Yeah. It was hard. Before I started working with you guys, I didn't have much connection to the kids in this county. But now? I do. I care about you. About your families. And I want to make sure that if you ever find yourself struggling with a decision, you lean on each other. You ask for help. You remember that you don't have to face anything alone."

The weight of his words lingered in the air. After a few moments, the boys nodded, one by one. The conversation continued, shifting toward how they could look out for one another, how they could communicate when something felt off. And when it was time to head out, the tension had eased.

As Pete led them toward the van, he felt something settle in his chest... hope.

Angie glanced up as the door to the Careway community room swung open. She had been setting out hot chocolate for the kids, and tea and coffee for the adults, when she caught sight of Pete and the boys filtering in. Normally, they entered with an energy that filled the space—laughing, nudging each other, launching straight into conversations with their adopted grandparents.

Tonight, though, something was different. Pete gave her a warm smile as he approached, but there was a heaviness to it, like his mind was elsewhere. And the boys, who were normally a pack of motion, were quieter and more subdued. A few offered halfhearted greetings, but most just gravitated toward their usual spots, hands in pockets, shoulders slightly hunched.

The grandparents noticed, too. George, already seated and waiting for Tony, exchanged a glance with Harold. Rosetta, ever perceptive, raised an eyebrow at Mike before glancing at Angie, silently asking if she knew what was going on. Angie shook her head slightly, then turned to Pete.

"Everything alright?" she asked softly.

Pete hesitated before answering, running a hand over the back of his neck. "Yeah. Just... a heavy conversation before we got here."

Angie nodded, glancing at the boys again. She could see it in their eyes—uncertainty, maybe even a little worry. Whatever Pete had talked to them about had made an impact.

She clapped her hands together gently. "Alright, everyone, let's get settled. I think a couple of you forgot to say hello," she teased lightly, hoping to pull them out of their quiet state.

That did the trick, easing the tension. Darius gave Bertram a sheepish smile before sitting beside him. Kyron and Caleb slid into their seats near Harold. But the usual liveliness was still missing.

It was Marty who finally broke the silence. He adjusted his glasses and leaned forward, looking directly at Jimmy. "Alright, son, what's got you all looking like somebody just told you Christmas got canceled?"

That made a couple of them chuckle, but only briefly. Jimmy hesitated, glancing at Pete before exhaling. "It's just... we were talking earlier. About making good choices. There was a kid ... um... a high school kid. He got in a car with some guy he didn't really know, and they turned out to be a gang member. The car crashed, and..." He shrugged, as if unsure how to sum it all up.

"Drugs," Rasheem muttered. "Money. The whole thing was messed up."

"That coulda been any one of us," Curly added, his voice quiet.

A ripple of understanding passed through the room. Some of the grandparents exchanged looks, and Angie could tell they were weighing their words, remembering their own youth.

Marty was the first to speak. He looked at Jimmy with a wry smile. "You think this is new? That back when we were young, the world was all rainbows and sweet tea?" He chuckled, shaking his head. "Son, when I was your age, the world was changing fast. I served in Vietnam but came home angry. Decided that normal society wasn't for me. I worried my parents silly when I didn't want to get a job and work nine to five. Hell, I went to Woodstock, if you can believe that."

"They won't know what Woodstock was!" Hannah said, shaking her head. She looked at the other kids. "It was a four-day music festival of hard rock, anti-war, drugs, drinking, and... um... other things."

Eyes widened around the table. "No way," Tony said, his usual skepticism creeping in.

"Oh yes," Marty said with a knowing smile. "And let me tell you, I made a few mistakes in my time." He let that settle before adding, "But I also had people who looked out for me. People who reminded me that I had choices."

Rosetta nodded. "It's all about who you keep around you. In the sixties, drugs were easy to get. And if you didn't have the right people watching your back, well..." She shook her head. "But I was lucky. I had family, friends who worked hard and never let me slip too far down the wrong path."

Harold leaned forward, his voice steady. "Money was

tight for my family back then. I grew up in Baltimore. Some people turned to drugs, others to alcohol. Me? I worked. Didn't have time to get into trouble because I had to help put food on the table. And you know what? I never regretted that choice."

"It's not just about staying away from the bad," Bertram added, looking at Darius. "It's about knowing where to turn when things get hard."

A quiet settled over the room again, but this time, it was thoughtful. The boys weren't just listening; they were absorbing the stories, realizing that the people in front of them hadn't always been old. That they had been young once, making their own choices, some good, some bad.

Jimmy leaned forward, glancing at Marty. "So… what kept you from making bad choices?"

Marty smiled, his face lined with time, but his eyes still sharp. "The people I surrounded myself with. It all comes down to that, son. You run with the right people, you'll find your way through just about anything. You run with the wrong ones? That's when life gets dangerous."

Heads nodded around the table.

Pete, who had been quiet for most of the conversation, finally spoke. "And that's exactly why we have this group. So that no matter what, you have people to turn to. People who care about you."

The boys exchanged looks. "So you all are like our safety net, huh?" David murmured.

Hannah smiled, placing a hand over his. "Absolutely."

For the first time that evening, the tension eased. The room didn't feel so heavy anymore. The past and present had come together in a way none of them had expected, and Angie could see the way the boys sat a little straighter, their expressions a little lighter.

A bridge had been built tonight. And not just between

the boys and the seniors. As she looked over at Pete, her heart squeezed with an emotion that she hadn't realized was growing. She was falling for this handsome, kind, and honorable man. Smiling, she stood and began serving the cookies she'd brought.

31

Pete's eyes blinked open, and for a moment, he just lay, letting the warmth of the morning and the softness of the sheets settle around him. He didn't need to shift to know he wasn't in his bed. Angie's sheets were softer and smoother, wrapping around him like a whisper. The pale blue walls and lace curtains didn't belong to his world but were integral in hers. The way the light filtered through them softened the morning, making it feel less like a harsh wake-up call and more like a gentle welcome to another day with her.

And then there was her warm and faintly floral scent that had sunk into her pillow and into his skin. The silk of her hair brushed over his arm, and her body curled into his like she belonged there. Like she belonged to him.

He loved this. The ease of it, the rightness. He wanted to wake up like this every morning for the rest of his life. *Was it too soon to say that? To even think it?*

But he didn't have a blueprint for love. His parents sure as hell hadn't modeled it, and the only real examples he had came from friends—friends who didn't exactly sit around talking about feelings and forever. But the way he felt with her? The way she made everything seem brighter, lighter, even when they weren't talking? *I want this for always.*

A soft sigh stirred the air between them, brushing over his skin. She moved, shifting her body closer and pressing against him like a perfect fit. He held his breath, waiting for the first glimpse of her eyes.

Angie's lashes fluttered, her eyes slowly blinking open, unfocused for a second. And then—there was that flicker of honesty in her expression before she was fully awake but knew she was with him. And when she did, her entire face softened. A slow, lazy smile curved her lips, beaming up at him like she held the sun inside her. She was beautiful. His heart gave an aching clench in his chest.

He rolled onto his forearms, hovering above her, giving her space but not too much. Her body knew his now and responded before she was even fully aware. Her thighs parted in a way that made heat rise sharp inside him as his hips were cradled.

His hands cupped her face, thumbs tracing the curves of her cheeks, memorizing how she felt beneath him. His breath hitched as her hands slid over his back. Her fingernails gently scraped over his skin, sending tingles throughout his body.

"Good morning, beautiful," he murmured, his voice rough with sleep and need. Her knee was less swollen, and her joints were less painful. He was learning the little tells her body or expression would give when she was in pain.

She started to reply, but he was already kissing her, swallowing the words, stealing her breath, letting his body say what he wasn't sure he knew how to put into words.

She moaned into his mouth, sending a fresh wave of heat rushing through him. Her fingers tightened against his skin, pulling him closer, letting her body tell him what she wanted.

And he gave it to her. With a slow, unhurried roll of his hips, he pressed into her, feeling her body welcome him in a way that made his chest go tight.

Her hands clung to him, her lips trembled against his, and she breathed his name in a way that let him know he was someone special. It no longer mattered if it was too soon. He was a goner.

Pete had never been a man to overthink things. Life came fast, and you either grabbed hold or got left behind. But this feeling in his chest was flaming out of control like a wildfire. It filled all the empty spaces he didn't even know existed before Angie. And he'd never felt this way before.

She lay on the bed underneath him, and he drank her in. Her hair was spread out on the pillow, a little wild from his hands. Her lips were still swollen from his kisses. Yet there was hesitation in her eyes, like a battle deep inside. He wasn't about to let her fight alone.

"You're thinking too much," he murmured, keeping his weight off her chest. He kissed her lightly, then pulled back, keeping her eyes on him. "I can see that little crease right here—" He smoothed his thumb between her brows. "Tell me what's racing through your mind."

Angie exhaled a soft, unsteady breath, her fingers digging into his shoulders. "It's just... this seems like we're going at the speed of light. My feelings... they don't make sense to happen so quickly."

Pete felt a slow smile pull at his lips. "Does it have to make sense?"

She blinked up at him, and he saw the battle still waging in her gaze. Logic and reason on one side, and the undeniable feelings between them on the other.

"Angie," he said, voice steady as a promise, "I don't know much about love. Didn't see it modeled when I was growing up. But, as an adult, I've seen most of my friends fall in love, and sometimes very quickly. That tells me that love doesn't run on a clock. It's not always convenient, and it sure as hell doesn't wait for us to make sense of it. I've seen friends fall on a first date or after years of knowing each other. It comes when it comes. I know what I feel, and I'm not about to argue with this." He finished, unsure he'd ever said so much at one time. Certainly not about feelings.

Her breath hitched, and he felt the tremor in her chest as she lay underneath him. "But how do we know it's real?"

Pete kissed her lightly, his touch grounding them both. "Because it is real. Just like I know how to breathe, I know I want to be with you no matter what. I don't need time to tell me what I already feel in my heart."

She searched his face, and he let her. He wanted her to see that he had no doubts or hesitations. All she would find in his eyes was steady certainty.

Finally, Angie smiled, and the sun shone brighter. "Are you always this convincing?"

Pete grinned. "Only when it matters."

She framed his face with her hands, her thumbs sweeping over his stubbled jaw. Her touch was warm, and her eyes were filled with something that made his chest tighten again. "You matter to me, Pete."

That was all he needed. He bent, capturing her mouth with his, hoping she felt words he hadn't said yet. This was their time, and as far as he was concerned, they were happening now.

After they'd made love, showered, and dressed, they ate breakfast quickly before needing to head to work. "I have to run home to feed Queenie," he said, filling his travel mug of coffee.

She walked over and rested her hands on his waist while dropping her forehead to his chest.

"What's the matter, babe?" he asked, setting the hot mug onto the counter.

She leaned back and smiled while shaking her head. "Nothing."

"Uh-uh," he retorted, then chuckled at her incredulous expression. "Don't say 'nothing' when there's something on your mind."

Her eyes twinkled, but she pressed her lips together as though she still wasn't sure if she should say anything. He waited, willing to give her the time to decide, even if it made him late.

"I just wish you didn't have to leave," she finally said.

He waited, still patiently, knowing there was more to come.

"I suppose that sounded dumb, didn't it?" She sighed, then said, "I know you only live about fifteen minutes away, but right now, that seems huge. I wish we lived closer, that's all."

"How close is closer?"

This time, her smile widened. "Oh, I don't know. Maybe... here? Sometime. Once we know that Queenie would be happy."

Those words were almost as sweet as her saying she loved him... almost. He grinned and said, "I'm all in, Angie. Now we just have to see what Queenie says."

Her laughter reached her twinkling eyes as she nodded. "I'm all in, too. And whenever you want, we'll let Queenie try out this place."

The air was thick with the scent of gasoline and fried food. The neon glow from the convenience store sign flickered, giving the front of the store a happier appearance than the shadows and cracked pavement in the back alley. Pete pulled the SUV behind the gas station, easing it into the same familiar spot near the overflowing dumpster.

Jacko was careful... always made them come to him. Sure enough, a few seconds later, the rusted back door creaked open. Jacko stepped out, dragging two overstuffed bags of garbage in each hand. Hefting them over his shoulder, he let them slam into the dumpster with a grunt, then wiped his hands down the front of his stained shirt.

He shuffled toward the SUV with a tired sort of swagger. Jeremy popped the passenger door open and slipped into the back seat, letting Jacko slide into his spot up front.

Pete exhaled sharply. "What have you got for us?"

Jacko's lips curled into something resembling a smirk. "Damn, I don't even get polite conversation anymore? You just jump straight to the action without foreplay."

Pete fought the urge to shudder. He did not need the mental image of what type of foreplay Jacko might engage in. "Just get to it."

Jacko sighed dramatically, then twisted around in his seat so he could see both of them. His expression was half amused and half confused... the usual mix when he was in one of his moods.

"Word is, G-Shine wants to use the Eastern Shore as their transport route from Pennsylvania to North Carolina. They want the whole track themselves."

Pete kept his face impassive, but Jeremy let out a scoff from the back. "Okay, tell us something we don't know."

Jacko held up a finger. "I was getting there. See, OGD ain't happy about G-Shine trying to take the whole route. They got a guy, calls himself Flame. Apparently, he was originally working with Ciao... you know, that dumbass who wrecked his car—"

"We know who Ciao is." Pete interrupted, his patience thin.

Jacko huffed. "Man, you take the fun out of telling my story."

Neither detective reacted. Jacko sighed again, more put-upon this time, before continuing.

"Fine. Okay, where was I? Oh, yeah. When Ciao got arrested by you all, Flame figured there was no reason he couldn't take over the route from North Carolina through his home turf in Norfolk, then straight up to Pennsylvania. It pisses all over G-Shine's plans, but if he pulls it off, he moves up in his orbit."

Jeremy leaned forward slightly. "We know someone named Flame. We're looking for him."

Jacko shrugged, rolling his shoulders like the weight of the conversation was an inconvenience. "Can't say I've ever met him myself, but I hear he's an ugly fucker." His chuckle turned into a raspy coughing fit. He hacked into his sleeve, his whole body shuddering as he struggled to catch his breath.

Pete grimaced. "You'd live longer if you quit smoking."

Jacko wheezed out a laugh. "Yeah, I heard you the first hundred times you told me that." He finally managed to suck in a steady breath before continuing. "Anyway, figured you boys should know. Word on the street is that Flame's been hanging around up here. Supposedly, he's got some relative in the area. Probably gives him a reason to be here, so it's less suspicious. Can't say I've seen him, but I don't stick my nose where it don't belong—especially not where I live. I'll leave that up to you all." He coughed again. "I'll tell you one more thing. Word has it that Flame is a helluva lot more ambitious than Ciao."

With that, he shoved the door open and climbed out, leaving behind the stale scent of sweat and unwashed body odor. The door slammed shut with a heavy thunk.

Pete exhaled through his mouth, trying to erase the stench. "Christ."

Jeremy slid back into the front seat, only to wrinkle his nose. "We need to start getting out of the vehicle before we talk to him."

Pete barked out a laugh. "Damn straight. Now, I gotta get my SUV detailed before I take Angie out."

Jeremy grinned, shaking his head as Pete pulled away from the gas station. The conversation with Jacko had been barely useful, but something about this whole situation sat wrong with him. As they headed back to the station, the weight of it settled deep in his gut. Flame was here. And not just because he'd come with Lashawn. And that meant trouble was coming.

32

JIMMY

Jimmy sat with the other boys on the bus, still riding the high of having passed his math test. Laughter filled the space around him, the kind that came easy after a good day.

"I think I'm gonna go check on Mr. Marty," he said to Darius, shifting in his seat as the bus slowed at their stop.

Darius nodded, his expression turning thoughtful. "I noticed he didn't seem to be feeling great the last time we talked to him."

"That's what I thought, too. If we go check on him now, then I'll have the rest of the evening."

The bus lurched to a stop, and nearly all the kids in their section piled out. Their apartment complex wasn't the nicest place around, but it was home. His mom worked hard to make sure their unit stayed clean and welcoming, even if the outside could use a fresh coat of paint and some better lighting.

Jimmy waved to the others as he stepped off, then headed down the breezeway to his apartment to get his bike. His mom was afraid someone would steal it, so almost everyone kept their bikes locked inside their homes. It didn't take too long to pedal to the Careway Senior Apartments. Jimmy liked the way the U-shape allowed a little garden in the middle. Marty lived in the end unit to the right.

He felt his bike was safer here than his own apartment building, but he still locked it to one of the small trees before making his way to Mr. Marty's door. He knocked and waited. No answer. Frowning, he knocked again, harder this time. Mr. Marty had trouble hearing, and Jimmy knew he was supposed to be working on getting a hearing aid.

The door swung open, but instead of Mr. Marty, a younger man stood in the doorway. Someone Jimmy had never seen before. He was dressed in a red tracksuit with a black ball cap. His look might be casual, but Jimmy recognized the brand, and it was more than his mom could afford.

"Uh... I just came to see Mr. Marty..."

The man didn't say anything. He just stared at Jimmy, eyes cool and unreadable. But from inside, Mr. Marty's familiar voice called out. "Oh, that's Jimmy, my friend. Let him in, Tamarcus."

The door opened wider, and Jimmy stepped inside, relieved to see Mr. Marty settled in his recliner.

"I didn't mean to disturb you. I didn't realize you had company."

"This is my nephew. Well, I suppose my great-nephew," Mr. Marty said with a chuckle. "He lives in Norfolk and has come to visit me recently."

Jimmy turned back to Tamarcus and stuck out his hand. "Nice to meet you. I'm Jimmy."

Tamarcus let the moment stretch, leaving Jimmy's hand hanging for just a few seconds too long. Then, with a grin that showed off a gold tooth, he clasped Jimmy's hand and gave it one hard shake before letting go.

Something in Jimmy's gut twisted. He didn't like him. "Well, I guess, Mr. Marty, I can—"

"Come sit down, Jimmy." Mr. Marty waved a hand toward the sofa. "It's always a treat to have you stop by."

Jimmy hesitated. Tamarcus was still watching him, expression unreadable but unmistakably guarded. The energy in the room felt off. "It's okay. I'll let the two of you visit," Jimmy said, taking a step back. "I'll come by later, maybe tomorrow."

"Sounds like a good plan," Tamarcus said. They were the first words he'd spoken to Jimmy, and the tone was not friendly.

Jimmy didn't miss the tension in his voice. Nodding, he turned toward the door, giving Mr. Marty one last glance before stepping out into the breezeway. He rode his bike back to his apartment complex, not surprised to see Jalen, Rasheem, and Darius walking down the outside stairs toward him when he arrived.

"Was Mr. Marty not home?" Rasheem asked.

"Yeah, he was, but he had company."

"Company?" Jalen frowned. "I didn't know he had visitors."

"His nephew or great-nephew or something like that," Jimmy said. "The guy gave me the feeling he didn't want me there. I don't know… I just didn't get good vibes off him."

"Was Mr. Marty okay?" Darius asked.

"Yeah, he seemed fine. Actually, he seemed happy to have company. I just got the feeling his nephew didn't want me around. I'll go back tomorrow and check on him."

Jalen exchanged a look with the others. "If you got a bad

feeling about him, is that something we should talk to Mr. Pete about?"

Jimmy sighed, running a hand over his head. "I don't know. Just because I don't like someone doesn't mean they're a bad person. And Mr. Marty seemed okay."

"It'd be nice if they lived closer, then we could watch out for our grandparents all the time," Darius suggested.

They all nodded, and while Jimmy liked the idea, he decided that he'd bike over to visit Mr. Marty more often.

The afternoon air had cooled as the sun dipped behind the apartment buildings, casting them in shade. By now, David, Tony, and Caleb had joined them. Curly's mom had sent a container filled with cookies to share, and they were enjoying their afternoon snack.

Jimmy sat on the steps with his arms resting on his knees, watching as the elementary school bus rumbled up to the curb. The doors hissed open, spilling out a group of younger kids, their laughter and chatter breaking up the quiet hum of the neighborhood.

Across the way, Robert stood at the end of the building, hands tucked into his pockets, waiting for his younger brother and sister. The afternoon sunlight cast a long shadow behind him, stretching across the pavement. From Jimmy's angle, it looked much heavier than just his silhouette.

Darius, sitting beside Jimmy, exhaled heavily. "I wonder what that was like for him—to get arrested," he mused. "I know Mr. Pete said we shouldn't talk about what happened, but he always seemed real nice to me."

"He just lives a couple of doors from me. Remember when we were all in elementary school together? I think he's nice," Jalen said, leaning back on his elbows. "He just made a bad choice."

They fell into silence as Robert gathered his siblings

and started up the stairs at the far end of the building. When he glanced their way, his expression was guarded, unsure. But when Jalen lifted a hand in an easy wave, Robert hesitated only a second before offering a small, tentative smile in return. Then, cautiously, he lifted his hand and waved in return.

Jalen hopped up, jogging down the breezeway to meet him. "If you wanna hang out with us, we're just chilling."

Robert glanced at his brother and sister, making sure they were headed inside safely before nodding. "Thanks. Maybe I will. I just gotta get them settled and make sure my granddad doesn't need anything."

Jimmy watched as Robert walked away, something thoughtful settling in his chest. Maybe things weren't as simple as they used to be when they were all in elementary school. Perhaps none of them had the luxury of seeing the world in black and white anymore. What happened to Robert could have happened to any of them.

He shifted slightly on the stoop, stretching his legs out as a black sedan with dark-tinted windows rolled into the parking lot, moving to the far side of the last building. The driver alighted, and Jimmy was surprised to see it was Tamarcus.

"That's him," Jimmy said in a whisper that came out much louder than he'd intended.

The other boys got quiet and looked at him.

"Don't act like you're staring, but that black car at the end... that was Mr. Marty's nephew."

"Who's he visiting here?" Caleb asked.

"I don't know. He's talking to those two men," David said.

"I know them," Darius piped up. "They live in the very

last building. My mom said to stay away from them because she doesn't like the way they look."

Rasheem nodded. "They look sneaky when they walk around. That guy who got arrested used to talk to them when he was around."

While a few of the boys kept their backs to Tamarcus so it didn't look like they were all staring, Jimmy kept his eye on him.

Tamarcus's gaze skimmed over the block, taking in every detail, as if he were memorizing it, cataloging things no one else noticed. Jimmy wasn't sure what to make of him.

"I've seen that guy," Tony said. "Not much, but enough to recognize that black car. He always walks around like his shit don't stink."

Jimmy continued to stare. The uneasy feeling grew.

Darius, Rasheem, and Jalen had gone quiet beside him, their conversation tapering off as Tamarcus's gaze flicked their way. It was brief but heavy, and enough to send a cold prickle along the back of Jimmy's neck.

As quickly as it came, Tamarcus turned his head like they were nothing more than background noise. Then he strode away from the two men and climbed into his car.

The Virginia plates gleamed as the engine roared to life. Then, with a sharp jerk of the wheel, Tamarcus peeled off down the street, tires screeching loud enough to send a couple of startled birds flapping from a rooftop.

Jimmy exhaled through his nose. "Idiot."

Darius stretched his legs out, his expression contemplative. "He sure don't act like Mr. Marty's nephew. Mr. Marty is nice. That guy is... I don't know... looks like a gang member. Red and black. Like one of the Bloods."

Before Jimmy could dwell on it, Robert reappeared, his hands stuffed deep in the pockets of his jeans as he walked toward them. He stopped at the base of the steps, glancing between Jimmy and the others. "Y'all still out here?"

Jalen shrugged. "Where else we gonna be?"

Robert let out a chuckle but didn't argue. Instead, he rocked back on his heels, his gaze drifting down the breezeway that ran the full length of the apartment building. "Feels weird, ya know?" he said after a moment. His voice was lower now, more thoughtful. "Not hanging with the high school crowd right now."

"You okay... you know... after what happened?" Jalen asked, his tone careful.

Robert huffed out a breath, his jaw tightening before he nodded. "Yeah. Some of the older kids tried to act like I was either a badass or a dumbass. Sure wasn't the first, but I was the second." He heaved a sigh, rubbing the back of his neck. "I gotta make better choices. Can't keep doing dumb shit and expect things to change."

Jimmy pushed up from the steps. "Tomorrow, I'll go back to check on Mr. Marty."

"We can go with you," Darius offered.

Robert shifted, hesitating.

"You can come with us," Jimmy said, his invitation quiet but confident.

Robert studied him for a beat, then narrowed his eyes slightly. "You all are part of that group the detective has going, right?"

"Yeah," Jimmy said, "but it's more than that."

Robert tilted his head, about to ask for clarification, when the sudden sound of running feet had them all turning.

Mike, Kyron, and Curly came barreling up the breezeway, their energy a sharp contrast to the weight of the conversation.

"Hey, guys," Mike called out, skidding to a stop. "Whatcha doing?"

"We're talking about going to check on Mr. Marty and the other adopted grandparents tomorrow," Darius said. "Robert's coming, too."

Robert frowned slightly. "I'm not part of the group."

"That doesn't matter," Jalen said. "Mr. Pete... um, Detective Pete, tells us to know who we can trust and hang out with those people. We've got some of the older people in those senior apartments who are kinda like adopted grandparents. They help us, and we help them."

Robert nodded slowly. "That's cool. My real grandpa lives with us, so I have that built in."

"Yeah," Jimmy said, "but you can never have too many people on your side." He jerked his chin toward the breezeway. "We'll meet here after the school bus drops us all off."

Darius looked at the boys who had just joined them. "Jimmy said Mr. Marty had a nephew visiting who looks like a jerk."

Jimmy shot him a look and rolled his eyes. "Yes, but we're not gonna say anything to him. After all, it's his relative."

"I know," Darius grumbled. "I was just letting them know that we're kind of like the undercover eyes for our grandparents."

Robert finally smiled, shaking his head, but there was something lighter in his expression now—like maybe for the first time in a while, he wasn't standing on the outside looking in.

As the group gathered and started down the breezeway together, Jimmy's focus remained elsewhere. Because if Marty's grand-nephew kept coming around to talk to some men who weren't trustworthy in their complex,

Jimmy needed to know why. And whether they should be worried.

The air smelled of fresh-cut grass as Jimmy and the others rode their bikes toward Careway Senior Apartments. Their bike wheels hummed against the pavement as they avoided the potholes. The ride was just over a mile, and the younger boys easily kept pace, their laughter ringing out as they lightheartedly teased each other.

Since Jimmy wasn't tied up with spring sports this year, he had more time to visit, and over the past few days, he'd made the trip whenever he could. But today was special since they all went together.

When they rolled up to the apartments, Rosetta was already outside in the garden, rocking in her chair like she'd been waiting for them. Her sharp eyes caught sight of them before their sneakers even hit the ground.

"Well, look at y'all, coming round like the sunshine," she called, grinning wide. "I wasn't expecting company today!"

Jimmy smiled as he kicked his bike stand down. "We had some time and figured we'd drop by."

Rosetta's whole face lit up, and she pushed herself to her feet. "That calls for cake, then!" She didn't wait for a response before turning back into the apartment, calling over her shoulder, "Y'all come on in!"

Inside, the apartment smelled of cinnamon and vanilla, and it reminded Jimmy of his apartment when his mom had time to bake cookies. Before they even had a chance to settle, Rosetta was already on the phone with Hannah.

"You better get over here. We got visitors, and I know you got something sweet in that kitchen of yours."

It wasn't long before Hannah arrived, carrying a tin of

fresh chocolate chip cookies that still held warmth from the oven. The boys didn't hesitate, diving into the treats, their chatter filling the room as they swapped stories with the women.

After a while, they made their rounds, checking in on the other residents. They didn't knock on George's door since Hannah mentioned he was at a doctor's appointment. Bertram and Harold were at their usual spot by the window, playing cards, their makeshift poker chips nothing more than dried pieces of pasta.

"Y'all ever gonna bet with something you can eat?" Darius teased, peering over Harold's shoulder.

Harold grunted, never looking up from his hand. "Boy, these noodles been sitting in that jar longer than you've been alive. They're worth more than a meal now."

The boys laughed, but soon, Jimmy's focus shifted to the one person he really wanted to check on... Mr. Marty.

The old man's eyes twinkled when he spotted them. "Well, I'll be. Thought I might've scared y'all off with all my stories last time."

"Nah," Jimmy said, shaking his head. "We like your stories."

Marty gave a pleased grunt and motioned for them to sit. After a few minutes of talking, Jimmy lingered as the others made their way toward the door. His voice dropped, turning more serious.

"Has your great-nephew been by again?"

Marty's expression tightened, his mouth pressing into a thin line before he let out a slow sigh. "Not much. Once a week, if that."

Jimmy frowned. "Was he around more before?"

Marty shook his head. "No. Truth be told, I'd almost forgotten my stepsister even had a grandson. He showed up outta the blue months back, said he was doing business over this way and that his grandma mentioned me."

Jimmy studied Marty's face. "What kind of business?"

"I don't rightly know," Marty admitted, rubbing his chin. "But whatever it is, it must be doing well. Boy's got himself some fancy shoes, and that car he drives up in? That ain't no used junker, that's for sure."

Jimmy nodded, filing the information away. He didn't know what kind of business required expensive shoes and unannounced visits, but something about it sat wrong in his gut.

"Well, I'll check in again soon," Jimmy promised. "I'll see you tomorrow at the meeting."

Marty clapped a bony hand on Jimmy's shoulder, his grip firm despite his frailty. "You're a good young man, Jimmy. Never had kids of my own, but I'd be proud to claim you as family."

Jimmy swallowed against the warmth that rose in his chest, then grinned. "Thanks, Mr. Marty."

As he stepped outside, the boys crowded around, their curiosity sparking like flint.

"What'd he say?" Darius asked, glancing back at the building.

Jimmy relayed the conversation, his voice dropping when he mentioned Tamarcus.

Darius smirked. "You gonna be like a superspy and keep watch?"

Jimmy chuckled. "Something like that. Now that I know what car Tamarcus drives, I can check if it's here before coming up."

Mike frowned, glancing around. "Not a lot of good places to hide here, though. We stick out with these bikes."

Jalen jerked his chin toward the back. "Maybe we can stash them somewhere."

Curious, they hopped back on their bikes and pedaled to the rear of the building. The grass was mowed, and the building's overhang shadowed the area. Each apartment had a back door that opened to a sidewalk running along the rear of the building. Their trash cans were standing next to the doors like sentinels.

"I don't think anybody comes to the back much," Curly muttered, eyeing the neat yard that was empty.

"Probably leftover from the hotel before this place became apartments for older people," Jimmy guessed. He glanced around, then nodded. "But no one's back here. If I ever need to hide my bike, this is the spot."

The others murmured their agreement, and with a silent pact sealed, they rode off toward home, the weight of their new plan settling in their minds like a secret worth keeping.

33

Jeremy gripped the steering wheel of the county SUV, his eyes scanning the stretch of two-lane highway that cut north through the heart of the Eastern Shore. Gray clouds loomed low overhead, casting the flat fields in a silvery haze. Beside him, Pete sat silently, flipping through the notes they'd scrawled from the morning's dead-end interviews.

They had spent hours chasing whispers, trying to pull something solid out of the fog surrounding Tamarcus Waters. Norfolk PD hadn't seen him in a while. He wasn't living where he used to or haunting the same places. The informants for the NPD could only say that Flame was moving up. The word on the street was that Tamarcus was climbing within the ranks of the OBG, stepping into power. That kind of rise didn't happen quietly. Yet... here they were. Still no face, no recent photo. Just rumors.

Cedric had reluctantly agreed to let them float the idea of a deal to Lashawn, hoping maybe, just maybe, the man would be desperate enough to talk. But desperation hadn't even brushed Lashawn's hardened exterior.

Jeremy remembered the way Lashawn had sneered, one side of his mouth lifting in something close to amusement.

"I can do my time and live like a king on the inside," he'd said, voice rough with disdain, "or I can be dead the first night. You go figure which one I want."

Now, a new call had them heading thirty minutes inland. A possible gang-related shooting. Drugs involved. Jeremy pressed harder on the gas, the SUV chewing up miles of cracked pavement. The air between him and Pete was quiet as the silence filled with shared thoughts and unspoken theories.

They saw the pulsing red and blue lights before they reached the scene, a swirl of chaos illuminating the parking lot of a run-down laundromat tucked just off the highway. Jeremy pulled in behind an ambulance, gravel crunching under the tires, and both men stepped out into the damp air.

Deputies from the Accawmacke Sheriff's Office had already cordoned off the scene, the familiar yellow tape fluttering in the wind. Jeremy offered a chin lift to a few of the uniforms as he and Pete made their way toward the cluster of responders. The laundromat stood in the background, its flickering neon "Open 24 HRS" sign casting a jittery glow.

Their captain, Terry, was mid-conversation with Sheriff Liam Sullivan when they approached. Both men turned, nodding in greeting.

"What have you got?" Pete asked, his gaze still taking in the scene.

Terry blew out a heavy sigh, the kind that carried the weight of too many crime scenes. "Two shots to the head through the driver's window. Close range. Execution style. The guy never had a chance. His gun was still in the seat next to him."

Pete's gaze slid to where a K9 unit circled the crime scene, the dog tugging its handler toward the rear of the vehicle.

"Drugs?"

"Traces," Terry confirmed. "Dog found a small stash of powder. One of the detectives identified it as coke. So far, only found in the trunk."

Jeremy stepped in closer, brow furrowing. "Do we know who the victim is?"

Terry gave a solemn nod. "Pennsylvania plates. Driver's license says Jacob Parsons. Same Blood ink on his knuckles as Lashawn. We'll know more once the medical examiner gets a look."

The laundromat stood like a relic from another time, its paint peeling, its windows fogged with years of grime. Still open for business… In this area, many people didn't have washers and dryers in their homes, so there was always a need. Pete looked around the lot, instinct already ticking. "Witnesses?"

Terry's expression shifted slightly, just enough to signal something more. "That's what I thought you'd be interested in. A couple was inside, doing laundry. They said they were watching when the victim's car pulled in. The engine was still running. He was looking down, possibly texting. Then a black sedan with tinted windows pulled up beside him. Passenger side window came down, shots fired. Clean, fast. No one got out."

Pete and Jeremy shared a look. Terry continued, "The woman screamed and dropped to the floor. Her husband pulled her behind the counter. No security cameras outside, unfortunately. Just one inside."

Jeremy shook his head. "Guess the owner only cares who's stealing quarters."

Terry smirked. "That'd be my guess too."

He gestured toward the street. "The ambulance has already taken Jacob's body to the morgue. Cora said she was going to get started on him straight away. You can check in with her on your way back."

Pete noticed Jeremy's mouth curved at the mention of Cora's name. He knew he'd do the same if someone talked about Angie.

Turning back to Terry, Pete said, "Can we talk to the couple?"

"Yep," Terry said, jerking his thumb over his shoulder toward the laundromat. "I told Liam to keep them here. I figured you'd want to see if you could get anything out of them that his detectives didn't. You two know more of the players."

"Okay, Terry. Thanks," Jeremy replied, giving a nod of appreciation.

"I'm heading back down to North Heron. If you end up needing backup, just give me a call."

Pete tilted his head, studying Terry. Their captain was usually composed, but something in his tone seemed rushed.

"Everything all right?" Pete asked, voice low.

Terry offered a tired half smile. "Got a call from the school. My daughter is sick, and of course, the one person who usually helps cover for me is out too."

Jeremy waved him off. "Don't worry about it. We've got this covered."

With a few quick chin lifts and murmured goodbyes, they watched Terry retreat across the lot, slipping into his SUV and pulling away, tires spitting gravel behind him.

Jeremy and Pete turned toward the laundromat, their boots crunching over the pavement. The victim's vehicle sat crookedly in a space just left of the front window, engine now silent. The driver's window was shattered, with the glass sprayed all over the front seats, dashboard, and console. Along with blood.

Jeremy spotted the K9 unit nearby—a tall man with a neatly trimmed beard holding the leash of a German Shepherd who paced, alert.

They walked over. Pete extended a hand. "Pete Bolton. This is Jeremy Pickett. Drug Task Force."

The handler shook it firmly. "Carlos. And this here is Birdie."

Jeremy gave the dog a small nod, then smiled faintly. "She found traces?"

"Yeah. Led us straight to the trunk. We did a full search, since nothing was visible at first. I had her double-check the back and front seats too. Still clean. One of the detectives finally used trace paper and picked up a little powder in the trunk. Likely a carry situation... maybe a poorly sealed baggie leaked during transport."

"Got it," Jeremy said. "Appreciate it."

Carlos gave a nod, and the partners continued inside.

The laundromat smelled like fabric softener. The old tile floor was chipped in places, and the plastic chairs had seen better days. The machines were all silent, but the warmth of their use still permeated the air.

Along one wall, seated on a molded plastic bench, a couple sat close together. The man had his arm protectively around the woman, and she was clutching a paper cup of coffee with both hands as if it were the only thing keeping her grounded. Her dark eyes were red-rimmed, her mascara faintly smudged.

A female deputy stood nearby and straightened when she saw them approach.

She gave a respectful nod. "This is Juan and Tina Ramirez."

Jeremy offered a gentle smile and pulled a chair up

across from them, lowering himself slowly so he didn't feel towering. "It's good to meet you. I'm sorry it's under these circumstances. I'm Detective Jeremy Pickett, Drug Task Force. This is my partner, Detective Pete Bolton."

The couple nodded. Tina gave a small, nervous smile, while Juan kept a steady hand on her shoulder.

Pete took the seat beside Jeremy. His voice was calm, his presence grounding. "I know you've already been questioned. I imagine it's exhausting to go over this again, but we'd appreciate it if you could walk us through what happened one more time. Sometimes a small detail, even something that seems insignificant, can help us make a connection."

"I understand, sir," Juan said. His voice was quiet, thoughtful. "It all happened so fast."

"Just start from the beginning," Pete encouraged. "Tell us what you remember."

Juan glanced at his wife, who gave him a small nod of encouragement.

"We'd just finished loading the dryers," Juan began. "We would have about an hour to wait before everything would be ready. I thought about running down to the gas station for lunch, but Tina..." His eyes softened as he looked at her. "She said she thought it might rain. We walked over to the front window to check the sky. Just standing there, talking about what we might get to eat."

Jeremy leaned in slightly, his voice low and steady. "Do you remember what time this was?"

Tina lifted her head slightly, her voice still shaky but certain. "It was right at five minutes until noon. I know because I checked the time. The weatherman said it might rain this afternoon, and I remember wondering if we'd make it home before it started."

"That's good to know," Jeremy said gently. "What did you see?"

Juan shifted in his seat and glanced out the laundromat's large front window. "A car. A black car," he began, his voice low and steady, but tight with unease. He nodded toward the victim's vehicle, still surrounded by detectives and evidence markers. "It rolled up and parked just where it's sitting now. I don't think the driver ever planned on coming inside. But I watched, just in case. I didn't want to leave Tina if a lone male was going to be doing his laundry here at the same time."

Pete gave him a respectful nod. "Smart thinking."

"He looked like he was using his phone," Tina added. Her fingers tightened around her coffee cup. "I couldn't actually see a phone, but his head was down, like he was reading or texting. And I noticed the license plate—Pennsylvania tags. I thought maybe he was lost, maybe looking up directions."

Jeremy scribbled that down, then looked up. "And then?"

Juan exhaled, his jaw tightening. "Another car came flying into the lot. Tires squealed as it stopped right up alongside the driver's side. Passenger window was already down. And then… he lifted a gun."

Juan's eyes unfocused, as if he were watching the whole thing again. His hand curled slightly on his thigh.

"It took me a second to understand what I was seeing," he continued. "Then he opened fire. I heard the glass shatter in the other car, but he kept shooting. Tina screamed and dropped. I hit the ground, too, and crawled to her. I pulled her behind the counter over there for folding clothes."

Pete kept jotting, his pen moving steadily as the couple recounted the chaos.

"Then it was quiet," Juan said. "Just like that. The tires squealed again. When I peeked over the edge of the counter, the second car was gone. And I couldn't see anyone moving inside the first one."

Tina nodded, her voice softer now. "Juan told me to call 911. He stepped out to check, but…"

Juan nodded. "He was dead. The man… he was on his side, not moving. I didn't know what to do. Open the door? Not touch anything? I… I… I had no idea."

Jeremy glanced at Pete, both reading the silent pain in the couple's expressions. Neither had expected to witness a murder that day. Most people never did.

"No words were exchanged?" Pete asked.

Juan and Tina shook their heads in unison. "No. He just drove up and started shooting."

Jeremy leaned forward. "Tell us about the second vehicle. What did it look like?"

"Black sedan," Juan said. "I didn't really look too close. Everything happened so fast. But it had Virginia tags."

"Do you remember anything about the license plate? Even just part of it?" Pete asked.

Tina's brow knitted as she stared at the floor, then looked up suddenly. "Two Xs. I remember that. Right at the beginning. I don't know why it stuck with me, but it did. That's all I saw. He wasn't there more than a few seconds before I dropped down."

Jeremy nodded, encouraging. "That's helpful. Anything you can tell us about the driver?"

Juan shook his head. "Windshield was dark. Could barely make out the shape of a person inside."

Jeremy tilted his head slightly. "But earlier, you said it was a man."

Tina opened her mouth, then paused, her confusion flickering across her features.

Juan frowned. "We assumed. But honestly? I couldn't tell. When I think about it now… I couldn't see clearly. It might not've been a man. The shape was there, but the windshield was dark. I didn't think it was legal to have a windshield so dark." His hand trembled slightly as he wiped it down his jeans.

"Anything about the shooter?" Pete asked gently.

Juan's head snapped up. "Glasses."

Pete blinked. "You saw that?"

Juan nodded slowly. "You couldn't see much, just an outline. But when he turned his head slightly, just before firing, I saw the side of glasses on his face. Then his hand lifted with the gun, and that was all I could focus on."

"Sunglasses?"

Juan's brow furrowed. "I don't know."

They tried for more, but the details had been muddied by fear and adrenaline. Eventually, Jeremy and Pete handed over their cards and thanked the couple, reassuring them they'd done more than enough.

Outside, the late afternoon light had dulled into a steel-gray sky. Pete glanced at his watch and sighed. They still needed to oversee the forensics team as they processed the car, then swing by the hospital. Cora would be deep into the postmortem by now. And somewhere in the back of his mind, he knew he needed to call Angie to cancel their Thursday night plans with the group. He hated that more than anything.

As they walked toward the taped-off car, Jeremy glanced over. "First impressions?"

Pete didn't hesitate. "Why do I feel like Tamarcus Waters was just here on the Eastern Shore… taking out more competition from up north?"

Jeremy gave a dry chuckle, but there was no humor in it. "I was thinking the same damn thing."

34

Angie sat at her desk, poring over the ESAAA budget, wondering how to squeeze blood from a stone when her phone buzzed. It was buried on her desk, but she shuffled some papers around to find it. She glanced at the screen and grinned, seeing Pete's name on the caller ID.

"Hey," she said, tucking the phone between her shoulder and ear as she leaned back in her chair, feeling her hips ache in protest.

"Angie, I hate to do this, but I have to work late. There's no way I can get to the Y in time to work with the kids." Pete's voice was laced with frustration, and she heard people talking in the background.

Angie straightened and shook her head with a small smile. "Are you okay? Is something happening?"

"Yes, we're fine," Pete said, his voice low but steady in her ear, a slight tension just beneath it. "But there's been an incident up near the north end of Accawmacke, close to the state line. Jeremy and I are dealing with it."

Angie heard what he wasn't saying just as clearly as

what he did. She already recognized the tone. He was giving her as much as he could, without crossing lines he'd drawn to protect both his work and her peace of mind. She respected that.

She leaned back in her chair, cradling the phone between her shoulder and cheek. "What do you want to do about tonight?"

He sighed, then said, "I can message the boys. Let them know we'll have to cancel."

"Do you think they'd mind doing chair yoga instead?"

There was a brief pause, and then his chuckle warmed her chest. "No, not at all. They'd probably get a kick out of it, especially if they're with the adoptive grandparents. That crew knows how to make anything fun."

She smiled, imagining the boys sprawled out with exaggerated poses, the older folks egging them on with lighthearted competitiveness and laughter. "I'll still pick up my group for the Y. I can take one of the bigger ESAAA vans, then swing by for the boys, too. If they're game for chair yoga, I'll give them their usual hangout time at the YMCA, then drive everyone home."

Pete exhaled slowly on the other end of the line, the sound curling into her like a tender hesitation. "Do you think that'll be too much on you?"

She softened her voice, lacing it with just enough tease to draw him back from worry. "Too much? You forget who you're talking to? I've already wrangled my crew into a van. What's a few more kids? They're good boys. They'll fall in line."

"You sure?"

"Positive," she said firmly. "They'll love it. And the grandparents will get such a kick out of having them in the class."

He chuckled again, the sound a little more relaxed this time. "Chair yoga? Wish I could see that."

She could imagine his amused brow lift through the phone. "Oh, they'll go for it," she replied confidently. "And if I know the kids, they'll make a competition out of it before the first leg lift."

Pete let out another sigh, softer now, a trace of warmth behind it. "If you're sure... I just don't want you overdoing it."

"I won't. Honestly," she added, voice dropping into something more sincere, "I think I need it, too."

There was a pause. "Are you okay? Are you hurting?"

Her chest tightened with something sweet. There had been a time when hearing someone questioning her pain level would have made her feel exposed. She hated feeling vulnerable. But not with Pete. Her RA was part of her reality, but so was he. And his concern didn't weigh her down. It held her up.

"No worse than usual," she admitted. "But I've been stuck in my office chair for hours. My body's reminding me that I need to move. And hydrate."

"You do," he said gently. "So drink some water. Stretch a little. Be kind to yourself, sweetheart."

She smiled, touched by the tenderness threading through his voice. "I will. I promise."

There was a moment when neither of them spoke, as they shared a breath across the distance. Then he sighed again, his voice dropping to a rough whisper. "Thanks, Angie. I owe you."

She leaned her head back, a playful smile tugging at her lips. "You do," she teased. "But I'll let you make it up to me later."

"If I make it back in time, I'll come to the Y. Meet you there."

She heard the lingering uncertainty. "No worries," she said, with quiet confidence. "I have it all covered. And I can swing by and feed Queenie, too. You just take care of you."

"You do the same, babe." His voice had a little gravel in it now, that edge she loved. "And thank you."

After they disconnected, Angie couldn't stop the soft and lingering smile that bloomed across her face. She already missed the idea of seeing Pete tonight, but at the same time, there was a quiet contentment in knowing where they stood.

They hadn't made a big declaration. They didn't need to. Somehow, they'd just become a couple. One day, she was teasing him over coffee, then the next day, they were texting good night like it was the most natural thing in the world. Now, even if he wasn't beside her, he was with her. The thought stayed in her mind all through the afternoon, making even the drudgery of budget reports and expense columns feel bearable.

By the time she waved goodbye to her staff in the late afternoon sunlight, she was practically humming with purpose. She headed straight to his place, unlocking the door with the spare key he'd given her. It was a simple gift, made in case he needed a backup person to feed his cat. But the gesture had meant more than he'd ever said out loud.

The house greeted her with a hush until Queenie emerged from the back room like a queen returning from court with a loud meow.

"Hey, Queenie Girl," Angie said, crouching down with a fond smile.

The aging cat responded with a loud, throaty meow before weaving herself through Angie's ankles in greeting. Angie reached to scratch gently behind the cat's ears, affection curling in her chest. Pete could be the very definition of no-nonsense. But then he'd adopted this older rescue with arthritis and a crumpled ear as if it were the most natural thing in the world. She loved how he gave quietly, not trying to impress anyone.

She found Queenie's dish, portioned out her dinner, and stood by as the cat buried her nose into the soft food with eagerness.

"Good girl," she whispered, fingers brushing Queenie's back before she locked up behind her.

The drive home was peaceful, the late sun casting long golden rays across the farmland. As she pulled into her driveway, she spotted her grandparents out in the yard. Just the sight of them brought a warmth she'd never stop being grateful for.

She greeted them both, savoring the comfort of their familiar hugs. They moved to the porch, where three lemonades already waited on the small table. Angie raised a brow. "Were you expecting company?"

"Of course we were," Grandma Dorothy said, as if it were the most obvious thing in the world. "You."

Laughing, Angie settled onto one of the vintage rockers, sipping the lemonade.

Grandpa Stan shot her a knowing look, a glint in his eye. "Seems like that nice young police officer you're sweet on has been around a lot lately."

Before she could respond, Grandma Dorothy gave him a light swat on the arm. "Stanley, don't you go embarrassing her."

Turning to Angie with a conspiratorial wink, she added, "Although… I wouldn't mind if he came by for dinner one evening."

Angie chuckled, a blush rising to her cheeks. "Well, I'm pretty sure you'll be seeing a lot more of him, so yeah… dinner can be arranged."

"Oh, good." Dorothy clapped her hands lightly. "Then things are progressing?"

"They are," Angie said with a nod. A small pause. "I guess it's moving kind of fast…"

Dorothy's voice was warm and sure. "Honey, when it's right, you just know."

Stan nodded beside her. "Your grandma and I knew on our first date."

Angie leaned forward, heart soft. "Really? Tell me more."

But Grandpa Stan glanced at his watch and shook his head with a grin. "We would, but isn't this your night at the Y?"

"Oh! Shoot!" She sprang up, kissing their cheeks before dashing toward the house. "Love you both!"

A quick change into leggings and a loose, comfortable top, a fast bite to eat, and Angie was out the door again, heading back to the ESAAA center to grab the larger van.

As she pulled up to Careway Senior Apartments, her group was already gathering on the curb. She climbed out and opened the side door, helping each one aboard with practiced ease. Mr. George peered at her from the passenger seat, fiddling with his hearing aid. "This is the big van. Everything all right?"

Angie gave him a reassuring smile. "Just a change of plans. The kids are joining us for yoga tonight."

Ms. Hannah clapped delightedly. "Oh, how wonderful! It's about time they saw what we get up to!"

Mr. Marty grumbled something unintelligible but gave a sly grin. "We'll see if they can keep up."

Angie chuckled as she pulled out onto the road, taking the scenic back route toward the pickup spot. As she approached the familiar lot, she saw the boys waiting, their lanky frames casting long shadows in the fading light.

They hopped on board with easy smiles and quick greetings, immediately buckling themselves in like they'd done it a hundred times.

Jalen leaned forward slightly. "Mr. Pete messaged us. Said you were picking us up." With a curious tilt of his head, he asked, "Who's gonna watch us in the gym?"

"You'll be joining us for chair yoga," Angie said, glancing into the rearview mirror just in time to catch their wide-eyed expressions.

"Chair yoga?" Mike asked, like she'd just told him they were going ballroom dancing with nuns.

From behind him, Ms. Rosetta chimed in, her tone dry but amused. "Don't knock it till you try it."

Inside the YMCA, Angie led the group through the familiar halls, the kids accompanying the older adults with a mix of curiosity and skepticism. The room they entered was flooded with late afternoon light, airy and welcoming, the scent of lavender diffusers lingering in the air. Rows of sturdy chairs replaced traditional yoga mats.

The boys looked around, surprise on their faces. Rasheem eyed the setup with a skeptical frown. "So… we just sit there?"

A low chuckle came from Mr. Bertram. "Oh, you'll see."

The instructor walked into the room. She was a petite woman with silver-white hair pulled back in a neat bun, her posture impossibly elegant. She carried herself with a graceful calm, her presence soft but commanding.

"Angie!" she greeted warmly, eyes sparkling as she took in the newcomers. "And today, you brought reinforcements?"

Angie grinned. "Change of plans. Think you can handle a few extra limbs in the room?"

The instructor gave a theatrical sigh, then smiled. "Absolutely. The more, the merrier."

As the boys grabbed chairs and settled in beside their grandparent matches, Angie watched with a full heart. It was one of her favorite sights—these little blended families being stitched together by kindness and time.

The instructor clapped her hands, calling the class to order. "Let's start with a few deep breaths. In through the nose... and out through the mouth."

A hush fell over the room as everyone followed her lead. Eyes closed, chests rising and falling in unison. An occasional snort or chuckle erupted from the boys, but they soon got into the rhythm.

Darius peeked one eye open and whispered, "So far, so easy."

Angie pressed her lips together to hold back a laugh.

Soon, they were rolling their necks, stretching their shoulders, and reaching their arms up and over in a slow wave of movement. The boys fidgeted at first, glancing sideways at their elder counterparts for cues. But when the instructor called for lifted legs and firm posture, things got real.

"Whoa," Curly muttered, wobbling in his chair. "This is harder than it looks."

"Balance is key," Mr. Harold offered, lifting his leg with slow, practiced control. "Use your core."

"Core?" Kyron echoed, eyes narrowed.

"Your middle," Mr. Marty explained, patting his own stomach. "Muscles in your belly and back. That's where your strength comes from."

Jimmy wasn't about to be left behind. He sat up straighter, bracing himself and lifting one leg with exaggerated precision. "Like this?"

Ms. Hannah clapped. "Look at that! You're a natural!"

The class moved on with a rhythm all its own. There were moments of serious effort—gritted teeth, trembling limbs—and just as many bursts of laughter. Mr. Bertram stole the show with a dramatic Utkatasana that had half the class giggling, only for him to wink when he said, "That was my fierce pose!"

The other boys declared they also wanted to try it, each making a concerted effort. By the time they reached the final stretch, Angie's muscles were tingling. She leaned back in her chair, turning slightly, and paused.

There, in the doorway, stood Pete.

His shirtsleeves were rolled to his forearms, and his hair was pushed back as though his fingers had just been dragging through it. Something in his expression made her breath catch. He hadn't said a word yet, just stood there, arms folded loosely across his chest, eyes scanning the room full of kids and elders bent in gentle concentration.

Then Tony spotted him. "Mr. Pete! You made it!"

David grinned. "We're basically chair yoga champions now."

Pete chuckled and stepped inside, the sound like a ripple in still water. "That so?"

Angie reached across the empty chair beside her and patted the seat, eyebrows raised in challenge. "Have a seat, Detective. You might learn something."

He hesitated just long enough for the boys to start goading him, then gave her that slow, sideways grin that never failed to make her stomach flutter. He dropped into the chair with a grunt and rolled his shoulders, mock serious. "Alright. Show me what you got."

The instructor, never one to waste a teaching moment, added a final stretch to the session, this one just for him. Pete did his best to mimic the move, but his long limbs and not-so-flexible frame betrayed him, earning chuckles from both kids and elders alike.

Easy, genuine laughter bubbled up around the room. It

was the kind of expression that came when people felt safe and connected. Angie glanced sideways at Pete. Their eyes met across the heads of giggling boys and beaming seniors.

He mouthed, *"Thank you."*

She didn't reply. She didn't have to. The smile she gave him said everything.

35

JIMMY

The tires of Jimmy's bike hissed against the sidewalk as he and Robert coasted the last stretch toward the Careway complex. A few gulls screamed overhead, circling lazily in the pale blue sky. The afternoon sun glinted off the windows of the low brick buildings, but Jimmy barely noticed. He was too focused on the tight feeling in his chest, the way it always hit him when they rounded that last bend near Mr. Marty's.

Robert rode beside him, quiet, looking ahead, his expression unusually tense. That was when Jimmy saw it. The black sedan.

It sat in the parking lot like it belonged there, polished and sleek. Its presence twisted something in Jimmy's gut. He coasted to a slow stop and put a foot down near the edge of the sidewalk, eyes narrowing.

"There it is," he muttered. "That's the car."

Robert braked beside him, gaze flicking toward the vehicle. "You sure?"

"Yeah. He's been by a couple of times to see Mr. Marty." Jimmy's voice dropped. "But I don't like him. He gives me that... bad feeling." As if summoned, the front door of the building creaked open.

Jimmy tensed. Tamarcus stepped into view, striding up the walkway like he owned the place. His black cap was pulled low, and the glint of a chain caught in the sunlight as he moved. He rapped on Mr. Marty's door twice, then grabbed the doorknob and walked right in.

Jimmy's mouth went dry. "That ain't right."

"Duck down," Robert hissed, already dragging his bike behind the overgrown hedge beside the building. Jimmy followed, heart pounding. They crouched low, out of sight, the muffled slam of the door still ringing in their ears.

Robert kept his head down. "That's him."

Jimmy blinked. "What?"

Robert's voice dropped to a whisper. "That's the guy I saw with Lashawn."

Jimmy turned sharply. "Lashawn?"

"The one who was driving when I was with him. The one who wrecked his car with all that stuff in it."

"Oh shit, man," Jimmy cursed, his chest heaving as worry began to slither through him.

Robert nodded once. "Same guy. I didn't know his name then. But I saw Tamarcus with him... kinda hanging in the background. I thought maybe he was under Lashawn."

Jimmy stared at him, stunned.

"But I said no," Robert added quickly. "I'm not about that anymore. I told Detective Pete. I told Jeremy, too. They got Lashawn now—but Tamarcus wasn't there that day, but I know they're looking for him."

Jimmy let out a slow breath, everything shifting inside his chest. "And now he's here. With Mr. Marty."

Before Robert could respond, the sound of tires and chattering voices rolled in from the sidewalk.

Darius and Mike arrived first, kicking up bits of gravel as they dropped their bikes. Curly, Kyron, and Rasheem followed close behind, then Jalen, Caleb, Tony, and David. The entire crew had biked over to see the grandparents.

Jimmy stood and waved them over fast. "Back here. Quiet."

They ducked behind the building one by one, crowding into the narrow space between the hedge and the brick wall. They were a flurry of legs and arms as their voices dropped to urgent whispers.

"What's going on?" Tony asked.

"Who's in there?" added David.

Jimmy leaned in. "Tamarcus. He's in with Mr. Marty right now."

Robert crossed his arms. "He's dangerous. I saw him with Lashawn. He's part of it. The drugs, the gangs… all of it."

That shut everyone up.

Rasheem frowned. "Why would Mr. Marty let him in?"

Jimmy shook his head. "He don't know. He just thinks Tamarcus is some long-lost great-nephew."

The boys all stilled as the sound of footsteps came from around the corner. Barely breathing, the boys all looked at Jimmy as though he was now their leader. He tried not to make a sound as he listened to the steps stop just around the corner. Then a knock on the door, and a familiar voice drifted through the air.

"Hey, Mr. Marty, it's Angie!"

Jimmy's eyes snapped to the walkway as he peeked over the shrubs. Ms. Angie was at Mr. Marty's door, her tote bag slung over her shoulder.

"Wait!" Tony gasped. "She's going inside!"

Robert surged forward a step but stopped, too far away to reach her in time without blowing everything.

The boys all froze, helpless, as the door opened again. Tamarcus was the one who answered it. And Angie stepped right inside. The door clicked shut.

"No, no, no," Jimmy muttered, fists clenched. "She doesn't know. She's in there with him."

Robert pulled out his phone fast. "I'm calling Pete."

Everyone waited, watching him, holding their breath.

He frowned. "Voicemail."

He swallowed hard, then left the message in a low, urgent voice. "Detective Pete, it's Robert. Tamarcus is here. Um... not at my place but in Mr. Marty's place. The guys are with me. Uh... and Ms. Angie just walked in too. You gotta get here. Please. Call me back."

He ended the call and looked around at the others. The younger boys were wide-eyed, the older ones visibly rattled.

Jimmy's heart thudded so hard it felt like it echoed in his ears. Angie and Mr. Marty were in that room with someone they knew wasn't safe. They were crouched behind the shrubs at the end of the building, next to Mr. Marty's apartment. Jimmy's eyes kept darting toward the parking lot, visible through the small gaps between the branches. The black sedan hadn't moved, but it was hidden in plain sight. "We can't just sit here," he said under his breath, more to himself than the group.

Robert looked up. "We called Pete. What else—"

"I can't wait," Jimmy cut in. His jaw was tight. "Ms. Angie's in there. She doesn't know. She thinks Tamarcus is just family or something."

He stood abruptly, brushing dust off his jeans. "I'm going in," he said. "At least they won't be in there alone."

Some of the boys started to argue, but Jimmy was already pointing. "Darius, Robert—you two go back around, stay by the back wall near the end unit. That's Mr.

Marty's place. I'll see if I can get to the bathroom window to tell you what's happening inside."

Without another word, he jogged around the side of the building, sneakers thudding softly against the pavement. He reached Mr. Marty's door in seconds and swallowed deeply before knocking. He heard Mr. Marty call out, "Come on in!" and then turned the knob and stepped inside.

The small apartment smelled faintly of the strong peppermint lotion Mr. Marty used on his joints. Sunlight streamed through the front window, catching on Ms. Angie as she looked up from her seat on the sofa. She smiled, her pen pausing mid-stroke.

"Well, hey there, Jimmy."

Mr. Marty sat across from her, his eyes bright and his grin wide. "I'm gonna get my new hearing aid!" he boomed. "Ms. Angie's helpin' me finish the paperwork for the doc tomorrow."

Jimmy gave them both a quick smile, but his attention was already shifting.

Tamarcus stood a few feet off, leaning near the window, shoulders tight. He wasn't smiling. His fingers twitched, his leg bouncing, eyes flicking back and forth between the door and the room's occupants. His jaw clenched like he was barely holding something together.

"Hey," Jimmy said carefully, stepping farther in. "Just came by to check on you, Mr. Marty."

Tamarcus didn't say anything.

Jimmy walked past them, forcing his steps to stay calm. "Mind if I use the bathroom?"

Marty waved a hand. "Course, son. Through my bedroom."

Jimmy walked through the bedroom and shut the bathroom door behind him. It was big enough for a person who used a wheelchair if necessary, but he didn't look around. Instead, he quickly darted to the window. Carefully sliding it open, he peered out into the back.

"Psst!" he hissed.

Robert and Darius rose into view from behind a trash can.

"He's real twitchy," Jimmy whispered. "I don't think he likes Ms. Angie being here. Mr. Marty just likes having people so he doesn't suspect anything. Call Pete again. If he doesn't pick up, call 911."

Darius nodded and took off running around the corner to get out of sight.

Robert looked at the younger kids now crowding around. "Get to the other people you know live here. Tell them to stay inside and stay out of sight yourself."

Within seconds, the group of boys exploded into motion, scattering like startled birds. "We'll go to George!" Caleb whispered and ran away with Curly and Rasheem.

"We'll get to Bertram," Jalen said, grabbing Kyron by the sleeve and pulling him along.

"What about Ms. Hannah and Ms. Rosetta?" Mike asked.

"You three go to them," Jimmy whispered through the open window, hoping his voice didn't carry to the room behind him.

Mike, Tony, Darius, and David turned and ran toward the back corner to go to the other side to get to Hannah's and Rosetta's apartments.

Robert stayed. "I'm coming in. Move back."

Robert climbed through the window with Jimmy's help as he prayed that they weren't making too much noise. He flushed the toilet as Robert's feet landed with a thud on the floor. Then Jimmy turned on the water at the sink, hoping that sound would also drown out any noise they were making.

He whispered, "Stay here. Only come out if the way is clear. Then you can hide in… uh… the closet."

Robert nodded, and Jimmy opened the door, breathing easier when he found the bedroom empty. He stepped back into the living room and tried to act normal, but Tamarcus's head snapped up the moment he reappeared.

The man's eyes were too wide now, his skin glistening. Something had shifted. "You got a lotta friends, huh?" Tamarcus said suddenly, his voice sharp, his gaze narrowing.

Jimmy froze and glanced out the window. He looked across the wide garden area and caught sight of the four younger boys entering Ms. Hannah's and Ms. Rosetta's apartments. He had no idea what all Tamarcus might have seen of the other residents' front doors from his view at the window. Swallowing deeply, he also spied Mr. Bertram walking to the parking lot.

Tamarcus had his back to the window now, and Jimmy felt his heart beat so hard he was sure everyone could hear it. He smiled at Ms. Angie, who was staring at him. Another glance out the window showed Mr. Bertram backing his car out of its spot and parking it behind Tamarcus's vehicle. If he wasn't so scared, Jimmy might have laughed aloud.

Mr. Marty blinked. "You okay, son?"

Jimmy jumped but nodded his head. "Yeah… just, uh… I ate too much pizza earlier."

Tamarcus didn't take his eyes off Jimmy.

Ms. Angie glanced up, brow creasing as she looked up at Tamarcus. She opened her mouth but didn't get a chance to speak.

36

TAMARCUS

Tamarcus paced slowly near the window. His heart thumped in an uneven rhythm as the stale scent of lemon cleaner, peppermint, and old age itched under his skin.

This was supposed to be a quick stop. In and out. He could tell his grandma he checked on her brother, but more importantly, it gave him a solid hiding spot for an hour while the heat cooled on the highway. The backroads around the senior complex made it easy to lay low when the highway was crawling with local and state police, known for their notorious speed traps. It's the only way this back-ass county could bring in any money.

But when he stopped by, he hadn't counted on company. He snorted softly. *I'm a drug transporter creating a route for the OGB Bloods of Norfolk, and my fucking plans are unraveling. Goddamn Lashawn... goddamn kid and a goddamn do-gooder.*

Marty didn't matter. Half blind, half deaf, and smiling like this was a family reunion. Tamarcus had never met the man before this past month. Only heard of him from his grandma, Marty's stepsister. A throwback. A safe spot. Nothing more.

But the woman was a different story. Marty had introduced her as Ms. Angie. She sat stiffly on the worn sofa next to Marty's recliner, a stack of neatly arranged forms in her lap. She didn't seem to let his negative vibes scare her off. She calmly filled out paperwork like she didn't even feel the tension choking the room. She kept looking at him, though. Every time he shifted, she clocked it. Not nosy, just… observant. Watching.

She didn't flinch like the others usually did when he walked into a room, and her determination unnerved him. He had expected silence or fear. Instead, her resolve pissed him off more.

She adjusted her stupid purple glasses and offered Mr. Marty another gentle smile as she flipped to the final form in the stack. "Almost done, sir," she said. "This one just needs your signature, and you'll be all set to take it to your hearing doctor tomorrow."

Marty beamed from his recliner like a schoolkid with a gold star. "I'm finally gonna be able to hear Rosetta fussin' at George from halfway across the garden again!"

Tamarcus didn't give a fuck about the old man's hearing aid. He'd die soon, and no one would care if he could hear or not.

What did matter was the kid. The tall one with sharp eyes and twitchy nerves. He'd been here the other day. Now, suddenly popping in and pretending like this was a friendly visit, Tamarcus didn't trust him.

Tamarcus also didn't believe in coincidence. He waited, arms crossed, heart crawling up his throat. The kid had gone into the bathroom. And hadn't come back.

He couldn't shake the cold certainty that both the kid and Angie had seen him up close. Tamarcus now felt exposed, no longer an unseen ghost in an old man's apartment.

This place was supposed to be off-grid. A ghost lane. A clean thread through the Eastern Shore to Pennsylvania. If he got the line tight, the whole route would belong to OGB. They wouldn't need G-Shine's weak-ass boys from up north anymore. Tamarcus had promised his set's president he could make it work on his own. He didn't need Lashawn dragging heat around every corner, nor any other G-Shiner who came down.

He'd worked too damn hard to lose it here, surrounded by lace curtains and hearing aid forms. And now that woman and kid had looked at him like maybe they knew something. Like they felt something.

If this goes sideways, I ain't just burning a hiding spot. I'm burning my shot with OGB. I burn this, I'm done.

Tamarcus shifted his weight, fingers twitching near the edge of his hoodie. His hand brushed against the waistband of his red tracksuit, where the Glock sat like a stone. Cold, heavy. Familiar. The weight felt like it had doubled in the last sixty seconds.

He heard the sound of the toilet flushing and then running water from the sink. Jimmy stepped back into the living room, offering a wobbly smile, but he was even more twitchy than before. Tamarcus's head snapped up the moment the kid reappeared.

He heard it then—a wail outside. Distant. But getting louder. Sirens.

His body moved before his brain did. The Glock came free from his waistband and into his hand, small and lethal and shaking slightly in his grip.

He wasn't going down. Not here. Not like this.

37

Angie had laughed softly at Marty's exuberance over the hearing aids he would be getting soon. This was why she did what she did—these small wins for the people who still had a lot of life in them but now found some everyday things to be challenging. But even with a smile on her face, she was acutely aware of the man standing to the side. Her pen hovered as she double-checked a date, but she glanced up, still seeing him stare at her.

Tall. Young. Dressed sharp, but not Sunday sharp. City sharp. Black hoodie under a red jacket, black cap turned backward, silver chain glinting like a warning light. There was a hardness in his eyes that didn't match the warmth of the senior apartment. Gangster. That was the word that popped into her head.

Marty had introduced him as his great-nephew and seemed thrilled to have a visitor. "Ain't that somethin'? Come all the way out to check on an old man."

Tamarcus hadn't smiled. Didn't sit. He just hovered near the window, shifting from foot to foot like his skin didn't fit right. Something about the way he watched the window, barely glancing at his uncle, made her spine tighten. But she didn't show how it rattled her.

Angie had felt the sharp edge of fear. His eyes barely met hers, and when they did, they held no warmth. Grammy Ellen always said you could tell a lot about a person when looking into their eyes. She had a feeling Grammy Ellen wouldn't trust Tamarcus. Nor would Pete.

Jimmy had arrived, his face flushed, and his usual confidence tamped down. His smile seemed forced. Angie watched as Jimmy glanced at Tamarcus, then at her, then excused himself to the bathroom.

Still, she kept her tone light. "I'm almost finished helping Mr. Marty with some paperwork for his new hearing aid."

Tamarcus still said nothing, but kept his eyes now toward the bedroom where Jimmy had disappeared. She looked that way, then back at Tamarcus. His jaw was locked, shoulders coiled tight. His eyes didn't leave that hallway.

Something was wrong. Angie's pen stilled on the form.

Jimmy came back out a minute later, posture stiff, eyes scanning the room before they landed on her. He tried to smile, but once again, it didn't reach his eyes.

That was when she heard it—the low whine of a siren in the distance. Faint at first, but growing louder. Angie turned her head slightly toward the window.

In the split second it took to glance, she saw the flicker of relief cross Jimmy's face.

But Marty was frowning now, struggling to sit forward in his recliner. "You hear that? You think that's—?"

Angie reached to place a calming hand on his arm. "It's probably nothing. Let's just—"

"Don't move."

The voice was sharp. She turned, breath catching in her

throat. Tamarcus held a gun. Small. Black. Steady in his hand. But his eyes were wild.

"Don't move," he repeated, louder. "I swear to God."

Marty stiffened. "What the hell's goin' on?"

Jimmy stepped forward instinctively, moving between Angie and the weapon. "Don't—don't hurt anybody. Just—"

Tamarcus's hand twitched.

Marty's eyes flared wide. "You get that thing outta my house!" He reached for his cane, his gnarled hand gripping it like a sword. "I didn't fight in Vietnam just to sit here and let some fool wave a piece at me in my own damn living room."

Before anyone could stop him, Marty stood with more strength than any of them expected and whacked Tamarcus on the leg.

"Dammit!" Tamarcus roared, lifting his hand and hitting Marty in the head.

Marty swayed and fell backward, unconscious.

"Mr. Marty!" Angie gasped, rushing forward—

Tamarcus's arm shot out, snatching her by the wrist. "Come here, bitch!"

"No! Let go of me!"

"Shut up! You're coming with me."

The gun pressed into her side. Angie froze. Her heart pounded against her ribs as Tamarcus hauled her toward the door. Her gaze hit Jimmy's.

Jimmy tried to grab her, screaming, "No!"

Tamarcus lifted the weapon and pointed it straight toward Jimmy. Angie pushed his arm down as he fired, and the bullet hit the floor. Jimmy dove behind the table, and a teenage boy she didn't know ran from the bedroom, his gaze wild-eyed, darting around.

"Robert! Down here!" Jimmy cried.

Tamarcus opened the front door and jerked on Angie's

arm, dragging her along. He was strong, and her knee buckled, keeping her from digging her heels in to slow him down.

Several people were now outside screaming. She spied some of the kids and seniors coming out of their apartments. Another gunshot cracked the air, and Angie screamed as the crowd scattered like birds under fire. Doors slammed as the kids were hustled back inside.

Tamarcus dragged her toward the black sedan. But when they reached it, he stopped. "Shit!" he barked.

The car was blocked in. A big, ancient Buick was parked directly behind it, and she recognized it as Bertram's. Not understanding how it came to be there, she tried to wrench her arm from his grasp. He yanked her back, fury radiating off him like a furnace.

Red and blue lights flashed around the corner. Sirens were now right there, tires screeching. Tamarcus spun around and dragged her back toward the apartments.

"No—let me go!" Angie twisted, but his grip was like iron. Her knee completely gave out, and she dropped to the ground.

He dragged her until they were at Marty's door. Tamarcus tossed her to the floor. She looked behind her, but Jimmy had disappeared. So had the other boy, and when she looked toward the recliner, Marty was also gone.

Her attention darted back to Tamarcus. She could hear shouting, commands being yelled, and footsteps thundering down the walkway.

Tamarcus jerked the curtains closed over the front window, and Angie scooted farther away, trying to stay out of his way. Her heart crashed like thunder, and her chest heaved with each breath. She wasn't sure if she was going to die at this moment, but she wasn't going to make it easy for him.

38

Pete's SUV screeched to a halt at the edge of the Careway Senior Apartments. Jeremy was already out of the passenger door, weapon drawn but lowered, eyes sweeping the quiet complex. A few unmarked vehicles followed in behind, deputies piling out with grim, tight expressions.

Pete had gotten the voicemail from Robert three minutes before the dispatch call came in. He didn't need more details—the names Tamarcus, Robert, and Angie in the same sentence lit a fire in his gut he hadn't felt since Cora had been held hostage in the hospital's morgue. He now knew how Jeremy had felt.

He scanned the U-shaped curve of the buildings. It was quiet for a few seconds, then suddenly erupted. A few of the seniors popped their heads out of their apartments, and he spied some of his kids peeking out as well.

"Back inside, now!" Pete shouted, bending low to race to the closest apartment. "Bertram! Harold! Get them inside and lock it down. Go! Get into Rosetta's or George's, I don't care which. Just keep them together and away from the front."

The kids turned and raced back inside, with the exception of Caleb, who darted out, ducking and weaving as he ran to Pete. "Hey!" he called, breathless, pointing toward the other side. "They're still inside! Mr. Marty's apartment! Tamarcus has Ms. Angie in there!"

"Got it! Now, get back behind the deputies' vehicles!" Pete's jaw locked as adrenaline surged through him.

"Jimmy still there?" he asked.

Caleb nodded fast. "Jimmy and Robert are there too. Said he was gonna protect her. There's a back window that goes into the apartment's bathroom. You can't see it from the living room, but the back door is visible."

He radioed, "Multiple hostages inside apartment 101."

Jeremy stepped beside him. "We need to get to the back."

Pete didn't wait. He and Jeremy took off at a dead run, boots pounding the narrow concrete strip as they raced around the back corners of the building. The trimmed grass behind the units was silent, broken only by the humming of old AC units and a few flapping trash can lids.

"Marty's on the far end," Pete muttered, his eyes flicking to every movement, every possible angle. As they rounded the last corner, two back doors cracked open— George and Harold again, peeking out, heads low.

"Stay inside!" Pete snapped, voice low but firm. "Lock it up. Don't come out again, you hear me?"

George gave a tight nod and was pulling the door shut when there was movement at Marty's window. Robert crawled through and turned to assist someone else.

Pete raised his weapon instinctively, but froze as he registered who it was. Robert was helping Marty to the outside. Robert looked to the side, and his gaze begged for assistance. "Help!" Robert whispered. "He's hurt—he's bleeding!"

Pete signaled to a deputy, who ran over. "Get rescue here. Have them come to the back."

While the deputy made the call and signaled the other law enforcement in the area, Jeremy helped get Marty out of the window. As soon as the older man was clear, Pete could see Jimmy on the inside.

"Jimmy," he breathed.

Robert had his shoulder under Marty's arm, struggling to keep him upright. Pete looked over his shoulder to see Bertram hustling down the back sidewalk. George was already at the door, rushing forward with Bertram. Together, they helped Marty into the neighboring unit, their movements fast but careful. Marty's face was pale, blood in his hair, his eyes dazed as he mumbled something about not being able to hear right.

Robert stood, his face tight with fear and effort as he looked up at Pete. "What do I need to do?"

"Get into that apartment with them and stay there until it's clear," Pete ordered, pointing at George's back door.

Robert hesitated. "But Jimmy's still in there," he whispered, pointing at Mr. Marty's apartment.

Pete said, "You did good. Now keep doing good by following orders, okay?"

Robert nodded and followed Bertram into George's apartment.

Pete and Jeremy rushed forward to Marty's window again, still seeing Jimmy inside. "What happened?"

"Marty got hit in the head. Tamarcus dragged Angie outside and then back in because Bertram parked behind him and blocked his car. Now, he's got her inside again. Tamarcus has a gun. He fired inside but didn't hit me 'cause Ms. Angie pushed his arm. Then he fired again outside to scare everyone."

339

Jeremy swore under his breath. Pete's stomach clenched.

"Can we go through the back door here?" Jeremy asked, inclining his head toward Marty's rear entrance

"No… it's visible from the living room. This bathroom only leads to the bedroom."

"Okay, come on out—"

"No, you get in. I'll stay here," Jimmy insisted.

Pete didn't have time to argue, so he crawled through the window, which was just barely big enough for a large man in full tactical uniform. Once in, he turned to Jimmy. "Give me the layout."

"No halls in this place. Bedroom leads into the dining area. The kitchen is next to that and is open to the living room."

Pete radioed the instructions to the other law enforcement. "Suspect. Male. Gang leader. Armed. He is in the end unit of Careway Senior Apartments. Maintain the lockdown at the Careway Assisted Living next door. Suspect has hostage. Female. In living room."

He bent low to hold Jimmy's gaze. "Get out of here now. You've done all you can. And you did good, man. Couldn't have done better."

Jimmy nodded, and Pete added, "Get out and go to George's back door. The ambulance is on the way."

With that, Jeremy helped Jimmy out the window before he climbed inside with Pete.

Jeremy turned to Pete. "You okay?"

"Not even close."

Jeremy nodded. Then they moved forward, slowly opening the bathroom door. The bedroom was clear, and they stepped silently inside. From the living room, a male voice shouted and cursed.

Angie's voice followed, muffled, tense but not panicked.

No matter what happened in the next five minutes, Pete was going to get Angie out of there. Even if he had to walk through gunfire to do it.

Pete eased into the bedroom, shoulder brushing the doorframe, every sense on edge. The room was dim, lit only by the daylight seeping in through the curtains. He crouched low, eyes narrowing.

Tamarcus was pacing, cursing under his breath, his voice sharp and agitated. Pete couldn't make out every word, but the tone said enough. Tamarcus knew he was backed into a corner.

Pete couldn't see Angie. For one chilling beat, he feared the worst, but then Tamarcus stopped pacing, standing just at the edge of the window, holding the curtain open with two fingers as he peered out. His other hand still gripped the gun.

Pete tracked his movements, slow and quiet, staying in the shadows. Then Tamarcus said something, voice lower, directed downward. Pete's chest tightened. *She's on the floor.*

He shifted slightly, angling himself for a better view. Tamarcus leaned again toward the curtain, peeking through the edge, just a sliver. He was probably watching the squad cars forming a perimeter beyond the garden and seeing his precious plan go up in smoke.

Pete's pulse beat steadily in his ears. His body was still, calm, but his mind calculated every inch of cover, every second between movement and engagement. He glanced back, caught Jeremy's eyes, and gave the hand signals. Behind him, Jeremy crept back into the bathroom. A beat later, Pete heard the faintest murmur of Jeremy whispering into the radio.

"Suspect still armed. Standing near the front window.

341

Civilian female hostage on the floor. Hold position. Standby for breach."

Pete moved into position behind the bedroom doorframe, raising his service weapon slowly. He was angled just enough to see Tamarcus's profile and the gun in his hand—but Angie was still out of view.

Then suddenly he could see her. She shifted while still on the floor and turned her head, just enough for their eyes to meet. Even from across the room, Pete could see the fear flash in her eyes, but then hope.

He couldn't risk spooking Tamarcus but prayed she'd understand. *Stay down, sweetheart. Just a few more seconds.*

Tamarcus turned from the window again and resumed pacing. He muttered louder now, swearing about "this hick-ass town" and how "nobody gets to screw up my deal, not after everything I worked for." He stopped in front of Angie, his shoes just inches from her.

Pete's finger tightened slightly on the trigger.

"Get up," Tamarcus snarled. "You're my ticket outta here. You're gonna walk with me nice and easy, and nobody's gonna shoot a pretty bitch."

Pete's breath hitched. *No fucking way.* He adjusted his grip and tracked the angle of Tamarcus's arm.

And then, as though her knee couldn't hold her weight, Angie dropped and landed flat on the floor. Pete couldn't tell if it was on purpose or not, but in that split second, the line between him and Tamarcus cleared.

Pete took the shot. Tamarcus jerked hard, his right shoulder snapping back—the one holding the weapon. The Glock dropped from his hand and hit the floor with a dull clatter. He screamed and staggered back, his hand clutching his shoulder as blood poured.

Pete was already through the doorway. "Angie!" He was at her side in an instant, pulling her behind him, shielding her body with his as Jeremy came in like a storm from behind and tackled Tamarcus to the ground.

The apartment exploded with shouting—Jeremy barking commands, Tamarcus screaming in pain, other voices crackling over the radio. Pete stood, still half shielding Angie, as the front door burst open. Deputies poured in. Detectives followed. Relief mixed with the flood of movement.

Pete helped Angie sit up, his heart hammering. "You hurt?"

She shook her head, stunned. "Just—my knee. Twisted when he was dragging me outside." Her breath came fast and shallow, but her hand curled around his forearm like she was grounding herself there.

"I'm here," he murmured, crouching in close. "I got you. You're safe now."

"Marty?" she cried.

"Okay… the kids got him out. He's at George's place."

"The kids?"

"All okay," he assured, realizing as he said the words, he was assuring himself as well.

Outside, sirens wailed closer. Pete looked through the now open door as an ambulance pulled into the garden loop just as Bertram flagged it down. Paramedics ran into George's place to get to Marty. Pete saw the kids come pouring out of the apartments across the garden. Darius, Jimmy, Robert, Jalen, Mike—wide-eyed and wild with emotion.

The seniors followed, staying with the kids. Other seniors who lived there but weren't part of their group joined the others.

Hunter Simmons jogged over as the deputies had Tamarcus handcuffed to a gurney being loaded into the back of an ambulance. He ordered the deputies to stay with him and make sure they followed legal procedures at the hospital. "We don't want that asshole getting off on a technicality."

Pete knew Hunter would have raced over to help no matter what, but the fact that Belle, his wife and mother to his children, was in lockdown at the nursing home next door would have had the big man on edge.

Terry and Colt hustled over to oversee the scene and check on everyone.

Pete stepped out of the front door with Angie in his arms. The kids raced over, all clambering to make sure she was okay.

A second ambulance rolled up. Angie hesitated. "I don't—"

Pete just shook his head. "You're going. You're gonna let them check that knee. No arguing."

She looked up at him. Her eyes filled with tears, and she nodded. She looked over at the kids and seniors. "Thank all of you so much. Marty and I are okay because of you."

Pete kissed her forehead, brief and protective, just as the paramedics rolled up with the gurney. As they rolled her toward the ambulance, Pete looked around—the chaos giving way to relief, the senior community gathering to witness what had just unfolded. He caught Jimmy standing next to Robert. He offered both a chin lift. They grinned, their chests heaving with nerves and adrenaline. Then they smiled.

Jeremy said, "Go with Angie. We'll process the scene and get all the witness statements."

Terry agreed. "This will take a while." He chuckled. "You go be with your girl while we deal with it."

"I need to make sure the kids get home—"

"We'll call their parents before we talk to them, then we'll get them home safely," Terry assured. "We certainly want them safe and the DA not to have any reason to object to our investigation."

Bertram, George, Harold, Hannah, and Rosetta moved closer. "We won't let the kids out of our sight until their parent or guardian cómes," they promised.

Nodding, he let out a sigh of relief, but in his chest, the pounding hadn't stopped. He'd come too close to losing something he didn't even realize he needed so badly.

39

By the time the last car pulled away from the driveway, Pete leaned his shoulder against the doorframe and took a long breath. The kind of breath you only let out when the chaos finally gives way to stillness. The house was quiet now.

Sunlight streamed in through the front windows, warm and golden, dust motes floating lazily in the air. The smell of cookies and muffins lingered—Bess had brought enough for a small army. Belle had brought flowers, the bouquet now offering a sweet scent. Somewhere in the kitchen, a card from Cora and Jeremy rested beside a wrapped tin of herbal tea. Mark and Karen had stopped by too, with Karen not letting Angie get away with anything less than elevated rest and perfectly timed ice packs.

It had been a steady stream of hugs, chatter, tears, and can-you-believe-it stories all day long. And Angie had smiled through every second of it with her leg propped on a pillow, the wrap firm around her swollen knee.

Now, though, the house had hushed.

Pete crossed the room slowly and sank beside her on

the sofa, careful not to jostle her leg. The cushions cradled them as Angie let out a soft sigh, leaning against his side.

"Still good?" he asked, glancing at her knee.

She nodded, eyes soft. "Sore. But manageable. I mean, Cora and Karen checked it. That's what happens when you have friends who are physicians and nurses. If I survive their care, I can survive anything."

He smiled, wrapping one arm around her shoulders and the other around her waist. "You were a damn hero."

"Pete, honey, I was just in survival mode. But thank God, I had backup." She looked up at him with that look that always leveled him—the warmth in her eyes hit deeper than anything he'd ever felt before. "Those kids... the seniors... together they were so much more than just a hero."

He glanced around the room. Earlier, throw pillows had been tossed to the side, mugs were half full on coasters, and paper plates of goodies had been left with nothing more than a little residual powdered sugar. But Angie's parents and grandparents had cleaned every surface before they offered final hugs with tearful thanks to him and then heartfelt hugs to Angie.

"Your folks," he said softly. "Your grandparents... they're something else."

Angie's eyes went glassy for a second. "Yeah. I'm lucky."

He hesitated, holding her tightly. "You know... I've always done better alone. Just how I'm wired, I guess. But somehow you and your people—you've pulled me in like it was always meant to be that way."

Her lips twitched. "Well... I think you and I are fated to be."

He let out a soft laugh, the kind that started low and ended with something like awe. "The timing might suck, but I have something to talk to you about."

Eyes wide, she stared, uncertainty filling her expression. "Okay. That sounds ominous, but okay…"

"I got a call from my landlady the other day. I didn't say anything about it. I… uh… I wasn't sure how to bring it up."

"Pete, honey, just talk to me. Please."

"She's decided to sell the house. She wanted to give me the first chance to buy it, or I could find another place to rent."

Angie's tongue swiped her bottom lip. "Okay…"

"The thing is that I don't mind buying since I know I'm staying in the area. But… honestly, my rental house was good enough in the past, but it's not what I want to buy."

Now, her brow furrowed, but she nodded.

"I could buy a place, ask you to look with me, and then we could move in together," he continued, now feeling his heart pounding more as the anxiety rolled over him.

She opened her mouth, then closed it, pressing her lips tightly together.

"But you love this place with your grandparents next door and your parents just a few houses down the street. And I know you don't want to give that up… and honestly? I don't want you to."

"So… what are you thinking about doing?" she asked, a tremor running through her voice.

He sucked in a deep breath, then swallowed. "Angie, sweetheart… what do you think about me just staying here?"

She blinked, then gasped. Her lips curved as her eyes widened. "You mean like—move in? Here? With me?"

"Yeah." He nodded, heart now galloping. "Not just sometimes at your place and sometimes at mine. But here… home. Together."

The air rushed from her lungs, and she tilted her head, her brow furrowing. "I don't know…"

He froze, and his heart plunged. Then the sparkle in her eyes caught his attention.

She smiled and shrugged. "I'm uncertain if Queenie will give up your bed."

He laughed, shoulders loosening as everything inside him settled into place. "She'll share. As long as you don't try to move her blanket."

Angie grinned. "Fine. But you're on litter box duty."

"Deal."

They sat in silence for a moment, wrapped up in each other as the light stretched long across the floor, the last shadows of the day fading into peace. Her head leaned on his shoulder, her fingers laced gently with his.

He turned to her, voice low. "I love you, Angie."

She looked up at him, eyes shimmering. "I love you too, Pete."

The kiss was soft, slow, unhurried—like neither of them needed anything more than this right now. Not safety, not heroics, not even words.

Just this moment. The warmth of a sunlit room. The hush after a storm. The quiet promise of forever.

The smell of grilled burgers and charcoal drifted lazily through the backyard, mingling with the scent of blooming roses and freshly cut grass. Angie stood near the picnic table, one hand resting on her cane, the other wrapped around a lemonade. Her knee was still tender, but she didn't care because everything else in her world was perfect. Preteens and teens darted through the yard in a flurry of shouts and laughter.

"Kyron! Quit throwing corn cobs like they're grenades!" Angie called, half laughing as Pete swiped one off the grill just in time.

"I wasn't gonna hit nobody!" Kyron shouted, grinning.

Robert sat in one of the folding chairs beneath the oak tree, watching the chaos with quiet amusement. Next to him, Caleb and Jimmy were deep in conversation—probably rehashing the Great Rescue for the hundredth time.

"Hey, Jimmy," Tony yelled, "tell it again—how you got Mr. Marty out and didn't even trip!"

"Yeah!" Darius added. "And how Pete shot the guy right in the arm!"

"I was there, too!" Jalen shouted. "I saw it!"

"Oh Lord," Rosetta said, waving her lemonade as she joined Angie by the table. "These boys'll be seventy and still telling this story. By then, Tamarcus will be ten feet tall and shootin' laser beams."

Angie laughed, her cheeks flushed from the heat and happiness. Hannah and Harold were gathering paper plates, and Bertram was sneaking his second slice of peach pie. George had somehow gotten hold of the Bluetooth speaker, and one of the kids showed him how to use it to play old Motown, his feet tapping like he wanted to teach the boys how to do the twist.

And Marty sat in a shady spot near the hydrangeas, cane across his lap, beaming like the sun itself. His bandage was gone, his hearing aid freshly fitted, and Hannah hovered like a mother hen.

Pete came up behind her and wrapped an arm gently around her waist.

"You good?" he murmured.

She leaned into him, smiling. "I'm great."

He pressed a kiss to her temple and passed her a deviled egg from the tray in his other hand. "Your grandma's been watching me like a hawk. I think she's testing my commitment to you by food quantity."

"She is," Angie deadpanned. "Next is her potato salad."

"God help me."

Queenie—their cat now, though Pete still pretended she was too spoiled to share—was sprawled under the patio table, her tail flicking lazily as she watched a butterfly.

Angie looked around and let the moment settle into her bones.

Her grandparents Stan and Dorothy were chatting with her parents near the patio, while Grammy Ellen swayed in a rocker, humming softly to the music. The seniors were all telling the tale of how the kids "saved the day," each version more dramatic than the last. And Pete was beside her at their home.

She looked up at him. "We really did it, huh?"

"We did," he said. "And I'm not going anywhere."

Angie smiled, heart full.

Behind them, Rasheem ran past with Mike, chasing Curly and Darius. A football sailed over the grill. Someone shouted about lemonade refills. Queenie yawned.

The music rose, the laughter swirled, and Angie let herself sink into the pure joy of it all.

It wasn't just happily ever after. It was exactly right.

Get ready for the next Baytown Hero!
Falling For a Hero

ALSO BY MARYANN JORDAN

Don't miss other Maryann Jordan books!

Baytown Boys (small town, military romantic suspense)

Coming Home

Just One More Chance

Clues of the Heart

Finding Peace

Picking Up the Pieces

Sunset Flames

Waiting for Sunrise

Hear My Heart

Guarding Your Heart

Sweet Rose

Our Time

Count On Me

Shielding You

To Love Someone

Sea Glass Hearts

Protecting Her Heart

Sunset Kiss

Baytown Heroes - A Baytown Boys subseries

A Hero's Chance

Finding a Hero

A Hero for Her

Needing A Hero

Hopeful Hero

Always a Hero

In the Arms of Hero

Holding Out for a Hero

Heart of a a Hero

Hidden Hero

More Than a Hero

Falling For a Hero

For all of Miss Ethel's boys:

Heroes at Heart (Military Romance)

Zander

Rafe

Cael

Jaxon

Jayden

Asher

Zeke

Cas

Lighthouse Security Investigations

Mace

Rank

Walker

Drew

Blake

Tate

Levi

Clay

Cobb

Bray

Josh

Knox

Lighthouse Security Investigations West Coast

Carson

Leo

Rick

Hop

Dolby

Bennett

Poole

Adam

Jeb

Chris's story: Home Port (an LSI West Coast crossover novel)

Ian's story: Thinking of Home (LSIWC crossover novel)

Oliver's story: Time for Home (LSIWC crossover novel)

Lighthouse Security Investigations Montana

Logan

Sisco

Landon

Hope City (romantic suspense series co-developed
with Kris Michaels

Brock book 1

Sean book 2

Carter book 3

Brody book 4

Kyle book 5

Ryker book 6

Rory book 7

Killian book 8

Torin book 9

Blayze book 10

Griffin book 11

Saints Protection & Investigations

(an elite group, assigned to the cases no one else wants…or can solve)

Serial Love

Healing Love

Revealing Love

Seeing Love

Honor Love

Sacrifice Love

Protecting Love

Remember Love

Discover Love

Surviving Love

Celebrating Love

Searching Love

Follow the exciting spin-off series:

Alvarez Security (military romantic suspense)

Gabe

Tony

Vinny

Jobe

SEALs

SEAL Together (Silver SEAL)

Undercover Groom (Hot SEAL)

Also for a Hope City Crossover Novel / Hot SEAL...

A Forever Dad

Long Road Home
Military Romantic Suspense

Home to Stay (a Lighthouse Security Investigation crossover novel)

Home Port (an LSI West Coast crossover novel)

Thinking of Home (LSIWC crossover novel)

Time for Home (LSIWC crossover novel)

Letters From Home (military romance)

Class of Love

Freedom of Love

Bond of Love

The Love's Series (detectives)

Love's Taming

Love's Tempting

Love's Trusting

The Fairfield Series (small town detectives)

Emma's Home

Laurie's Time

Carol's Image

Fireworks Over Fairfield

Please take the time to leave a review of this book. Feel free to contact me, especially if you enjoyed my book. I love to hear from readers!

Facebook

Email

Website

Made in the USA
Las Vegas, NV
30 August 2025